Emilia blinked ~~...~~ fear still in her pale blue eyes.

"What's wrong?" Dane asked her.

Clasping her baby son tightly against her with one arm, she gestured with her other hand at the window. "Someone was there—trying to get in."

He glanced at the window. "Nobody's there."

"There was," she insisted, her voice tremulous. With fear or doubt?

He glanced around the room, at the teenage girls who struggled to comfort crying babies and toddlers. One of the girls shook her head. "I didn't see anyone."

Emilia reached out now and clasped Dane's arm. His skin tingled beneath her fingers. "There was someone there—trying to open the window."

He nodded. "I'll check it out." But she held tightly to his arm, so he couldn't pull away—so he couldn't escape her and all those crying children.

If he didn't leave soon, he might do something stupid...like reach for her again, like try to hold her.

* * *

Be sure to check out the previous books in the exciting Bachelor Bodyguards miniseries.

* * *

If you're on Twitter, tell us what you think of Harlequin Romantic Suspense! #harlequinromsuspense

Dear Reader,

I am so excited to bring you another book in my Bachelor Bodyguards series. In the last book, *Nanny Bodyguard*, Nikki Payne finally met her match and became a full-fledged bodyguard. But she isn't the only employee in her brother Cooper's division of the Payne Protection Agency; he hired guys from his former Marine Corps unit. Working together, they rescued Emilia Ecklund from captivity and reunited her with her baby.

Unfortunately, the drama isn't over for poor Emilia. She doesn't know if she's losing her mind or if someone's gaslighting her. Feeling she already put her brother Lars and Nikki through enough, she turns to determined bachelor Dane Sutton for help. Lars is suspicious and angry over the relationship between his sister and his best friend, and he understands how Cooper felt when he started seeing Nikki as more than his friend's little sister.

Since I have three older brothers, I can identify with Emilia and Nikki having to deal with overprotective males. But sometimes I think my three older sisters are more protective, though—even now. Family is everything to me. That is why I have so much fun writing about the Payne family. I hope you enjoy this latest installment in the series.

Happy Reading!

Lisa Childs

SINGLE MOM'S BODYGUARD

Lisa Childs

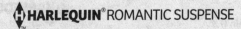

Recycling programs
for this product may
not exist in your area.

ISBN-13: 978-1-335-47453-7

Single Mom's Bodyguard

Copyright © 2017 by Lisa Childs

Printed in U.S.A.

Ever since **Lisa Childs** read her first romance novel (a Harlequin story, of course) at age eleven, all she wanted was to be a romance writer. With over forty novels published with Harlequin, Lisa is living her dream. She is an award-winning, bestselling romance author. Lisa loves to hear from readers, who can contact her on Facebook, through her website, lisachilds.com, or her snail-mail address, PO Box 139, Marne, MI 49435.

Books by Lisa Childs

Visit the Author Profile page at Harlequin.com for more titles.

For my family. Thank you all so much for
your unwavering love and support!

Chapter 1

The crying awoke Emilia—as it always did. But it sounded as if it were coming from a great distance instead of just down the hall. Why did it seem so muffled?

She knew better than to put anything in the crib with the infant. She wouldn't take any risk with him ever again. "Blue…" she murmured as she jerked fully awake.

Throwing back the blankets, she jumped from the bed and ran from her room, hitting her shoulder against the jamb as she exited. Pain radiated down her arm.

This was real. This wasn't a dream like all the times before she'd heard that faint cry, when she had reached for her stomach, for her child—only to find her womb empty, her baby gone…

Except that hadn't been a dream, either. That had been the horror she'd lived for weeks until she and her son had been rescued.

Her feet slipped on the hardwood floor as she hurried down the hall toward the bedroom on the other side of the bath. She banged into that jamb, too, while rushing into the nursery. A breeze rustled the wispy blue-and-white-striped curtains and rattled the blind pulled over the window.

The open window.

She hadn't left that window open. She was always so careful to make sure that it was shut and locked. She wouldn't have…

She could barely hear the crying now. It was far in the distance. "Blue…"

Was he gone, too?

Her legs trembled, nearly folding beneath her, as she walked toward the crib. Dread gripped her. She was afraid to look, afraid that it was happening all over again.

She had lost her little boy once. She couldn't lose him again. Her hands shook and she wrapped her fingers around the top rail of the white-painted crib. And finally, she forced herself to look.

Her heart lurched, swelling with love, as it did every time she gazed upon her child. He lay on his side, his eyes closed, his little fist clenched as if he was ready to start fighting bad guys—just like his uncle.

Relief slipped from her lips in a long, shuddery breath. He was fine. Blue was fine, sleeping peacefully. There were no tears on his cheeks, which had finally begun to fill out. He looked happy and healthy.

And she'd thought she was, too, now that she had him back. But she could still hear the crying. Maybe it was coming from another house. But it hadn't sounded that way when she'd first heard it. It had seemed to come from down the hall.

And it sounded that way again but now the direction

had changed, as if it were coming from her room. She had cried herself to sleep a few nights, thinking of the mistakes she'd made, the mistakes that had nearly cost her Blue and her brother and the woman he loved and Emilia's own life, as well.

She had almost lost everything. But thanks to her brother, Lars, and Nikki Payne and Lars's friends, Blue was safe. Emilia was safe. She had lost nothing.

The sound of crying persisted. It sounded like Blue's cry. But he was still asleep. She reached down for him, tempted to hold him and assure herself he was all right. As her fingers brushed across his back, he murmured and a soft sigh slipped through his rosebud-shaped lips.

He was too peaceful. Disturbing him would be selfish. She had promised herself she wouldn't be that kind of parent, the one her father had been when he'd deserted his sick wife and kids.

No. She had to leave him alone, had to let him sleep. Most new parents would have been envious of how much her son slept. But she knew he did that because he hadn't had anyone there for him those first few weeks of his life. He hadn't had anyone that cared enough to come when he'd cried. And her heart broke over that, over knowing that she had already let down her son. She wouldn't do it again.

She forced herself to step away from his crib. Along with the crying, the breeze reached her, stirring her nightgown as it did the curtains and the blind. Shivering, she lifted the blind and slid the window closed, locking it. As she did, she remembered checking that lock earlier—when she had first put Blue down in his bed. The window had definitely been closed and locked.

Who had opened it?

Lars wasn't home. He'd moved in with Nikki nearly a week ago. Emilia had had to convince him that it was okay, that she would be fine without him.

But she wasn't fine. She was scared. Someone must have been inside the house. Who and why?

Was someone after her baby again? She turned back toward the crib. She wanted to lift Blue from it, wanted to hold on so tightly to her little boy that no one could get him away from her—ever.

But she resisted that temptation. Instead she settled into the rocker recliner in the corner of the nursery. With that crying echoing inside her head, she wouldn't be able to get back to sleep anyway. She would sit vigil, watching her son to protect him.

But from what? If someone had unlocked and opened the window, they would have had to be inside the room. So why hadn't they just taken Blue if he was what they really wanted?

She was probably just being paranoid because of what had happened. The adoption lawyer who'd stolen her baby was dead. To save Nikki, Lars had been forced to kill him. Myron Webber wasn't coming back. He wasn't taking her baby or anyone else's.

Maybe his was the crying she heard—as he burned in hell. Maybe he was haunting her. What he'd done to her had certainly been haunting her. Maybe that was all it was: flashbacks and nightmares from what had happened.

Because why would someone break in only to open a window? It made no sense.

It made more sense that she had left it open, that she hadn't locked it.

But that wasn't the case. Was it?

Had she kept everything she'd thought she was losing only to lose her mind instead?

He must have lost his damn mind. That was the only reason Dane Sutton had for deciding not to quit the Payne Protection Agency. He'd been all set on turning in his resignation to Cooper Payne, his boss and a fellow former Marine. But Cooper had persuaded him to give the job a chance.

Yet it wasn't the job Dane didn't like: it was everything else that encompassed the Payne Protection Agency. Family. Romance. Love.

He had vowed long ago to have nothing to do with any of those things. He'd tried family once, although it hadn't been his choice. Abandoned as an infant by a teenage mom who left him in a school bathroom, he'd been adopted by an older couple. But like his young mother, they had also realized they weren't really interested in being parents. So because he'd had this example, Dane had no idea what a family was actually supposed to be.

He hadn't liked what he'd witnessed with the Paynes. They interfered in each other's lives and even in the lives of the people who worked for them. They tried to bring everyone into this *family* of theirs. He suspected it was probably more like a cult, though. He shuddered just thinking of it. It wasn't safe for him to stay.

But something had compelled him to stick around River City, Michigan, and the Payne Protection Agency.

Friendship.

That, he was very familiar and comfortable with. The guys from his unit were his best friends. Now his boss and coworkers. He hadn't been able to leave them behind during a mission. And he couldn't leave them now.

But he would just have to be very, very careful he didn't wind up like Lars, the blond giant of a man who was sitting beside him in a Payne Protection Agency vehicle, holding a ring over the console. Dane was behind the wheel of the black SUV.

"So tell me—what do you think?" the guy eagerly asked him, his pale blue eyes bright with something almost like giddiness.

Dane sighed. "You know I love you, man, but only as a friend. I gotta turn you down."

Lars swung his free hand into Dane's shoulder. The tap probably would have knocked a smaller man through the driver's door, but Dane was nearly as big as his friend. "I'm damn well not proposing to you."

"Phewwww," Dane said. "You made me nervous. I thought I was going to have to go through that whole 'it's not you, it's me' speech."

Lars chuckled. "Yeah, you've given that speech a few times."

"So have you," Dane reminded him.

Lars hadn't been any more eager for romance or love than Dane was. In fact, with his sister missing, falling in love had been the last thing on Lars's mind.

Until he started at Payne Protection.

The security agency might guard people's lives but they were hell on hearts.

Lars glanced down at the ring he held out, and for a second the brightness of his eyes dimmed. "Do you think she'll give me that speech?"

Dane's stomach tightened into knots. He hated this stuff, hated seeing his friend so anxious. Lars had already suffered enough when his sister had gone missing and been presumed dead. It would be so much worse for him if he were to be turned down now by the woman he loved. "Maybe you should wait. You two haven't been together very long. And Nikki has made it clear she wants nothing to do with marriage."

"With weddings," Lars corrected him. "She doesn't want a wedding."

"What the hell's the difference?" he asked as he fumbled with the bow tie at his neck. That damn thing was cutting off his circulation.

Lars snapped the case closed on the ring and reached across to adjust Dane's tie. "This. The monkey suits, the dresses, the pomp and ceremony—this is the wedding. It's one day. The marriage is the life."

"So you think she's fine with the life and just wants to skip the day?" Dane hadn't always been the greatest at math but one day seemed a hell of a lot easier to get through than a lifetime.

Lars sighed wistfully. "That's what I'm hoping."

Dane couldn't blow smoke and offer his friend false assurances. He always had to tell the truth—unless he'd been sworn to keep someone else's secret. "That's a hell of a risk you're taking."

"Proposing?" Lars asked. "What's the worst that can happen? She can say no."

Dane figured it was a bigger risk if she said yes. But he just shrugged.

"And if I'm late to her mother's wedding, she's sure to say no," Lars said as he shoved open the passenger's door. "We better get inside the chapel."

Dane stepped out of the driver's side and walked around the truck, but he hesitated before heading up the steep steps to the double doors of the little white chapel.

His heart pounded slowly and heavily with dread in a chest that felt constricted in that damn tuxedo.

"I don't know why I'm here," he said. "I get why you are. You're dating the bride's daughter. But why was I told I needed to attend?"

It hadn't been an invitation. It had been a command.

Lars stopped halfway up the stairs and turned back toward him. "You haven't heard about what happened the last time the bride and groom were in this chapel together?"

Dane shook his head. Unlike Lars, he was trying to keep his distance from the Paynes. He didn't want to be sucked into their little family cult. He wouldn't have even been here if Cooper hadn't made it an assignment.

"The whole wedding party was taken hostage and the groom was shot and nearly died."

Dane shuddered. "Talk about bad luck. Shouldn't they have taken that as an omen and forgotten about trying to get married again?"

"Woodrow Lynch wasn't the groom that day. He was the father of the bride," Lars explained. "He's also a former FBI chief who's made a lot of enemies over the course of his career."

Dane glanced at the other people, all dressed up, heading into the church. Could one of them be a threat? "So he thinks there might be another attempt to kill him?" He studied the people more carefully, looking for not so carefully concealed weapons.

Lars gripped his shoulder and drew his attention back to him. "It's possible. That's why I wish Emilia wasn't working today."

Dane froze. "Emilia?"

"Yeah, she works for Penny Payne," Lars said, pulling his hand away to gesture at the church Penny had converted into her full-service wedding planning venue. "Didn't I tell you that?"

Dane had been trying to avoid any mention of Emilia. She had been the focus of his world for too many weeks when she'd been missing. That was why he'd been so fascinated with the photo Lars had given him to help find her. That was the only reason....

But why was his pulse quickening? Why could he feel his heart pounding faster and harder now?

"No..." Dane murmured but his reply wasn't just for Lars. It was for himself. No.

He couldn't see Emilia. He already saw her too much— every time he closed his damn eyes.

"She insisted on coming today," Lars said, his voice gruff with frustration and concern. "She said it was the most important day for her boss and she wouldn't miss it even though I tried to tell her it might not be safe."

And Emilia had already been through so much. Dane understood his friend's fear. Hell, he even shared it.

"Nikki was one of those hostages last time," Lars said, his fear making his deep voice even gruffer. "She was nearly killed. So I'm going to need to keep an eye on her."

"She's going to hate that," Dane reminded him. Nikki Payne was fiercely independent. There was no way she was saying yes to Lars's proposal.

But before he could offer his friend any more advice, Lars continued, "So I'm going to need you to keep an eye on Emilia. You need to make sure nothing happens to her." Lars's brow was furrowed, his concern for his sister apparent.

Dane couldn't refuse his request any more than he'd

been able to ignore Cooper's order to attend the wedding. Yeah, friendship had already caused him enough problems. He wanted nothing to do with family, romance or love.

"I also need you to talk to Emilia," Lars said, "and make sure that, after everything she went through, she's really okay."

"Why wouldn't she be?" Dane asked. "Myron Webber is dead. He can't hurt her anymore."

"Just because he's dead doesn't mean he's not still hurting her," Lars said. "She woke up with nightmares for weeks after we rescued her."

"PTSD?" he asked.

Lars nodded. "I think so. But I never really experienced that myself. That's why I need you to talk to her."

"Why me?" Dane asked.

"I bunked next to you for months at a time," Lars reminded him. "You have as many nightmares as she does."

Dane tensed. "I don't talk about that stuff…" Not with his friends. He certainly wasn't going to talk to some young woman who already had enough nightmares of her own. "I can't help her."

Lars studied his face for a while before uttering a sigh of resignation. "Fine. Just watch out for her, make sure she doesn't get any more nightmares from whatever the hell might happen here today."

Just what kind of weddings did Penny Payne plan that people risked developing PTSD after them?

A lot of weddings had taken place in Penny Payne's Little White Wedding Chapel. Some real. Some staged to flush out serial killers. Some hadn't taken place at all. Brides had changed their minds. Or gunmen had taken the church hostage before the wedding was able to take place.

Penny wasn't worried about this bride changing her mind. She stared at her reflection in the oval mirror in the bride's dressing room.

Was it ridiculous that she wore a gown?

It wasn't white. At fifty…something…and with four grown kids, that would have been ridiculous. But the tea-length, lacy bronze dress looked like a wedding gown. For the second time in her life, Penny was a bride.

Her first groom had been a boy. Together they'd grown up. And he had become a man—one who'd made mistakes. One mistake had brought a child into the world with another woman. One had gotten him killed.

She had survived both of his mistakes. But then she'd spent the next nearly two decades afraid of making a mistake of her own. So she'd focused on her kids and her business and she'd protected her heart—until that day she'd nearly lost her chapel to those gunmen.

Her kids—the ones she'd given birth to and the ones she'd claimed as hers—had saved everyone that day. But Penny had still lost something she had never intended to risk again.

Her heart.

But this groom she could trust. He wasn't a boy. He was a man. Woodrow Lynch wouldn't make mistakes that would hurt her. He loved her as much as she loved him.

No. She wasn't going to back out and neither would Woodrow. Penny wasn't worried about that. She wasn't even worried about all the minute details of a ceremony that she usually insisted on overseeing herself.

She didn't need to do that anymore, not since she'd hired Emilia Ecklund. The beautiful blonde appeared next to her in the reflection in the mirror. She carefully pinned the tiny bronze lace veil onto Penny's coif of auburn curls.

"You look so beautiful," Emilia told her with such awe that Penny couldn't doubt her sincerity. She was such a sweet, sincere young woman. "Everything's ready."

Penny's heart lurched. Not with nerves over the marriage. She knew that would be good. But now a few doubts flickered in about the wedding details. Emilia had seemed kind of distracted the past few weeks. Penny opened her mouth to ask a couple of questions, just to confirm.

But Emilia shushed her with a smile. "Everything's ready," she repeated with calm assurance. There was not even a trace of nerves in her soft voice or on her beautiful face.

Penny believed her. Emilia had been about to graduate with her bachelor's degree in hospitality and event planning when her world had been turned upside down. After her rescue, she had been working hard to right her world again.

Maybe too hard.

Dark circles rimmed her pale blue eyes. Of course, she had an infant at home, too. New mothers rarely got enough sleep. That was probably why she'd seemed distracted lately.

Penny reached up and patted her cheek. "Thank you, Emilia, for making not just this day so special for me but for making my workload so much lighter since you started working for me."

Emilia's beautiful eyes glistened with unshed tears, but she blinked her long black lashes and cleared away the moisture. She smiled again, but it was as if she had to force up the corners of her mouth.

"Is everything all right?" Penny asked her.

"Yes, I told you it was," Emilia replied. "We're ready to start the ceremony. Are you ready?"

Penny sucked in a sharp breath. She was getting married again. She was pledging to share the rest of her life with another. She couldn't wait. "Yes, please send my kids in here. I am raring to walk down the aisle to my groom."

But as Emilia turned away to open the door, Penny caught her arm. The odd sensation raced over her—one of those god-awful premonitions she had that something was about to go very wrong.

Not today.

Of all days, not today…

"What is it?" Emilia asked. Alarm drained the color from her face. "Are you having second thoughts?"

"Definitely not," Penny said. "I can't wait to marry my soul mate. But…"

"I told you, everything's fine."

"I'm sure you did everything right," Penny said. "But I have that feeling…"

Emilia sucked in a sharp breath now. Penny had told her about the feelings that came over her, about her instincts that warned her when something horrible was going to happen.

"I'll double-check everything," her assistant assured her. "Don't worry."

She hurried away before Penny could stop her.

Penny couldn't shake the feeling that something bad was going to happen to Emilia. She hoped she was wrong. The young woman had already been through too much.

Chapter 2

Emilia's heart pounded as she gave in to the nerves fluttering inside her. This was it, her chance to finally prove herself to her benevolent boss. Penny had been so sweet to take a chance on her, to give her not just a job but the responsibility of overseeing the woman's wedding.

Nothing could go wrong.

But Penny's premonitions were legendary. When she had one of her feelings that something bad was about to happen, it always did.

So Emilia didn't waste time checking on the flowers. She already knew they were perfect. The minister had arrived, as had all the guests. The photographer had already begun taking pictures and setting up the camera to record the ceremony. The caterers were ready to serve for the reception in the banquet room in the chapel basement.

Emilia hadn't lied when she'd assured Penny that everything was ready. For the ceremony…

But Emilia had that sense of disquiet, too, the same way that Penny did. Something bad was about to happen. That feeling compelled her to quickly cross the foyer to the steps leading down to the nearly walk-out-level basement. This was where the offices were and the banquet hall and kitchen.

And the nursery…

Along with all the Payne babies, Blue was there, too. Two nursery workers—teenage girls—watched all the children. But they were only teenagers. If someone tried to take one of the babies…

They wouldn't be able to stop them.

But Emilia would.

She hastened her pace, her heels clicking against the stairs as she nearly ran down them. In her haste, she slipped. Her grasp on the railing kept her from tumbling to the concrete floor below. She steadied herself, finished descending the stairs and hurried down the hall.

Waiters and cooks milled around inside the banquet hall and the kitchen as she rushed past. Excitement hummed in the air. This was *the* wedding. The one everyone wanted to be absolutely perfect—because this was Penny's wedding.

They all loved Penny Payne.

Emilia hadn't known her as long as everyone else had, but she loved her, too. Loved her like the mother she'd never really had, because Mom had gotten sick when Emilia had been so young.

Penny was youthful and vivacious and affectionate. She was everything Emilia wished her mother had been and everything she wanted to be as a mother. Emilia didn't want to let down the woman she admired so much.

But at the moment the wedding was the least of her concerns. She had to make certain Blue was safe. He was what mattered most to her now.

"Emilia…"

A deep voice murmured her name. She ignored it. She had no time now for questions about the colors of the napkins or when to serve the cake. She would answer all those again after she held her baby, after she made certain that Penny's ominous premonition hadn't been about Blue.

She was in such a rush that she nearly passed the door to the nursery. But she drew up short and reached out, grasping the knob. Her hand trembling, she turned it and pushed open the door. Little kids chattered and laughed. A soft voice sang. Small hands clapped.

Like the kitchen and the banquet hall, this room was abuzz with excitement, too—the excitement of little kids and babies.

One of the teenagers glanced up from where she played patty-cake with a black-haired, blue-eyed toddler. So many of the kids looked like that, with the blue eyes and black hair of the Payne males.

"Miss Ecklund, is everything all right?" the babysitter asked. With black hair and blue eyes, she might have been a Payne herself. Some of the kids were getting older now.

"That's what I came to ask you," she said. "Is everything all right?"

The girl's brow furrowed. "With your son?"

"Yes."

Looking at her as if she were being overly anxious,

which she probably was, the girl nodded. "He's fine." She gestured toward one of the cribs against the wall. "He's napping."

Emilia stepped around children so she could get to her son. Like a few nights ago when she'd heard the crying, she approached the crib with fear and dread. And expelled a breath of relief when she found him sleeping peacefully.

She had overreacted to Penny's premonition. It probably had nothing to do with Emilia. With a family that comprised of all bodyguards, Penny's children were all exposed to danger.

Now Lars was a bodyguard, too. And she suspected he would soon be an official member of the Payne family if he was smart enough to ask the amazing Nikki to marry him. Her brother was smart.

She wished she was as smart as he was, as strong. She felt like she was losing her mind. But she'd rather lose that than her son.

He was here, though. He was safe just like he had been that night she'd been so worried she'd wound up bruising her shoulder crashing into doorframes. She glanced down at the bruise now. Maybe she shouldn't have worn a sleeveless dress. Or at least she should have remembered to put on the sweater she'd left hanging over the back of her chair in her office.

She hadn't needed to worry that night. Or now.

But yet she couldn't step back. She had a million and one things to double-check. And she didn't want to miss the ceremony, either.

She wanted to see Penny marry her soul mate even as she felt a pang of envy that she might never find hers. Her judgment was as poor as her mother's had been. Just like her father, Blue's father hadn't been a man she could count on. He'd wanted only one thing from her. And it hadn't been her heart.

Now her heart belonged to another male. To her son. She continued to stare down at her beautiful baby...until a shadow fell across him.

Then she glanced up at the window. Since this was the daylight section of the basement, the window was halfway up the wall. So she didn't see a face. She saw only legs standing in front of that window. Then she saw the black-gloved hands reaching down to try to lift the sash.

To try to get inside that nursery full of children.

And a scream slipped from her throat.

Her scream tore at Dane's heart, making it race with the fear he heard in her voice. Other cries echoed hers, startled cries of kids. He pushed open the door he'd seen her enter moments ago—as he'd followed her mad dash down the stairs and hall toward this room.

Toward her son...

He saw her hurriedly step back from the window with the baby clasped in her arms, nearly falling over the children sitting on the floor behind her.

This was Dane's worst nightmare. A room full of crying kids. But the fear he'd heard in Emilia's voice drew him to her side. "Emilia," he said.

After he'd seen her nearly tumble down the stairs, he'd called out to her in the hall. But she'd ignored him. She ignored him again.

So he reached for her. And yet when his hand closed around her shoulder, she flinched and jerked away from him. Now anger churned in his guts. What had happened to her those long weeks she'd been missing?

How badly had she been abused?

She had a bruise on her shoulder, which was bare. Her pale blue dress had thin spaghetti straps. If she'd gotten that injury in captivity, the bruise should have faded by now. Why did it look so fresh and painful?

She blinked and stared up at him, the dread still in her pale blue eyes.

"What's wrong?" he asked her.

Clutching her son tightly against her with one arm—maybe too tightly, if Dane could guess from how hard he was crying—she gestured with her other hand at the window. "Someone was there, trying to get in."

He glanced at the window. Sunlight glinted off the glass. "Nobody's there."

"There was," she insisted, her voice tremulous. With fear or doubt?

He glanced around the room, at the teenage girls who struggled to comfort crying babies and toddlers. One of the girls shook her head. "I didn't see anyone."

"There was a shadow," the other babysitter, the one with the black hair, said. "I'm not sure…"

If it was human, or just a shadow…

Emilia reached out now and clasped Dane's arm. His skin tingled beneath her fingers. "There was someone there trying to open the window."

He nodded. "I'll check it out." But she held tightly to his arm, so he couldn't pull away and escape her and all those crying children.

If he didn't leave soon, he might do something stupid…like reach for her again, like try to hold her like he had tried the night she'd awoken in the hospital, screaming. That had been a mistake on his part.

He wasn't made for comforting—women or kids. He couldn't give what he'd never received.

He glanced down at her hand on his arm, and she jerked it away as if embarrassed that she'd been holding on to him. As he passed her, she murmured, "Thank you."

He wasn't certain if there was really anything to check out. But when he headed outside, he found other bodyguards walking the grounds. His invitation really had been an assignment. Security was high at this wedding.

High enough?

Why would someone have been trying to get inside the nursery? Or had they just been looking for an open window to get inside the church undetected?

He walked around the white brick building to the back and found the window to the nursery. The woodchips beneath it had been disturbed, some brushed aside enough that he could make out a footprint.

He leaned down and peered into the window, and his gaze met Emilia's pale blue one through the glass. He nodded. And it was as if her shoulders slumped with relief when she should have been tensing with fear.

What the hell was going on with her?

Lars had been right to worry about her. Dane had thought that her brother had just become overly protective of her after the abduction. But maybe Lars wasn't being protective enough. She had that bruise on her shoulder, marring the pale silk of her skin.

"What are you doing?" Jordan "Manny" Mannes, the dark-haired bodyguard, joined Dane near the window. "I already checked that window. It's secure."

"It was you?"

"Yeah, I'm a perimeter guard," Manny said. "I thought you were interior."

Dane nodded. "Yeah. Yeah, I am."

"Then what are you doing out here?"

He glanced back at the window. "Someone saw you," he said. "And thought you were trying to get in, not making sure that no one else could."

After what she'd been through, it was no surprise that Emilia had suspected the worst. But was that because of her recent past or her present?

Manny leaned down and looked in the window, too. "Ah, I didn't even realize anyone was in there. Is that Lars's little sister?"

He said it like she was a child. But she wasn't a child. She was twenty-something and already a mother. She and her son were a ready-made family.

Dane waited for the shudder, but fear didn't grip him like it usually did whenever he thought of family. His experience with family had been nearly as bad as some of his missions with the Marines.

Where was that shudder? He needed the fear. It was all that had kept him alive during his deployments. Being afraid had kept him alert, had made him cautious.

He had never needed to be more cautious than now, when Lars had asked him to stick close to Emilia. He suspected he needed to be more afraid of the beautiful blonde than any enemy he had ever faced.

While his friend continued to lean over and stare into that window at Lars's sister, Manny straightened up. No. He hadn't missed her. If she had been inside the room earlier, he would have noticed her. Sure, she was off limits because she was Lars's sister. That didn't mean he would've failed to spot her, gorgeous that she was.

"No, man, I'm sure there was nobody in there when I checked that window earlier," Manny said. "The room was empty."

Dane shook his head. "How is that possible? She saw you just a few minutes ago and those kids were already inside the nursery then."

Manny tensed, every one of his bodyguard instincts at attention. "I checked that window over an hour ago when I first arrived at the chapel."

Dane cursed. "Did you see anyone hanging around this side of the chapel?"

He didn't even have to think about it. "Hell, no. I would have investigated if I had. It's just been me and Cole patrolling the grounds with a few of the guards from Parker's agency."

Each of the Payne brothers had their own franchise of the security business now. Parker, a former vice cop, had all former police officers on his team. Cooper's unit consisted of former Marines like himself, with the exception of his sister, Nikki, who was as badass as any Marine that Manny had ever known. Then Logan, the brother who'd started the security business, had all family members working for him. But that family was all inside the church for the wedding of the Payne matriarch.

A wedding that couldn't be interrupted. Manny cursed now. "I hope like hell we didn't miss someone getting inside who shouldn't be in there."

He wasn't sure if Dane heard him. His friend was still staring through that window, at Lars's sister. Friends' sisters were off limits to Manny, but Lars had broken that bro rule when he'd fallen for Cooper's sister.

Dane, though?

He was the last one Manny would have thought would break a bro rule. Or fall for anyone…

He was a bigger commitment-phobe than Manny and that was saying something. No. Something else about the blonde beauty had to be bothering Dane.

"If someone's trying to get inside the church, it's about the groom or bride, right?" Manny asked.

He had heard the story about the wedding party that had been taken hostage in the chapel, and that this groom had nearly died that day. Of course all of the hostage takers had died. None of them had survived to storm the church again.

That reason alone would keep anyone else from crashing this wedding. They wouldn't survive if they tried to break in now, not with so many Paynes and other body-guards present.

Dane must have come to that same conclusion because he shook his head and murmured, "No, if someone's trying to get into the church, I think it has something to do with someone else…."

With Emilia Ecklund?

But why?

She'd already been abducted and held hostage for weeks. And the man responsible for that was dead. Who could be after her now?

Chapter 3

Dane Sutton was staring at her through the glass, like she had begun to stare at herself in the mirror the past few days. With concern.

With fear.

She couldn't look into his dark eyes anymore, but it was hard to look away from him, hard not to look at him. He was so big. So handsome…

His features were chiseled. His dark hair almost shorter than the standard military brush cut. He wasn't on active duty anymore, but he still looked like a Marine. Still no-nonsense. To the point. That was why she hadn't been able to look at him anymore and see the doubts she already felt.

Was she losing her mind? Obviously it had only been the other bodyguard checking the window earlier. Nobody was after her baby.

She forced herself to release him and hand him back to one of the irritated babysitters. "I'm sorry," she murmured. "I saw the man."

The girl nodded and took Blue from her.

Emilia had to get back to the wedding. But she couldn't leave the nursery with the commotion she'd caused. Fortunately Penny—who thought of everything—had had the room soundproofed. Emilia must have left the door ajar when she'd rushed inside, or Dane wouldn't have heard her scream.

While his assurance to check things out had momentarily made her feel better, now she wished he hadn't heard her. He was certain to tell Lars how paranoid she was. And her brother already stared at her as if she was so fragile that she would shatter at any minute.

But she was stronger than that. She was capable. She didn't want Lars or Penny to think otherwise. So to quiet the startled nursery, she began to sing. She sang a popular kids' song from a musical she'd done in school.

The teenage girls looked more astonished now than they had when she'd screamed. The kids must have been equally surprised, for they'd all fallen silent with awe now.

Emilia smiled and headed toward the door. But then she saw that Dane had returned and was leaning against the jamb. He'd heard at least some of the song.

Heat rushed to her face, and she hurried past him. "I need to check on things now," she murmured. "Make sure the ceremony is going well."

Hopefully she hadn't missed it. She wanted to see Penny get her happily-ever-after. The woman had planned so many for other brides that she deserved the happiest ever-after for herself.

Dane kept pace beside her in the hall. He was so big, so tall and broad and heavily muscled, and the hallway was narrow enough, that his arm brushed against hers. Once their hips even bumped. She felt an arc of awareness sizzle between them, which was ridiculous. As ridiculous as she had been to scream moments ago.

"Don't you want to know what I found out?" he asked.

She sighed. "It was your friend," she said. "The other one I saw standing outside with you. He must have been who I saw. He must have been checking the window." She hadn't been able to hear every word they'd spoken but enough, with their hand gestures, to get the gist. "I overreacted."

"After what you've been through, that's understandable," he said.

She didn't want his pity, didn't want him looking at her the way Lars did. She wasn't fragile or weak. She wasn't crazy, either. "Penny had said she had a strange feeling."

Dane cocked his head. "What?"

"You haven't heard about Penny Payne's premonitions?" she asked with shock.

He shook his head.

"She always knows when something bad is about to happen."

"If she has that feeling today, maybe she shouldn't be getting married."

"This feeling wasn't about her," she said. The look on her boss's beautiful face had been about Emilia. Emilia knew that.

Her own instinct was already warning her, so it was especially unnerving.

"No wonder you're a little edgy," Dane said.

A little was an understatement. She felt as if she might never sleep again, not without hearing that crying.

"It's an important day," she said. "I need to make sure everything goes well." And she'd nearly blown that by screaming down the church.

Dane must have been the only one outside the nursery who'd heard her, otherwise her brother would have been there. Dane looked away from her now, and she saw that his hand was near his tuxedo jacket, as if he were about to reach for his weapon.

"What?" she asked. "What's wrong?"

"You were right," he said. "Manny did check the window. But it was when he first got here."

She tensed now. "And when was that?"

"Over an hour ago."

"So there was someone there when I thought I saw someone?"

He stared at her as if wondering if he could believe her, if he could believe that she had really seen anything at all. She had as many doubts as he had. But she stopped and turned back toward the nursery.

He caught her arm. "You had things to check on," he reminded her. "The ceremony…"

She shook her head. "Nothing is more important than my son." She would never let him down again. She couldn't risk losing him. "I need to watch over him." Or get him the hell away from the church.

But were they any safer at home?

Were they safe anywhere?

"Manny is watching him," Dane assured her. "I told him to stay right outside that window. Nothing will happen to Blue."

She turned back toward him. "You know my son's nickname?"

He nodded. "I know that. I don't know his real name."

"Lars."

"Good thing he has a nickname."

Since she'd always believed he and her brother were such great friends, she glanced at him in surprise at the snarky remark, but then she realized he was kidding. His face was serious, though. He really had the emotionless expression of a soldier. Or a bodyguard...

This job was perfect for him. But she didn't need a bodyguard. Or did she?

Was everything that was happening just in her head?

She would have to figure out that later. Right now she had a wedding to oversee. She hurried down the hall and up the stairs.

Dane stayed at her side, just like a bodyguard. "It wasn't that bad a joke, was it?" he asked.

Her lips curved into a slight smile. "Lars wrote about you during boot camp and your deployments..." So much that she felt as if she knew him already—or at least as much as Lars knew him—which by her brother's own admission wasn't totally.

Dane's an enigma, he'd written once. *I trust him with my life. But I never know exactly what he's thinking or feeling. Or if he feels anything at all...*

She understood that now.

"I really need to make sure everything's okay with the wedding." But when she climbed the stairs to the foyer, she found Nikki Payne looking for her.

"There you are," the petite brunette said. Her beautiful face was tense with anxiety.

"Is something wrong?" she asked. "Why hasn't the

ceremony started?" She knew Penny Payne hadn't changed her mind and that her groom would have no second thoughts about marrying such an amazing woman, either.

"We're not ready," Nikki said.

Emilia had thought everything was set to go. That she'd had everything in place. The minister. The photographer. The caterer.

Every detail.

Then she noticed the eerie silence but for the slight murmur of whispering voices, and she questioned, "Why hasn't the music started?" She had helped the musicians set up.

"The singer," Nikki said. "She hasn't showed up. We have the guitar players and pianist but no singer."

A big hand nudged Emilia forward. "Yes, you do. She can sing." She turned to Dane and shook her head.

It was one thing to sing to a nursery of children screaming their heads off. It was another to sing in front of a crowded church of quiet adults.

"You can sing?" Nikki asked, her brown eyes brightening with hope.

She shook her head again.

"I just heard her," Dane said. "She's amazing."

Her pulse quickened, and her heart warmed with pleasure that he'd thought so. But she shook her head again as nerves fluttered in her stomach. She wasn't certain if she was nervous about singing. Or about Dane standing so close to her.

Hell, maybe singing was one way to get him to leave her side.

"Would you do it for Mom?" Nikki implored her. "She

thinks the world of you. And she deserves this day to be incredibly special."

"My singing might hurt that," Emilia warned her. But then she sighed. She already knew she couldn't say no to Nikki. Lars's girlfriend was the only one who hadn't given her up for dead. "What song?"

She had expected a classic befitting Penny Payne. But her daughter named a newer pop song. It was about loving someone like you might lose them. She shivered. Penny had nearly lost her groom before he'd even been able to ask her on their first date. He'd wound up proposing instead. Emilia couldn't imagine a love like that, one where they had fallen so quickly for each other and had been so confident that it was the real thing.

But then Lars and Nikki had that same kind of love—that soul-deep connection. She glanced back at Dane, and something shifted in her chest. But his handsome face remained expressionless.

Unfeeling.

She doubted she would be lucky enough to find a love like Penny and Woodrow's or Lars and Nikki's for herself. No. She wasn't going to love a man like she was going to lose him. She would love her son like that—because she knew what it felt like—because she had already lost him once.

She couldn't lose him again.

If not one of the bodyguards, who had been outside the nursery window and why? Was someone trying to take her son? Or her?

She wasn't singing to him. She sang instead to the bride and groom. But her surprisingly sexy voice enveloped and overwhelmed Dane. His heart twisted in a tight fist of anxiety. Maybe it was her anxiety that he felt. Since she'd disappeared and Lars had given him that photo, Dane had had an almost eerie connection to her.

Despite what she'd said, he didn't think she was nervous about singing. Her voice was too clear, too strong—and so compelling that all the guests were riveted, staring up at her in awe. Dane couldn't take his gaze from her.

And maybe that was why he saw the fear he'd heard when she'd screamed in the nursery. Was it just post-traumatic stress disorder like her brother thought? But that bruise wasn't PTSD. Something had happened. She'd been hurt again.

Recently.

Heat rushed through him, his temper heating his blood and his skin. He wanted to hurt whoever had hurt her. First he had to find out who that was. Somebody slid into the church pew next to him and bumped his shoulder. Mentally cursing himself for not being aware of the person approaching, he reached for his weapon.

"Hey," Lars whispered. "You don't need that."

He wasn't so sure. Who the hell had Emilia seen outside the nursery window?

His friend emitted a soft gasp. "I forgot how she sings…"

"…like an angel," Dane murmured.

Lars glanced at him, his pale blue eyes narrowed.

A bead of sweat trickled down Dane's back, beneath his tuxedo jacket. The monkey suit was why he was so damn hot—because it wasn't like he was scared of his best friend. After nearly losing her once, Lars was bound to protect Emilia using whatever means necessary. Even murder…

Dane wouldn't hurt her. He wanted to make sure she didn't get hurt. Again.

Dane asked, "What happened to her shoulder?"

His brow furrowing, Lars glanced at him again then back at Emilia, who effortlessly held the last note of the song. Had her brother not noticed the bruise? But then, in a whisper, Lars replied, "She hit it on the doorjamb when Blue's crying woke her up."

That explained it, if Emilia had told her brother the truth. The tension clutching Dane's guts didn't ease at all. He suspected Emilia had left something out. Or maybe he was just thinking of all the abused women who claimed walking into doors had caused their bruises.

He needed to find out what was really going on with Emilia. Thinking of that—of sticking close enough to learn the truth and protect her—Dane's tension increased. This might prove the most dangerous mission he'd ever had.

Nikki Payne had spent most of her adult life dodging bouquets. This time, while the bride prepared to throw her flowers, Nikki was not hiding in the bathroom. She was out on the dance floor with the other single women. And as the brightly colored bundle of tiger lilies and calla lilies catapulted through the air, Nikki didn't duck behind any of those shrieking women. Nor did she keep her hands linked behind her back as she had every other time she'd been forced onto the dance floor.

Nobody had coerced her to join the others. Even as the maid of honor, she wouldn't have had to participate in this tradition. But she wanted to catch these flowers. So she lifted her hands in the air and actually elbowed aside some of those screaming single women to snag this bouquet from the air. Holding the flowers aloft, she let out a squeal of her own—of victory.

The bride, Nikki's mother, had tossed the bouquet over her shoulder. Now Penny turned fully around, and when she saw who'd caught her flowers, her eyes—the same brown as Nikki's—widened in shock. She wasn't the only one staring mutely at Nikki. Her brothers and sisters-in-law all gaped, their eyes and mouths wide.

Only Lars didn't look shocked. He appeared delighted, his sexy lips curving into a grin while his pale blue eyes sparkled. She loved him—so much. More than she'd thought it possible to love anyone.

She'd fallen for him when he'd been at his worst, desperate and guilt-ridden over the disappearance of his sister. He'd blamed himself for not protecting her even though he'd been deployed in a war zone at the time Emilia had gone missing. His sense of responsibility and honor had impressed her so much that Nikki had been unable to resist him.

And she couldn't resist him now as he dropped to one knee in the middle of the dance floor in front of her. Before he even opened his mouth, Nikki threw her arms around his neck. On his knees he was nearly her height.

"Yes!" she said. "Yes!"

"I don't believe it," a deep voice, belonging to one of her brothers no doubt, murmured. "I thought she'd be running the other way from that bouquet."

"And she's so impatient to say yes, she didn't even wait for him to propose," another brother chimed in.

Heat rushed to her face and she pulled back. "I'm sorry. I shouldn't have presumed—"

Lars pressed his fingers over her lips. "It's not like I'm down here looking for a missing contact," he assured her. "I'm on my knees because I thought you were going to make me beg you to marry me."

"And you were prepared to beg?" she asked in amazement. As well as having an overblown sense of responsibility and honor, he also had a lot of pride. Sometimes too much. But it was just another thing she loved about him.

He nodded. "I would do whatever it takes to convince you to be my wife, Nikki. I want to spend the rest of my life making you happy."

"You already make me happy," she assured him.

He tensed for a moment. Maybe he'd forgotten that she'd already said yes and thought she was going back to her earlier anti-marriage stance. She hadn't ever really been anti-marriage, though. She had been anti–getting hurt.

But just as she loved Lars, she trusted him more than she'd ever thought it possible for her to trust anyone. He wasn't going to hurt her.

"So you don't have to do anything to convince me to marry you. I'm ready," she said. And that was something she'd thought she would never say. She was ready to get married. Ready to be a bride and, more important, a wife.

His pale eyes glittered as if with a sheen of tears. She blinked furiously as tears of her own stung her eyes and tickled her nose. She would not cry, not in front of her brothers. Later, when she laid her head on Lars's mammoth chest, she would soak his skin with her happy tears. But she was too proud to give in to them now…until Lars popped open the velvet case and revealed the most beautiful ring she had ever seen. Stacy Kozminski-Payne must have made it. Logan's wife was so damn talented. As Nikki stared at the square diamond and twisted gold band on which it was mounted, a tear spilled over and trailed down her cheek—until Lars brushed it away.

"Oh, sweetheart," he said, his voice gruff with emotion. "I don't want to make you cry."

"Happy tears," she assured him. She suspected that was all she would cry once he became her husband.

"Good," he murmured. "Then I'm already doing my job."

"I'm not so sure about that," her brother Cooper, who was also their boss, called out. But he was over being mad at Lars for breaking the bro rule of not going after another friend's sister. She hoped.

Penny tapped her youngest son's shoulder and shushed him. "Don't interrupt."

"They interrupted your wedding," Cooper pointed out.

"Lars got my permission," Penny haughtily informed him.

In the past, Nikki would have been annoyed over the chauvinistic tradition of asking the parents for permission before asking the woman. But she understood that wasn't what Lars had done. He'd been asking permission to propose at Penny's wedding.

Of course, her mother hadn't hesitated to say yes and share her special day and spotlight with them. She had always been too selfless. But Nikki didn't mind being selfish right now—not as Lars slid that beautiful ring on her finger. Then he stood and swung her up in his arms before lowering his head to kiss her.

Passion and love overwhelmed her, and more tears leaked from beneath her closed lids. Those tears nearly turned to frustration when the kiss ended way too soon as well-wishers rushed the dance floor. Guys slapped Lars's back. Maybe her brothers slapped a little too hard. But Lars was bigger than all of them. The grin never slipped from his face so Nikki could tell he felt no pain.

Everyone hugged Nikki, who usually would have squirmed away from all the show of emotion. She wasn't a hugger. But she was too happy to mind the affection she was being showered with. Penny hugged her tightly.

"You really didn't mind him proposing here?" Nikki asked. She wouldn't have infringed on her mother's special day for anything.

Penny shook her head. "Nothing could have made this day more perfect for me."

Nikki snorted. "Of course not. You've wanted me to get married since the day I was born," she accused her mother.

Penny shook her head again. "No. I wanted you to find the man worthy of your love, the man who wouldn't betray your trust—who would cherish you forever. And, in Lars, you've found that man."

"Yes, I have," Nikki wholeheartedly agreed. Her fiancé was amazing. And soon he would be her husband.

Penny's new husband stepped forward and pulled Nikki into an embrace, as well. She had always respected the former FBI chief, but now she loved him, as well. He was going to be as wonderful a stepfather as he would be in his new position as chief of the River City Police Department.

"Do you want me to threaten him?" Woodrow Lynch asked. "Make sure he never hurts you?"

"He won't."

"He won't," Emilia promised as she stepped forward for her hug. "My brother loves you so much." Tears streamed down the blonde's face, washing away the makeup she'd used to disguise her dark circles.

Lars was already worried about his sister. And Nikki knew he wasn't just being overprotective. She was worried, too. And it wasn't just because of the dark circles. Since the young woman had an infant, she wasn't bound to get much sleep.

Nikki had other concerns, as well. The singer not showing up hadn't been the only thing to go wrong with the wedding. There had been countless other things Emilia had screwed up or, like the singer, that she'd canceled. As maid of honor and the daughter of the consummate wedding planner, Nikki had stepped in to fix those mistakes.

But why had Emilia made them? She didn't even seem aware that she had. What else was on her mind?

Was it just the ordeal she'd been through?

Or was something else going on?

Nikki had been reluctant to talk to Lars about it; she didn't want to worry him any more than he already was. But she noticed someone else carefully watching the blonde. And she suspected she and Lars weren't the only ones concerned about Emilia.

Dane Sutton was anxious, as well.

What the hell was going on with Emilia?

Chapter 4

How could she have messed up so badly? Emilia had been certain that she'd had everything under control. But she'd overheard the caterer and bartenders talking to Nikki about how Emilia had canceled their services just like she'd canceled the singer.

It wasn't true. But why would they all lie?

She looked at her cell phone now, scrolling through her call log. She had made calls at strange times. In the middle of the night, which was when the caterer and bartenders and the singer claimed she'd called and left voice mails canceling their services.

If Penny heard about any of it...

Emilia would lose her job.

At the moment, as she stared down at that phone log, she was more worried about losing her mind. She didn't remember making those calls. And she couldn't have done them in her sleep since she hadn't been sleeping. She'd been lying awake every night, listening to that crying that wasn't Blue's. Whose crying did she hear? Why was it haunting her?

She could hear it now…as she lay in her bed. Like always, she wasn't sleeping. Adrenaline from the wedding hummed through her veins yet. Despite all her sleepless hours, she wasn't tired. So much had happened tonight. Penny and Woodrow had gotten married, and the ceremony had been beautiful—apparently no thanks to Emilia. And then Lars and Nikki had gotten engaged. She'd known it was coming, but still it had taken her by surprise. It was all happening so quickly. Everyone was moving on with their lives.

Everyone but her. She couldn't get beyond the past, beyond what had happened to her all those weeks she'd been held captive without her son. Maybe that crying she heard was her own.

She felt like crying now, as her world began to crumble around her. If she lost her job…

How would she support herself and her son?

If everyone considered her an incompetent wedding planner, would they also consider her incompetent as a mother?

Was she?

She shivered as she allowed the thought to cross her mind. A chill passed through her body along with it. No. She would do anything for her son—even get help. Most of her life she'd turned to her brother when she'd needed help, except for when she'd discovered she was pregnant. He'd been deployed then and unavailable. While he was in the country now, he was equally unavailable.

Of course if she called him, he would rush immediately to her aid. But she couldn't do that to him. He'd already worried about her enough. For weeks he'd thought she was dead. She didn't want him to worry about her ever again. So to whom could she turn?

Not Nikki. She couldn't expect or ask the newly engaged woman to keep a secret from her fiancé. She would have asked her boss, but Penny was gone now for a long honeymoon.

Penny had trusted Emilia to keep the business running while she was gone. She probably shouldn't have done that. Undoubtedly she wouldn't have, if Nikki had shared with her how much the maid of honor had had to step in to make sure the wedding ceremony ran smoothly.

Emilia glanced down at her phone again, but she couldn't see the screen through the tears blurring her vision. She wasn't crying because she was sad or scared, though. She was crying because she was mad. There was no way she would have called and canceled those wedding services.

Sure, the numbers were on her phone. She couldn't see them now—through her tears—but she had seen them. Just because her phone had been used didn't mean she had used it, though. Someone else must have.

But how?

How had they used her phone in the middle of the night? She would have seen them—would have known. Unless...

She heard a noise, one she barely heard over the sound of the crying. But it was there—the telltale creak of a door opening. Someone was breaking into the house. Like they had broken in before?

Nightmares?

What the hell had Lars been talking about? Dane

didn't have nightmares. Sure, sometimes he woke up in a cold sweat with his heart pounding so hard it felt like his ribs might break.

But he was never able to remember what he'd been dreaming about, or if he'd been dreaming at all. He'd probably just been reliving some of those missions. Or maybe even things that had happened before that.

Like identifying his adoptive parents' bodies in the morgue after the terrible car accident that had ended their lives. He'd barely been eighteen at the time.

He hadn't thought about that in years, until that day he'd gone to the morgue to identify Emilia Ecklund's body.

But it hadn't been Emilia's. Just as he had that night, he expelled another ragged breath of relief that it hadn't been her. He had been relieved for Lars. His friend had already been in agony worrying about her. If he'd lost her forever…

Lars would have never forgiven himself.

But Dane had also been relieved for himself. He'd wanted to meet the young woman whose photo he'd been using as the screen saver on his cell phone. Of course he'd only been doing that so he would recognize the person for whom he'd been looking. Once she'd been found, he'd deleted it…

As his screen saver.

And yet he hadn't been able to force himself to send her photo to his recycle folder. He still had it on his phone—in its photo album.

Even though he'd seen her that day, looking beautiful in that pale blue dress that matched her eyes, he needed to see her again. So he reached out in the darkness, fumbling around for the cell sitting on the crate next to his king-size bed. Usually he loved having the extra space to sprawl out, like he hadn't been able to sprawl out all those months spent sleeping on cots. If they were lucky, they'd had cots. Sometimes they'd just had a hard floor or dirt.

Tonight his bed felt especially empty. He felt alone like he hadn't since he was kid. But he knew now that it was better to be alone like he'd been back then—with nobody to worry about, nobody to care about…

He'd already spent too much time worrying about Emilia Ecklund. Now he was worried again, especially after the newly engaged Nikki Payne had caught him alone.

Her concern furrowing her usually smooth forehead, she'd said, "Something's going on with Emilia."

"I know," Dane had readily agreed. "Lars is worried, too."

"Should we be worried?" she'd asked.

He'd shrugged then because he wasn't certain. Maybe she hadn't seen anything outside that window. Maybe she'd only banged into that doorframe like she'd told her brother because it had been dark and she'd been tired.

Nikki had told him about the other things—about her slipping up on her job—a job in which she had seemed to be taking pride. He doubted she would have messed that up purposely.

What the hell was going on with her?

He'd followed her when she'd left the chapel. He'd made certain she'd gotten safely inside her house with her son. But then he'd forced himself to drive away. She was fine.

Wasn't she?

He needed to see that picture. Not that seeing her

smiling face would make him feel any better. It usually made him feel worse, made his pulse quicken and his heart flip. But he didn't pull his hand away; he kept reaching for his phone. His fingers skimmed over cold metal, his gun. He always had it within reach, which had saved his life more than once.

That weapon wouldn't save him from Emilia, though. But how dangerous could she be?

She was his friend's sister. And unlike Lars, that meant something to Dane. That meant she was off limits.

And she had a baby.

Dane had no intention of being a father to anyone. He wouldn't make the mistake his adoptive father had. He wouldn't take on a responsibility he really didn't want. He wouldn't do to a kid what had been done to him.

No. Emilia Ecklund was no danger to him. But was she in danger?

The crate began to vibrate beneath his phone, and he finally found it. His screen lit up with the photo he had of her—because she was calling him. Lars had put her number in Dane's phone—just like he'd put his in her phone—in case she ever needed help and Lars wasn't available.

Feeling like he'd been sucker punched, he expelled a gasp of air. Then he pushed the button. "Hello?"

"Dane?" she asked in a raspy whisper.

A chill raced down his spine. "What is it?" he asked. "What's wrong?"

"I—I think someone's in the house," she whispered, her voice cracking with fear. "I heard the door open…"

He shivered again but kicked off the sheet that had tangled around his body. "I'm on my way," he promised. "Stay on the phone with me."

But the line clicked. Maybe she'd just been afraid that the intruder would hear her. Or maybe the intruder had already found her.

When he arrived at her house, Dane couldn't find her. Not that many minutes had passed since she'd called, but she was gone.

Maybe someone had dragged her through the front door that stood open. Or maybe she was hiding somewhere.

He hoped like hell she was hiding.

"Emilia…" he called out softly, not wanting to alert her intruder to his presence. But was his voice too low for her to hear him?

Because she did not answer.

He hoped that was only because she hadn't heard him. But as he stepped inside the house, a strange sensation passed through him. Maybe he was having one of Penny Payne's premonitions.

Because instinct warned him something bad had happened or was about to happen.

To him…

Emilia might not have heard him. But perhaps her intruder had.

For the second time that day, Penny stared at her reflection in a mirror. The first time she'd wanted to look beautiful. This time she wanted to look sexy.

A breeze fluttered through the white curtains, making them billow around the window. It carried the scent of hibiscus and the sea. While Woodrow had left it to her to plan their wedding, he'd taken charge of the honeymoon.

He'd found a beautiful beach house on a nearly deserted island. There were some other inhabitants, but she hadn't noticed them. She wasn't aware of anyone but her handsome groom. He was so tall. So fit. With short graying hair and kind, blue eyes. Not a bright blue like the Paynes', but a deep, soulful blue.

Woodrow had stepped outside for a few minutes. To give her time to get ready for their wedding night… But probably also to make a call. He wouldn't be able to stop himself from checking in with Nicholas Payne, from making sure his friend and former employee was managing the River City Police Department in the new chief's absence.

Penny had no desire to make calls. She had no desire for anyone but Woodrow. In the mirror, she could see how her face was flushed, her eyes bright.

Maybe that was embarrassment, though. She wore white now, a thin silk gown that skimmed her curves while leaving her shoulders bare. Would Woodrow find it sexy or ridiculous?

Because she knew her groom well, she smiled. She had no worries about how he would react when he saw her. But she was gripped by a sudden fear that chilled her skin despite that warm breeze. As she watched her reflection in the mirror, all the color drained from her face.

The door opened, but she didn't tense. She knew she wasn't the one in danger.

"Damn," a deep male voice remarked as a whistle hissed out with his breath. "I am a lucky man."

She was the lucky one.

He stepped closer—probably close enough to see her face—because then he dropped to his knees next to the chair at the vanity table.

"What is it?" Woodrow asked. "Who's in danger?"

His handsome face had turned pale, as well. "One of our kids?"

They weren't his kids or her kids. They were theirs, even the ones who weren't related at all to either of them. The orphans, the agents, the bodyguards...

They both loved and worried about them all.

She reached out and gripped his hand, and their matching wedding bands glinted in the light from the vanity table. She hadn't wanted diamonds, just simple gold. Stacy had designed a beautiful infinity pattern in yellow gold to represent their endless love.

But everything wasn't endless. Penny knew that too well.

"Who?" Woodrow asked again anxiously.

"Emilia..."

It was more than a feeling that she was in danger, though. It was a feeling that something bad had already happened. That no matter who they called to rescue her, that person would be too late to save her.

That person might be in danger, too—grave danger.

Chapter 5

Emilia had made a dangerous mistake. Instead of trying to get outside when she'd heard the front door open, she had grabbed Blue and headed up to the attic. This meant that she was trapped. She had no way out except past the intruder.

Then she'd called Dane, which had probably been another misstep. What if the intruder had heard her?

What if he knew where she was hiding now?

Fortunately her son was quiet, sleeping soundly in her trembling arms. He hadn't given away their presence.

But she might have.

Why had she called Dane?

Sure, she hadn't wanted to interrupt Nikki and Lars on the night they had just gotten engaged.

But why Dane?

She had the numbers of all Lars's friends. He'd given

her Cooper Payne's before he'd left for his last deployment. Cooper hadn't re-enlisted like the rest of his unit. He'd been home and able to help her.

If only she'd gone to Cooper instead of that sleazy lawyer.

She couldn't change the past, though. And Lars had made certain she had more than one man to call for help now. He'd given her the numbers of all his friends.

So why had she called only one man? Why had she trusted Dane, a man his own best friend had admitted he didn't really know?

Sure, he'd claimed he was on his way. But where was he coming from? How far away was he?

And why hadn't she just called 911?

Because she hadn't wanted it on record if there was no intruder—if that creak had only been in her head—like the crying.

What if she was losing her mind?

Why would she trust Dane Sutton to keep her secret? She couldn't even trust that he was really coming. There hadn't been just that one creak. After she'd heard the door open, she'd heard other noises—footsteps on the stairs, heading up to the second floor, to her bedroom and Blue's.

Was someone after her son?

She fumbled around in the darkness of the attic space, trying to find the cell phone she'd dropped. She hadn't imagined all that, the creak of the door and on the steps. She needed to call the police. She couldn't wait for Dane any longer.

But then she noticed the silence. It was eerily quiet. There were no sounds, not from the house or anything outside. Usually one of the branches of the trees hanging over the house brushed across the roof. But not now. Not even a cricket chirped.

Had she imagined it all? Was there no one inside? Of course that didn't mean that no one had been inside, just that he'd left. Maybe he hadn't been looking for Blue or her at all. Maybe he'd only been searching for her phone to make more of the late-night calls.

She expelled a shaky breath of relief. She and her son were alone. She could bring him downstairs and settle him back in his bed. But then a door creaked—the attic door. As it opened, a light flashed, the beam shining straight into her eyes.

Nearly blinded, she squinted and tried to peer around the beam. A hulking shadow loomed behind the light. But that wasn't what frightened her the most; it was the fact that the flashlight from which that beam came wasn't held in a hand. It was mounted to the barrel of a gun that was pointed directly at her.

A scream tore from her throat.

"Hey, hey!" a deep voice shouted. And the beam shifted, shining on the chiseled features of the man who held the gun. "It's me," he said. "Dane."

Instead of slowing, her heart raced faster. She could feel Blue's heart beating fast, too, as he cried. Her scream had startled him. He wasn't easily soothed. It was hard to comfort her son when she was still so scared.

Her hand trembled as she ran it up and down his back. "It's okay…" But she wasn't sure about that.

Something snapped, then light from an overhead bulb illuminated the rafters and wood of the unfinished attic space. "Are you really okay?" Dane asked as he holstered his weapon. "You're shaking."

As if afraid that she might drop her son, he reached out and took the crying child from her.

"What are you doing?" she asked.

Lars had remarked more than once that Dane Sutton couldn't stand kids. Why was he cradling hers so gently in those huge hands of his?

"You called me, remember?" Dane asked. "You said someone had broken into your house…" His voice trailed off and he stared at her oddly.

"What?" she asked. "Didn't you see anyone?"

He shook his head. "No. And the door jamb wasn't broken."

"No. They didn't break in," she murmured. "I just heard the door open."

He kept staring at her. She'd known his eyes were brown but she saw now, with the light glinting in them, that they were more golden than dark. "You didn't lock it?" he asked.

She shook her head. "No. No. Of course it was locked. I made sure that it was."

Hadn't she?

She reached out for her son, but her hands were still shaking. Not with fear now but with nerves.

His intense stare unnerved her.

"You can give him back to me," she said.

Blue had stopped crying, practically the moment Dane had taken him away from her. And he stared, too, up at the man holding him. His pale eyes were wide with awe. He should have been used to big men with his uncle being nearly the size of a giant. But maybe it wasn't Dane's size that awed him. It was his aura.

She felt it, too. She'd felt it the very first time she'd

met him. He was a man of power and control. A man who let little get to him or get in his way.

"I have him," he said, as if he didn't trust her with her own son. He turned and headed toward the stairs. "These steps are steep and narrow," he said.

"I know." She'd climbed them in such haste and fear that she'd nearly tripped up every one of them. She'd been carrying her sleeping son, so she'd been careful with him. "I brought Blue up here and never woke him," she said.

Dane ignored her and easily descended the narrow stairs. For such a big man, he moved silently, almost gracefully. He wasn't the one she'd heard walking around the house earlier. Heck, she'd thought she was alone when the door had opened, and he'd shone his light and his gun in her face.

"Which room is his?" he asked. He didn't wait for her answer before carrying her son right into the nursery.

She started to regret calling him. For one, he still didn't hand her son back to her. He cradled the baby in his palms. But maybe he forgot he held him since he wasn't looking at the child.

He kept looking at her. And that was the other reason she thought she shouldn't have called him. He kept staring at her so oddly, his caramel eyes darkening with his intensity.

She shivered and said, "Stop looking at me like that…"

"Like what?" he asked.

"Like I'm losing my mind." Because if he kept looking at her like that, she might start believing that she was. "And I'm not," she insisted, but her voice cracked on a note that sounded curiously close to hysteria.

Blue tensed and his little face screwed up as if he

were about to cry again. But Dane rocked him a little and murmured, "Shhh, little guy, it's all right."

Emilia shook her head and said, "It's not all right. Nothing's all right."

Dane's eyes darkened even more with anger. And finally he put down her son, laying him in his crib. Then he turned toward her and, despite the anger in his eyes, gently brushed his knuckles over the bruise on her shoulder.

"What's going on?" he asked. "Who's hurting you?"

She shivered even though his touch heated her skin and her blood. "I don't know."

"You don't know who's hurting you?" he asked skeptically, like he thought she was lying to protect someone. And she realized his anger was for that someone. "You don't know who did this to you?" He skimmed his fingertips gently over her shoulder again.

"No, no," she said as she realized what he was thinking. "Nobody bruised me." Again. She'd had her share of them from being held hostage back when she'd actually had the energy to fight. But then she'd gotten so sick.

If Lars and Nikki hadn't rescued her when they had…

She wouldn't have survived.

"You really ran into a door?" he asked, his deep voice full of doubt now.

She knew what it sounded like. But she wasn't involved with anyone. She might never be brave enough to trust anyone ever again.

"Yes," she said. "But it was because I heard crying—"

"Blue," he said and glanced down at the quiet baby.

She shook her head. "It wasn't Blue. I keep hearing this crying…" Tears stung her eyes. "But it's not Blue."

"A bad dream?" he asked.

"I'm awake," she said. "I feel like I'm always awake now."

A look passed through his eyes. It wasn't judgment. It was recognition. Did he also have trouble sleeping?

Lars wouldn't talk about his deployments—didn't want to share what were probably terrifying details with her. But she could imagine that whatever he and the other members of his unit, like Dane, had seen might haunt them.

What was her excuse?

Sure, she had been through some trauma, but only for weeks. Not months like Dane and her brother had endured. She doubted Dane would be any more willing to talk about their deployments than Lars was.

So she continued, "And even though I'm awake, I keep hearing that crying, but I can't figure out where it's coming from."

He was staring at her again like he suspected it was all in her head.

"Stop," she implored him.

He lifted his shoulders. "Stop what?"

"Stop looking at me like that." Tears stung her eyes. And now she knew where the crying was coming from, as a sob slipped through her lips. She was crying now.

And those big hands that had cradled her son so gently closed around her now, drawing her against his chest. "Shhh," he murmured, like he had to her son. His strong hands moved over her back now, sliding up and down as if petting her.

She found herself instinctively burrowing closer, seeking his warmth and his strength. He was so big. So strong. She felt safe.

He made her feel other things—things that frightened her even more than the crying and the creak of that door opening.

"It's okay," he murmured.

Like she had before, she protested, "No, it's not." Her words were muffled in his shirt and the hard muscles of his chest. It wasn't all right what she was feeling now—in his arms—the tingling, the heat, the desire.

She shivered, and his arms slid around her, holding her closer. Her heart pounded madly.

What she'd been thinking wasn't all right, either. That she was going crazy. But maybe she was crazy to be attracted to this man, who might be incapable of feeling anything at all according to his best friend.

Or maybe she was just overwhelmed. She hadn't dared share her problems with anyone yet. She hadn't wanted to burden them or make them think that she was losing her mind. It was different with Dane. Maybe with her voice muffled and her face pressed against him, she could tell him everything. She could let it all pour out.

Everything that had happened. Finding windows open that she swore she had closed. Hearing that door creak open. Finding those calls in the log on her phone—calls she would have never placed.

And when she finally lifted her face from his chest, his shirt was soaked with her tears. And his face was unreadable. Did he believe her?

Or did he think she was crazy?

He was crazy. Dane should have left the minute he'd found her and the baby safe in the attic. Then he wouldn't have held the baby.

Then he wouldn't have held her.

The night breeze blew through his damp shirt, chilling his skin. But that was good. He'd gotten too hot holding her, too edgy. And her tears…

All those tears had done something to him. He'd felt like he was drowning in them, like he couldn't get a breath in lungs that had felt so tight, so heavy.

He drew in a deep breath now. That pressure didn't ease any. He had to go back in that house, had to see her again. The minute she'd finished pouring out her heart and her tears he'd hurried outside. He'd told her that he was going to check everything out and see if anyone had broken into her house.

But he already knew nobody had broken in. The lock of that open door had born no scratches or gouges from someone picking it. The jamb hadn't been broken. Nobody had forced their way into the house. And yet she swore someone had been inside, that she'd heard footsteps on the stairs and the hardwood floors.

Was it possible?

When he'd followed her home earlier, he'd watched her go inside juggling the baby, a diaper bag and something that had looked more like a suitcase than a purse. A laptop bag? She'd had her hands full. She might not have closed the door tightly behind them.

But he'd sat there long enough, watching her house, that if it hadn't been shut tightly, it would have blown open then. Wouldn't it?

And what about the crying she claimed to hear that wasn't Blue's?

He tilted his head and listened. Maybe a neighbor had a crying baby. But while Lars had been living in the little bungalow, Dane had met the closest neighbors. An older couple lived on one side and a single man on the other. He doubted either had a baby staying with them.

He heard nothing now. Not even the sound of a TV despite the glare of one showing behind a window of the adjacent house.

Shining the flashlight on his gun barrel, he walked around the house. Like at the chapel, he found wood chips disturbed beneath some of the windows. Had someone been standing in them, looking inside? Watching her?

He shivered and it had nothing to do with his damp shirt. His blood was chilled now. He had that eerie sensation he'd had when he'd walked through the open door earlier into a dark house.

The house had been dark then.

But he'd watched her turn on every light before he'd driven away. She had had every light in the house shining as if she'd been checking to make sure no intruders lurked in any of the rooms. And she'd told him earlier, when she'd been sobbing against his chest, that the minute she'd heard the door open, she'd grabbed her son and headed up the attic steps. She'd had no time to turn off all those lights. Unless she'd done it earlier, after he'd left.

Somehow he suspected she hadn't. As spooked as she was, she probably left the lights on all the time and locked the windows. When he'd walked through the house, he'd noticed that all the windows had been unlatched, like the door had been unlocked.

When she'd turned on those lights earlier, she'd checked the windows. That was one reason he'd driven off because it had looked as though she'd made certain her house was secure. So why would that door have been open and the windows now unlocked?

The short hairs on the nape of his neck rose and the skin between his shoulder blades tingled. He felt like someone was watching him now. When he glanced up, he saw her clearly illuminated in the light behind her that she must have just turned on.

Like she'd turned him on when she'd clung to him, her face buried in his chest. Every word she'd spoken had sent a warm breath whispering across his skin.

He'd never been as aware of another person as he'd been aware of her. He hadn't just felt her breath on his skin; he'd felt her breathing, as her breasts had pushed against his chest. He'd felt her fear in every fast beat of her heart. And he'd felt her sobs in the moisture of her tears and in the breaks of her sweet voice.

And she'd wondered why he'd kept staring at her. Since finding her in that attic, looking so terrified, he hadn't been able to look away from her. He was staring again, he knew it. But he couldn't look away now, either.

With her blond hair glowing and her luminescent skin, she looked like an angel. He'd never seen a more beautiful woman. Or a more frightened one.

One hand was pressed over her mouth, as if holding in a scream. The other was pressed over her breast, probably her heart. She still wore that dress from the wedding, the pale blue that exactly matched the color of her wide eyes. Her thick black lashes fluttered up and down, breaking their locked stare.

He backed up away from the house. Away from her. But he couldn't leave even though every instinct was warning him to run from her.

Instead he walked around the house and back through that open door. She was holding it, though, and as soon as he stepped through it, she closed it behind him.

"What did you find?" she asked anxiously.

Not his mind. He must have lost that, since he'd ignored his instincts for the first time in his life. What would that cost him?

Only time would tell if it would be his life or something else…

Something he'd never risked before.

"What is it?" she asked, reaching for him. Just her fingers clasped his arm, but it felt like she had reached inside him.

He shook his head. He couldn't tell her what was really bothering him: her. Not when he was the one she'd called.

"Why?" he asked.

Her eyes glistened with the threat of more tears. "Why? I have no idea. I don't know why someone would break into the house. Why they would use my phone to make those calls…" She blinked furiously. "Why they would play that…crying…"

Was that what it was? A recording?

"Nobody broke in," he told her. "None of the locks was tampered with."

"But I heard the door open."

"It must not have been locked."

"I locked it," she said. And her voice was sharp now, decisive.

"You had your hands full," he said, "with the baby, his bag, yours…"

Her beautiful eyes narrowed with suspicion. "How do you know that?"

He shrugged off his slip. "Just assumed."

"How?" she asked. "You don't have a baby."

"No, I don't." And he had no intention of ever having one. With anyone.

"Then how?"

He sighed as he acknowledged that he was busted. "I followed you home from the chapel."

Her mouth opened on a soft gasp of shock.

So he hurriedly explained, "I'm not stalking you. I promised your brother I would watch you at the wedding, make sure you stayed safe."

"Oh," she said. "That's why…" Her chin lifted, and she bristled with pride now. "Then you know I locked the door and the windows." She gestured toward the one through which she'd seen him. "And now they're unlocked."

He nodded. "I did see you check the windows, but not the door." The solid steel exterior door had no window, so he hadn't been able to see through it.

"I locked it, too," she insisted.

"So how did someone get in?" he asked. "Does anyone else have a key?"

"Only Lars."

And her brother would give up his life for hers— nearly had. He would never do anything to upset her. Purposely. Asking Dane to watch over her might have upset her, though—or at least pricked her pride.

Her brow furrowed now. "But I lost my keys a couple of weeks ago. Well, just misplaced them."

"What happened?" he asked.

"I left them at the coffeehouse near the chapel. One of the baristas called me a couple of hours after I left and told me a customer had found them under a table."

"Do you mean you called them?" he asked. "How would they know they were yours?"

"The key for the office has the name of the White Wedding Chapel on it with the phone number," she explained. "I hadn't even realized I'd lost them. And…"

"What?" he prodded.

"I hadn't sat down at a table," she said. "I got a latte to go and was only near the counter."

He felt like he'd been punched again. "Someone could have taken them."

"But why return them?" she asked.

"If you'd known they were stolen, you would have changed the locks," he explained. "This way they had time to make another set and get yours back so you'd only think you'd misplaced them."

"But why?" she asked. "Why would someone want a set of my keys? Why would they come in here and not take anything? Just use my phone and…"

"Play that recording?" he prodded when her voice trailed off.

Her breath caught. "A recording? You think it's a recording?"

"Could be."

"But why? Why keep playing it all night, every night?" she asked.

He'd never been captured, but he knew guys who had been—like Gage Huxton, another Payne bodyguard. "Sleep deprivation is a form of torture," he said. "It's used to break someone."

That was why he had sworn, at the start of every mission, that if something went bad, he would not be taken alive.

"Break?" And her voice did again when she breathed the word. Her eyes were wide, the circles so dark beneath them. She had not been sleeping for a while. "Why?"

"Someone's trying to drive you crazy."

She expelled a shuddery breath. "I'm afraid it's starting to work."

* * *

The plan had been working. Emilia Ecklund was nearing her breaking point. All the crying wasn't just the recording; it was her, too.

But then she'd called someone tonight. And Dane Sutton had rushed to her aide. That had nearly messed up everything. What if he'd arrived a little faster?

The whole plan could have been destroyed.

The guy was big and armed—like her brother. It might have been better had her brother showed up. He would have been more concerned about her, about how distraught she was and he probably wouldn't have checked out the house as thoroughly as this guy had.

What had he found?

Had he seen any footprints? Any evidence that the sounds weren't just in Emilia's beautiful head?

Dane Sutton was a problem. A problem they would have to eliminate.

Chapter 6

Did Dane really believe her? Or was he only humoring his best friend's crazy sister? His face was so expressionless that she couldn't tell. He looked like a statue or a bust carved from granite. His features were that chiseled, his eyes that unreadable.

His stare made her shiver. But she hadn't been cold earlier—when he'd held her. Then she'd been hot, her body tingling with awareness. With attraction.

She sighed. "Yes, it's definitely working." She was losing her mind. She couldn't be attracted to her brother's enigmatic friend.

"You're too strong to let that happen," Dane said.

Despite her fears and nerves and sleeplessness, she laughed. "Strong?"

She had been going out of her mind.

"You survived weeks in captivity," he said.

If she'd been stronger, she would not have been in captivity. She would have freed herself instead of having to wait to be rescued.

"You survived nearly losing your son," he added.

A pang struck her heart, filling it with the fear she'd felt then when she'd thought she would never see her baby again. She glanced toward the stairs and thought of running up them, of grabbing up Blue from his crib, where he'd fallen back to sleep.

He was sleeping. He was safe. He was here—with her.

"I survived that," she agreed. "Once. I can't go through that again. If all of this—" she gestured at the windows and the door that she'd locked but the intruder had still managed to get through "—is so that I lose him."

"What makes you think that's what this is about?" he asked.

She shrugged. "You asked me earlier, why. That's the only reason I can think of. Blue is who matters most to me."

For once his face wasn't quite that unreadable. An expression passed through eyes that were once again a lighter shade of caramel. Skepticism.

She bristled and pulled her fingers from his arm. Why had she been hanging on to him? She hadn't even realized that she had been, that she'd been clutching at him like he was her anchor in a storm of fears and self-doubts.

But what she didn't doubt was her love for Blue. "I love my son," she said. "He matters most to me."

"You contacted an adoption lawyer," he said. "You must have been thinking about giving him up."

She sucked in a breath as pain and regret jabbed at her heart. "I was pregnant and alone and scared." But it was no excuse. She never should have made that call.

"So was my biological mother," he mused. "She gave me up. Actually she left me in a school bathroom."

"You're adopted?" she asked with surprise. Had Lars ever told her that? He'd said Dane didn't like kids, that he'd never wanted a family. Was it because he'd never had one?

He nodded.

He was what Blue might have become if she'd gone through with the adoption. Cold. Expressionless.

"I wouldn't have given him up," she insisted. "I knew the minute I'd made the appointment that it was a mistake." Guilt over making that call weighed heavily on her. She hoped Blue never learned what she'd done, what she'd momentarily considered.

"But you still met with the lawyer," Dane pointed out. It was as if he was determined to think the worst of her.

It shouldn't have mattered to her what he thought of her at all. But for some reason it did. Maybe because he was Lars's best friend or maybe because of how she'd felt in his arms.

Both safe and unsettled.

"I tried to break the appointment," she explained. "But he threatened to call the police or Social Services for a safety check if I didn't meet and talk with him. He said he needed assurances that I wasn't going to hurt myself like some young pregnant women do." Then he had hurt her instead. Stolen her baby.

Dane nodded, and yet she wasn't certain he really believed her.

"I'm telling the truth," she insisted and now frustration overwhelmed her. She needed him to believe her. "About everything. About my baby. About the crying. The calls."

"When I asked you why earlier," he said, "I was asking why you called *me*."

Her lips parted with a gasp, and heat rushed to her face. "Lars gave me your number. He said that I should call you if I needed help and he was…"

"If he was unavailable," Dane supplied the words she'd been unwilling to admit. "He would have come if you'd called him tonight. And he probably would have gotten here faster than I did."

"You got here fast," she assured him. His arrival had probably scared off her intruder.

"I wasn't fast enough to catch whoever you heard in the house," he pointed out. "Lars might have caught him."

She shook her head. "I'm not even sure if he and Nikki went home tonight or if they're out somewhere celebrating their engagement." She hoped they were out somewhere celebrating. They both deserved to.

He nodded. "That's true. They might not be home. It's good you called me instead. But Lars will want to know what's going on."

She reached out again and grasped his arm, which was so muscular, so hard, as if he really was carved from granite. "No, my brother can absolutely *not* know."

"Emilia—"

"You know Lars." Probably better than Lars knew him. "He can't know," she insisted. "He would overreact and move back in here. Or he would try to move me and Blue in with him and Nikki."

"That would be a good idea," Dane said.

"It would be a terrible idea," she said and cringed at the thought of her brother hovering protectively, like he had been since he'd found her. She had been relieved when he'd moved in with Nikki, until the crying started.

But she wasn't thinking of just herself. She didn't want him to put his life and his happiness on hold because of her. "He and Nikki just got engaged. They need this time alone—to get to know each other better."

"It was too fast," he said.

"No!" she said, jumping to their defense as they had to hers. As they would now if she told them she needed their help. "That's not what I meant. They're perfect for each other." The only other couple as perfect was Penny and Woodrow.

His brow furrowed slightly. "But you said they need to get to know each other better."

"What I meant was that they deserve to enjoy each other without worrying about me. I've already caused them too much trouble." Regret overwhelmed her, but she blinked away the threat of tears. "They were nearly killed because of me. I don't want them in danger."

Finally his expression cracked as his mouth curved into a slight grin. "So you'd rather put me in danger."

Her face heated even more, burning with embarrassment. She pulled her hand away from his arm again. Maybe it was touching him that rattled her brain so that she didn't know what she was saying. "Of course not. That's not what I meant."

"It's okay," he said. "I'm used to being in danger. And so is Lars."

"I know," she said. "But I don't want him to know. I don't want to put him through anything else."

Dane's face wasn't expressionless now as it twisted into a grimace. "Lars is my best friend. I don't want to keep anything from him."

"That's why you need to," she said. "You need to protect him."

"I need to protect you," Dane said.

She wanted to argue that she could take care of herself. But she couldn't. She didn't have a gun like he had. She had regained some of her strength, but she still wasn't strong enough to fight off an intruder. She needed Dane's protection.

Just his protection.

A ragged sigh slipped through his lips along with a curse.

She flinched, hating that she was becoming a burden to him. "I'm sorry…"

"You're right," he said almost begrudgingly. "I need to protect Lars, too."

Dane needed to protect his friend—from himself. If Lars knew his sister was in danger again, he would track down the person responsible and kill him. Dane couldn't take the risk of his best friend winding up dead or in prison.

And for some reason, Dane wanted to be the one to keep Emilia safe. He wanted to be the one to find out who was trying to hurt her. And he wanted to hurt that person—himself.

"I'm sorry," she said again, her voice soft as tears pooled again in her beautiful blue eyes.

He struggled to draw a breath into lungs that felt suddenly very constricted, as if there was a heavy pressure on his chest. "It's not your fault," he said.

"How do you know that?"

Because she was sweet. And innocent. And good.

Or at least that was what her brother thought. Maybe

Lars was wrong about her, though. Maybe there was more to Emilia Ecklund than anyone knew.

After all, she had a child and her brother hadn't even known she was dating anyone. Was she seeing someone now? Someone who might be trying to scare her?

He shrugged. "I guess I don't know that," he admitted. "All I know about you is what your brother has told me." And that was a lot. He had constantly bragged about his little sister.

Maybe that was why Dane had felt a connection with her. Before they had ever met, he'd felt like he'd known her. But he actually only knew what Lars knew.

"I'm sorry," she said again. But this time she was smiling. "Lars talks too much."

Dane nodded. "Definitely."

Would Lars speak to him again after Dane carried out his plan to keep both him and Emilia safe?

"You don't," she said.

He'd never really had anyone to talk to before. "That's probably why people tell me things," he said. "They know their secrets are safe with me."

He'd kept secrets for Lars. But could he keep secrets *from* Lars?

"You really won't tell him anything?"

He shook his head. "Not until I catch whoever's messing with you."

"How will you do that?" she asked.

In order to catch whoever was sneaking into her house, he only had one option. "I'll have to move in with you."

Her eyes widened, and she gasped. "That won't work."

"You can't stay here alone," he said. "Not with what's been going on."

"I can change the locks."

"And tip off the person that you're onto them? We'll never catch him then." Not that they'd catch him this way, either—with a man living in the house. But the only way Dane could make sure nothing happened to Emilia or her son was to be with her at all times.

"Lars will go ballistic."

Dane nodded. "Yes, he will. But we don't have another option, not if I'm going to catch whoever's doing this to you. I have to stick close to you."

"And everyone will wonder why you're doing that," Emilia said. "They'll realize something's going on. And they'll worry about me."

They were already worried about her. But because Dane kept secrets, he didn't share that. He also didn't want to upset her or make her feel worse than she already did.

But he had a solution to everyone's problems—everyone's but his. "Not if they think the only reason I'm sticking close to you is because I've fallen for you."

She laughed. "I must be going crazy. I thought you just said…" She laughed again, albeit a little hysterically. "Maybe you're the crazy one. Nobody's going to believe that."

"We'll make them believe it."

Her mouth stayed open, but her laughter dried up. Her eyes huge, she stared at him. Then she stammered, "H-how will we make them…?"

He moved closer to her, but she stepped back. And her eyes widened even more. He reached out and skimmed his fingertips along her jaw.

She shivered and whispered, "How?"

"Like this," he murmured and he lowered his head to hers.

* * *

When Lars stepped into the Payne Protection Agency conference room, everyone fell silent for a few long, awkward moments. He narrowed his eyes and glanced around the room—at his boss and coworkers—all of them friends. What the hell was going on?

Then a slow clap began, echoing throughout the room. Cole stood up, put his fingers between his lips and let out a shrill whistle. Lars wasn't sure why they were applauding, but he took a bow anyhow.

Cooper, at the head of the conference table, shook his head as if disgusted. But his mouth was curved into a slight grin. "Hey, since Romeo showed up, we can start the meeting now."

"Juliet isn't here," Manny murmured. He must have been referring to Nikki.

"She's checking on the wedding chapel while her mom's on her honeymoon," Lars explained. And he knew why. She didn't trust his sister right now.

Emilia was too distracted. What the hell was going on with her?

Had Dane had a chance to talk to her?

Lars settled onto the empty chair next to his best friend. But Dane didn't meet his gaze. He didn't even glance at him during the meeting Cooper led. The boss discussed assignments, which weren't in abundance at the moment. He was still building his business, and this was fine with Lars. This way, he had more time to spend with his fiancée as well as to check on his sister and nephew.

Since the night he'd gotten engaged, he hadn't had much time to look up Emilia and Blue, though. The past couple of days had passed in a blur of passion with Nikki.

But despite how happy he was, Lars was worried about Emilia.

He'd asked his friend to watch out for her during the wedding, which he had. But had Dane talked to her? Had he found out what was bothering her?

Lars wasn't the only one concerned about his sister. Nikki was trying to protect him, but he knew how she'd stepped in to save her mother's wedding ceremony. And now she was worried enough that she had skipped a bodyguard meeting to check on the wedding planning business.

What was wrong with Emilia? She loved Penny Payne; she wouldn't have consciously done anything to derail the wedding.

As preoccupied as he was with thoughts of his sister, Lars didn't realize the meeting had concluded—until Dane stood and headed toward the door without a word.

"Hey," he called out. But before he could scramble out of his chair, a big hand settled on his shoulder and shoved him back down onto the seat.

"What the hell's going on?" Cooper asked him. "Where is my sister really?"

"At the wedding chapel," he said.

Cooper snorted. "Yeah, right. Mom's been trying all Nikki's life to get her to help out at the chapel. You can't expect me to believe that. Did she come to her senses and dump you already?"

Lars snorted now. "That will never happen."

"She'll never come to her senses?" Cooper asked and shook his head as if disgusted. But it was clear now that he was just teasing.

"She'll never dump me," Lars said. "She really is checking up on the wedding chapel."

Cooper narrowed his eyes speculatively.

"Hey, she and I have a wedding to plan." And it couldn't happen a moment too soon for Lars. He wanted to make sure that Nikki didn't actually come to her senses and dump him. She could do so much better than him.

"You have some time to make those plans," Cooper said, and now his brow furrowed with concern. "Until we pick up some more cases."

"We will," Lars assured him.

"Hope the guys don't abandon ship," Cooper said, "because I can't keep them busy enough."

Lars glanced around and realized they were now alone in the conference room. Not just Dane but everyone else had left, too. "Don't worry," he assured his friend. "We'll be busy again soon."

Cooper nodded, but from the furrow between his dark brows, he didn't look convinced. "Will you talk to them?"

"Oh, I intend to," Lars said. He most especially wanted to talk to Dane, who curiously seemed to be avoiding him. Why?

After a short truck ride to Dane's apartment, Lars knocked on his door. "What the hell's going on with you?" he asked when Dane opened up.

Dane didn't even blink, just stood in the doorway staring at him. He held the handle of the door and the jamb on the other side, blocking Lars's entrance.

"What do you mean?" he asked.

"I asked you to check on Emilia for me and I haven't heard a word from you. I even came by here last night, but you weren't home." And because there was something furtive about Dane blocking his entrance, Lars pushed aside his friend and forced his way inside.

It wasn't much of an apartment really. It was a studio loft in an old warehouse. If not for Emilia, Lars might have rented a place like that himself, but he'd wanted to have room for his sister to stay with him. Now she was staying alone with her son.

And from the clothes overflowing Dane's duffel bag, it looked like he was packing to leave. "Where the hell are you going?" Lars asked.

Dane had tried to quit once. Now that there was less work at the agency, had he decided to leave?

"I'll be at the same place I was last night when you came by," Dane remarked.

Lars waited, but of course his stoic friend didn't freely offer any information. He had to prod him. "And where was that?"

"Emilia's."

Alarm squeezed Lars's heart. "So she is in danger!"

"No, she's not."

Lars tensed. "Then why else would you be moving in with her?" In addition to the duffel bag, there were boxes. "Why did you stay there?"

A thought immediately came to his mind. But he pushed it aside. No. Not Dane...

"She must be in danger," Lars insisted. "She's not been herself at all. That's why Nikki went to the wedding chapel instead of the meeting. She wanted to make sure Emilia was handling everything all right."

"If she's been a little distracted lately, it's my fault," Dane said.

Lars turned away from the bag and boxes to study his friend's expressionless face. "Why the hell would that be your fault?"

"Because she and I have been seeing each other."

Lars laughed. His friend had to be kidding. Dane had that weird sarcastic sense of humor. Fortunately Lars usually found him funny.

"I'm not kidding," Dane said. "We've been dating for a while now."

"No!" Lars exclaimed in anger. It wasn't possible. "You're joking."

Dane shook his head. "No. We've just been keeping it quiet because we didn't know for sure it was going anywhere."

Apparently it was going—with boxes and a bag of clothes—to Lars's house. Well, the house he'd rented.

"You're lying!" he growled, refusing to accept the betrayal.

Dane shook his head.

"You're going to wish you were lying," Lars threatened. "Or dead."

He couldn't believe that Dane—of all people—would take advantage of Emilia like this, when she was vulnerable.

"It's true," Dane said. "We've been seeing each other for weeks. And it's gotten serious. That's why I'm moving in with her."

"No!" Lars exploded in fury. "You're not going to be able to move at all once I get done with you." And he swung.

Chapter 7

"No!" Emilia screamed. But she was too late.

Her brother's fist connected with his best friend's jaw. A blow like that would have felled a lesser man. But Dane didn't even stumble back. He just shook his head as if a fly had landed in his hair.

Not that he had much hair, since the dark strands were buzzed so short. She had run her fingers over it the other night when he'd kissed her. Her skin tingled as she remembered the softness of his hair and the hardness of his body as it had pressed against hers.

Even though that kiss had happened a couple of nights ago, she could still taste him on her lips, still feel the sculpted hardness of his mouth moving over hers.

And the heat, it flashed through her now, like it had then. The desire overwhelming her.

But that had been one-sided. He'd kissed her, but only

briefly before lifting his head and stepping back. "We'll have to get used to doing that," he'd said. "If we're going to fool your brother."

It looked like he had fooled Lars all by himself. She had left Blue with Nikki and come to Dane's apartment to tell him she'd go along with his plan. But she could see now what a bad idea it had been, how it would drive a wedge between men whose friendship had helped them survive war.

"What are you doing here?" Lars asked her, his eyes bright with anger.

"What the hell do you think?" Dane asked him. "We're seeing each other."

She opened her mouth to admit the truth, but if she told him they weren't dating, she would have to explain why Dane had lied about it because she'd asked him not to tell Lars about the intruder and the crying.

Before she could say anything, her brother spoke, his voice a roar of anger. "I won't allow it!"

"Why not?" she asked, his attitude piquing anger in her now.

"Because friends don't date friends' sisters."

She snorted. "You're a hypocrite. You're engaged to Cooper Payne's sister."

Lars's skin flushed. "That's different."

"Why?"

"Because Nikki isn't…"

"Isn't what?" she prodded when he trailed off. What was he unwilling to call her?

His face flushed a darker shade of red.

"What?" she persisted. "Nikki isn't fragile like I am?" She was so damn sick of his treating her like she was made of glass. What would he do if he learned that she'd felt like she was losing her mind—over that crying, over her phone being used to make calls she never would have made…

He would smother her with protectiveness.

"Nikki isn't *vulnerable*," Lars said, "like you are. And if Dane was truly my friend, he wouldn't take advantage of your vulnerability."

He was a better friend than Lars knew. He was willing to lie to Lars to protect him. And in lying to him, he was risking their friendship.

But perhaps it was she who was risking their friendship by asking Dane to lie. The way Lars was talking about her convinced her she'd done the right thing, though.

"I am not vulnerable," she told her brother. But she heard the hollow ring to her protest, too. She knew better than Lars just how helpless she'd been. Until Dane had come to her aid, she'd been worried she was losing her mind.

Now that she knew she wasn't, she felt strong again. "No one is taking advantage of me," she said. If anything it was the other way around.

She was using Dane's friendship with her brother, exploiting Dane's sense of duty and protectiveness. She knew that was the only reason he was helping her since it was in his nature.

That kiss the other night—and how quickly he'd pulled away from her—had proven to her that he did not feel the attraction she felt for him. He was only doing a favor for his friend.

His stupid, stubborn best friend.

"Emilia," her brother began, and along with the concern in his voice, there was condescension. Like he knew more than she did.

And when it came to Dane, maybe he did. But he had shared with her that the man had no emotions, that he didn't get attached to people. Perhaps that was because he was adopted or because he was incapable of feeling.

That didn't matter. She didn't want him to fall in love with her. She only wanted him to protect her. And Lars.

In order to shield Lars, they needed to pretend that their relationship was real. That they were romantically involved. If Lars didn't believe that, then he would know that the only reason Dane was staying with her was for her protection.

So she pushed her brother aside and approached his friend. She skimmed her fingertips along his jaw, which was slightly swollen from the blow Lars had delivered just as she'd appeared in the open door. Pitching her voice low and husky with concern, she asked, "Are you all right?"

He nodded. And his caramel eyes darkened to the color of espresso as he stared down at her. "I'm fine."

"I'm sorry my brother's an idiot," she said.

And the corner of Dane's mouth curled up into a slight grin. Maybe he was enjoying messing with his best friend. He did have a slightly warped sense of humor.

She felt sick lying to Lars, though. But it was for the best.

And maybe so was this. She rose up on tiptoe and pressed her lips to that red mark on Dane's jaw. Then he moved and brushed his mouth across hers.

Her skin heated, and her heart began to race. And she forgot why she'd kissed him. She could focus on nothing but the sensations rushing through her—the heat, the fire, the desire…

* * *

Desire rushed through Dane just as it had two nights ago when he'd been stupid enough to kiss her. That had been a dumb idea then—to try to get her more comfortable around him so that they could fool her brother.

But he'd been fooling himself. He hadn't kissed her for Lars that night. He'd kissed her for himself, because he'd been wanting to ever since his friend had sent him that damned photo of hers that had so captivated him.

She was so beautiful. And sweet and soft. Her lips had felt like silk beneath his. Today they felt like warm silk moving over his mouth, parting for him to deepen the kiss. That night he'd held on to his control—barely. But he'd had to pull away quickly. He'd had to step away from her.

And when he'd settled onto the couch a short while later, he'd had to open the window for the cold air to clear his head, to clear the desire away.

His control was slipping now as he deepened that kiss, as he dipped his tongue inside her sweet mouth. And his arms slid around her, pulling her closer—for just a moment—before she was ripped away from him.

He'd forgotten Lars was there until the big man tugged Emilia away from him. This time, when the meaty fist swung toward him, he ducked and caught it in his hand. And no matter how hard Lars struggled, he held it tightly.

"I let you have that first one," he told his friend. "Because I probably had it coming." He hated keeping secrets from his friend. But Emilia was right. If Lars knew she was in danger, he would lose his mind just like she'd feared she was losing hers. "But that's your only freebie."

"I should tear you apart," Lars threatened him.

He should—if he had any idea the thoughts that had

flitted through Dane's mind during that kiss. He wanted Emilia, and not just to protect her. He wanted her in a way he couldn't remember ever wanting anyone else.

"No!" Emilia exclaimed. "You're going to get the hell out of here until you can get yourself under control and accept that Dane and I have something special."

Secrets and lies. That was all they had. And Dane had to remember that. That kiss wasn't any more real than the one the other night. It was just to fool her brother, which had apparently worked.

Lars was furious—so furious he couldn't fight—not when Emilia pushed him toward the door. She slammed it closed in her brother's face and turned the lock. Then her breath shuddered out, and she trembled.

Dane wanted to reach for her again, wanted to comfort her. Hell, he just wanted to kiss her again. But when he approached her, she whirled around before he could touch her.

"He can't ever find out the truth!" she said, her voice trembling with emotion.

Dane blinked, surprised by her intensity. He'd rather have all that intensity—that passion—focused on him.

"You have to promise," she implored him, "that Lars won't ever find out we're lying to him. That no one will find out."

"Eventually he'll find out," Dane said. It was inevitable.

She shook her head. "No, no. Why do you think that?"

"Because I will find out who is gaslighting you and stop them," Dane said. "And then Lars will learn what's been going on this whole time." And he would no doubt hit Dane again for not being truthful with him.

"That doesn't mean he has to find out we lied to him," she said. "I don't want him to know."

"Then maybe we should tell him the truth now," Dane said. While their relationships could still be salvaged.

"I thought that for a moment," Emilia said. "But then he started talking about how vulnerable I am. He would go crazy protecting me. And he'd probably wind up losing Nikki." She shook her head. "No. I can't risk it. You're right. This is the only way."

"To pretend we're together?"

She nodded grimly. She didn't seem any more willing to really fall for him than he was for her. "Yes, but I don't want him to learn we're just pretending."

"Then what do we do once we catch whoever's after you? Stay together? Get married?" That was out of the question. Dane had no intention of staying with anyone. Ever.

He really should have quit Payne Protection when he'd had the chance.

"That's not me," he warned her. "I'm not that guy. I'm not your brother. I won't ever be getting married or having kids. I don't want anything to do with that life."

"I'm not proposing," she said indignantly. She had some of her brother's pride. "At least I'm not proposing that we stay together. I'm proposing that once we figure out who's been messing with me, we break up."

So she didn't intend to hold him to their fake relationship. He should have been relieved, but he wasn't. Instead he felt again like he was about to undertake his most dangerous mission yet.

Manny had been looking forward to some downtime. Since coming back to the States after his last deployment, he'd been under fire—on the job—and even off the job. Instead of finally being able to relax, he found himself helping move boxes from Dane's apartment to his truck.

"What's going on?" he asked as he slid the cardboard across the truck bed.

Dane shrugged. "I don't know what you mean."

"Well, where the hell are you moving?" That wasn't what he really wanted to know. That wasn't why he'd come over to talk to Dane. He'd come to warn him about an imminent threat.

"I'm moving into Lars's old place."

"But his sister lives there—oh." Now he fully understood the conversation he'd had earlier with Lars, which was the reason he had come to warn Dane. "Really? You and Emilia?"

Dane didn't say anything.

But Manny hadn't expected him to say much. And maybe he didn't need to. He remembered how he'd stared at the blonde through that nursery window just a couple days ago. There had been something there, something between them. More than Manny had realized.

Obviously more than Lars had realized.

Dane snapped his tailgate closed and jingled his keys in his hand. "Thanks for the help."

Manny had only carried a couple of boxes. Dane didn't have much stuff. None of them did—except maybe Cole. But then he didn't carry his stuff around with them. It was back at the home to which he had refused to return. None of them had much property because during their deployments, they'd learned to travel light.

No one had traveled lighter than Dane. He hadn't wanted stuff or people burdening him. Now he was moving in with a woman and her baby?

It didn't make sense. No matter how beautiful Emilia Ecklund was...

"Lifting these boxes isn't anything compared to what Lars just asked me," Manny said.

At the mention of their friend, Dane tensed and rubbed his knuckles across a bruise on his jaw.

Manny had already figured out what was wrong between his friends.

A woman...

He made a vow to himself to stay the hell away from them. He didn't need the drama all his friends had gone through. He didn't need love.

Dane didn't ask what their friend had asked him. But Manny continued anyway, "Lars just asked me to help him dispose of a body."

Dane didn't ask who. He obviously knew.

But still Manny told him. "Yours."

Chapter 8

Emilia's breath caught, trapped in her lungs. Her heart swelled with love. Not just for her son. But for the woman holding her son. This woman was going to be the sister Emilia had always wished she had.

Not that she didn't love and appreciate Lars. But he had always been so protective, so fatherly. With her mom being so sick, what Emilia had really needed was a more feminine presence in her life. Although an aunt had helped take care of their mom, Emilia hadn't wanted anyone to take her attention away from their mother then. Since losing her mother, she had longed for that presence, until now.

Not that Nikki Payne was all that feminine. She was more like her brothers than she was like her mother, Penny. But she looked maternal now as she cradled the baby in her arms, making faces at him until his laughter gurgled out.

"You are so good with him," Emilia remarked, joining them in her office in the basement of the chapel.

Despite being in the basement, the office had a wide window, high on the wall, like the nursery, and was painted a bright and sunny yellow like the bride's dressing room. It was also right next to Penny's. Other people might have had a problem working in such close quarters with their boss. But Emilia loved it. She only hoped it would last.

What other slipups of hers had Nikki found? As she turned toward Emilia, her brow furrowed with concern.

Or had Lars called her?

"Is it true?" the brunette asked her. "Have you really been secretly seeing Dane since shortly after your rescue?"

She wished. A secret romance sounded so much better than what she'd really been going through. She opened her mouth, but she couldn't reply. Lying to Lars had been for his own good—to protect him from his overprotectiveness.

But lying to Nikki…

It just felt wrong, especially with how much Emilia admired the woman and appreciated everything Nikki had done for her. If Emilia told her the truth, Nikki would tell Lars. She'd have to because Emilia wouldn't ask the woman to lie to her new fiancé. She wanted them to build their relationship on the trust Lars had worked so hard to win.

"I didn't think so," Nikki remarked.

She must have mistaken Emilia's hesitation for a no. But Emilia shook her head. "We are involved."

And that much was true. At least Emilia considered them involved. The man was protecting her child, her life and her sanity.

And those kisses...

Her face heated just thinking about them. The first kiss had jolted her, like she'd touched a live wire. But the sensation had passed quickly because he'd pulled away so fast. But that kiss in his apartment...

That had been hot and passionate.

And just a ruse to fool her brother.

Her face heated even more, with embarrassment over the fact that she'd momentarily lost herself in his embrace, that she'd believed his passion was real. But the only real passion in that kiss had been hers.

"Oh, no," Nikki murmured. "You really are into Dane Sutton."

Emilia had to suppress the protest that sprang instantly to her lips. She wasn't into the man; she barely knew him. Even his best friends barely knew him.

Nikki nibbled on her bottom lip for a moment while she stared at Emilia. "I don't know if that worries me more or less."

"You don't need to worry at all," Emilia said as she stepped closer to her almost sister-in-law. She held out her arms for her son. "And neither does Lars."

Nikki hesitated a long moment before passing the baby back into Emilia's arms. She didn't know if it was because the other woman didn't completely trust her to hold him—like Dane hadn't a couple of nights ago—or if she was just reluctant to release him.

Nikki was known for being tough and no-nonsense, with no interest in marriage or children. That was obviously changing, from the ring on the finger to the soft kiss she pressed on Blue's forehead while settling him into Emilia's arms.

"Lars will always worry about you," Nikki warned her.

"Because he feels responsible for me," Emilia said. "Mom shouldn't have made him promise to take care of me. He was just a kid himself when she got sick. It wasn't fair to him."

"She didn't need to make him promise," Nikki said. "He would have done it anyway—because he loves you so much."

Emilia couldn't argue that; her brother did love her. And she loved him. That was why she didn't want him to worry about her. She may have made that situation worse, though.

"I know," Emilia said. "But he needs to realize that I'm not that little girl he used to buy dolls for." He'd saved his money to purchase those dolls and he'd been so happy to give them to her that Emilia had never admitted she hadn't liked them. Because they'd been so pretty, she hadn't felt comfortable playing with them. They had reminded her of their mother—someone she could see and not touch.

Would Dane be like that?

"I've made some mistakes," she admitted. "But I am an adult. I can take care of myself." She wished.

Nikki was studying her as quietly and intensely as Dane had.

"What?" she asked. "Have I made any more mistakes around here?" She suspected that was why Nikki was at the chapel today instead of at the Payne Protection Agency. She'd wanted to check up on Emilia and make sure she wasn't ruining the business her mother had worked so hard to build.

Nikki shook her head. But she didn't specify that she wasn't checking up on Emilia. Or if she'd found nothing wrong.

Emilia wanted to tell her that she hadn't made those calls—that someone had used her phone. But if she told her that, everyone would be worried. Now she was the only one.

"I won't make any more mistakes," she promised.

Nikki tilted her head until her auburn curls brushed her shoulder. "I hope you're not making one now—with Dane."

So did she.

Instinct had Nikki reaching for her holster as she walked toward the black Payne Protection Agency SUV that was parked at the curb outside the chapel. She wasn't working a case. She hadn't been threatened.

But yet she had this strange feeling, this sensation that someone was watching her. She glanced around, looking for Lars. He was so worried about Emilia that he might have been lurking outside the chapel to keep an eye on her.

But as she glanced around the area, she didn't see Lars's truck. Or Dane's. Or even another Payne Protection Agency SUV.

And if Lars had been present, she would have felt it. Her skin would have tingled and heated. Her heart would have raced. Actually, her heart was beginning to beat harder as that strange feeling persisted.

Was this what Mom felt when she had one of her premonitions?

No. This feeling was different; it wasn't about anyone else. It was about her, like she was being watched. Even though she couldn't see it, Nikki suspected someone was outside the chapel. But was he watching her or Emilia?

She opened the driver's door and slid behind the wheel. She glanced into the rearview and side mirrors, looking for any movement inside the vehicles parked along the street. But nobody sat within any of them.

Maybe there wasn't any danger outside the chapel. Maybe the danger Nikki felt was inside—was Emilia herself. Was she really all right?

She had been making so many mistakes and acting so strangely. Had being captured and almost losing her son affected Emilia more seriously than they'd even realized?

Nikki intended to find out. But she didn't intend to let Lars know about her concerns. Like his sister had said, he already worried too much. And Nikki loved him too much to worry him anymore.

She would find out whatever the hell was going on with Emilia—on her own.

As Manny drove off in one of the agency's black SUVs, Dane shook his head. His friend was actually concerned that Lars might do something to him—something like kill him.

Yeah, right...

Sure, Lars was pissed. Dane couldn't blame him. He didn't have a sister—at least not one that he knew about, but he wouldn't want a guy like himself dating her if he did have one. But he doubted Lars would actually kill him.

Not that he wasn't in danger. But that danger came from whoever was stalking Emilia. Because he needed to find out who the hell that was, he headed back into his place for the things he hadn't wanted to pack in front of Manny. He needed the surveillance equipment he'd picked up.

He wanted to catch whoever was after Emilia. He would probably have to do that first on video before he could do it in person, though.

He also had to hurry to get to her house before she came home from work. With Nikki hanging out at the chapel, Emilia had been safe there. She wasn't safe at home—not alone.

Someone had been inside her place, even when she'd been home. He couldn't risk her being there alone. So he had to grab the box that he'd pushed behind the couch when Lars had shoved his way inside earlier.

If Lars had seen the equipment, he would have known something was up. Hell, he probably already did. He was just too mad right now to realize that Dane would never willingly move in with anybody. He'd already refused to share that house Lars had rented with him.

Dane preferred to be alone. It was what he was used to. What he was comfortable with. Just like he'd warned Emilia, he was never getting married. Never having a family.

He'd apparently wasted that warning, though. She hadn't been interested in him, just in making sure her brother never realized they'd lied to him. She wasn't a risk to his bachelorhood. Once he caught her stalker, he could come back to his apartment and return to being alone.

But when he stepped outside the door with the box in his hands, he realized he wasn't alone. It was so dark that he couldn't see them. He knew they were there. With the box in his hands, he was too slow to reach for his gun, though.

A bag dropped over his head.

He laughed—at first. This was what he and his friends had done to Lars. They'd had a "blanket" party because the other guys had wanted to know what the hell was going on with him. Dane was the only one he'd told about his sister missing. And Dane had been sworn to keep his secret, the same way Emilia had sworn him to keep hers.

And just like he had for Lars, he would keep his promise to her. So it didn't matter what the guys did to him; he wasn't going to talk.

So he didn't shout in protest. He said nothing at all.

And neither did they.

Which raised the super-short hairs on the nape of his neck. These guys weren't his friends. For one, Manny couldn't keep his mouth shut this long.

And for another, the punch that jabbed into his ribs was harder than the one Lars had thrown earlier. Whoever had grabbed him wasn't just messing with him.

This attack was real. The blows kept coming. At least two men held him while at least another two threw those punches. And kicks.

Dane struggled against the arms holding him. And he began to fight. He just hoped he hadn't realized the danger too late. He wasn't worried about himself.

He was worried about getting to Emilia and the baby—about making sure they were safe. He guessed he was being attacked now because he stood between Emilia and whoever had been terrorizing the young mother.

He reached for his holster, but he couldn't pull his weapon. If his assailants were his friends being too rough, he couldn't shoot one of them. Hell, he couldn't shoot without knowing who he was shooting. What if these were just some dumb street kids jumping him?

Then they were strong as hell.

He grunted and cursed with each blow. Then he increased his struggle. He shook off the guys holding him. But the bag stayed on his head. He couldn't see who he was fighting.

But that didn't stop him from fighting.

He kicked and swung his fists. And as he connected, he heard grunts and curses ringing out around him. Then he heard the telltale cock of a gun.

No. He wasn't fighting his friends.

And this wasn't just a warning.

This was a hit.

Somebody intended to take him out. Just out of their way? Was Emilia the real target?

Chapter 9

Had Dane changed his mind?

Emilia couldn't blame him, not with how her brother had reacted to the news of their fake relationship. Maybe he'd decided that protecting her wasn't worth losing a friend. She understood that.

What she didn't understand was his not telling her in person.

She'd waited for him at her house, and she'd been a jittery mess of nerves. She wasn't sure what had unnerved her more—worrying that the crying would start again or that Dane was really moving in.

But he hadn't.

Then she'd begun to worry about him. Even if he'd changed his mind, he would have told her. But he'd seemed committed to helping her, so much so that he'd taken a blow from Lars that he easily could have avoided.

No. She had to find him. Had to talk to him.

She couldn't bring the baby along when she had no idea what she might find, so she'd asked Nikki if she could watch him again just for a little while. Her sister-in-law-to-be had shown up in short order, almost as if she'd been unusually close.

Was Nikki watching her?

"Where are you going?" Nikki had asked.

She could have lied, could have said she had an errand to run instead.

"I—I need to help Dane decide what he can move in here," she'd stammered the explanation.

If he was moving in at all...

Nikki had chuckled. "Does Dane have an ugly recliner or poker table he wants to move in?"

Emilia had only been in his place once. Even after Lars had left, she'd been too distracted from Dane's kiss to take in much of her surroundings. It had seemed kind of empty to her, though. Like he'd already moved out.

So why wasn't he here?

She'd only shrugged in reply to Nikki's question. Then she'd hurried out to her car and driven quickly over to his place. His truck was parked at the curb outside the old warehouse building.

Earlier that day, when Lars had beaten her to Dane's place, she hadn't noticed the outside of the building. She shuddered now as she looked at the stark metal structure. She had spent weeks in a place like this. Of course the warehouse where Dane lived had been remodeled.

The one she'd been held captive in had still been abandoned—but for her and her captors. The floor had been bare and hard, the building filled with broken-down crates. There had been no furnace to dispel the dampness and the chill that had penetrated deep into her flesh and bones. And no air conditioning to cool her off once the fever had set in.

She'd nearly died in that place.

As she remembered that, her skin chilled again, goose bumps rising despite the light sweater she wore with jeans. That was all over. She'd been rescued. She wasn't going back to that place, that hellhole.

And yet she didn't feel reassured. She was scared that she might be in nearly as much danger if she walked into this warehouse. The door stood open, but no light spilled from inside.

It was dark.

But the truck was there. Where was Dane?

Her hand shook slightly when she reached for the handle of the driver's side door. But she forced herself to push it open. As she stepped out of her small SUV, her legs trembled beneath her.

It was eerily quiet. And dark.

She'd probably waited too long before calling Nikki. But she'd kept thinking Dane would show up. Or call…

But he hadn't.

Why not?

His truck was still packed. The street lamp illuminated the boxes in the bed of it. So if he'd changed his mind about moving in, wouldn't he have unpacked it? And if he was here, wouldn't there be at least one light on inside his place?

Her heart began to beat faster as her fear increased. Her fear was for Dane now—not herself. What had happened to him?

"Dane?" she called out, but her voice barely rose above a whisper. She headed toward that open door. As she walked across the sidewalk, something crunched beneath the soles of her ankle boots.

She glanced down and noticed bits of glass and metal strewn across the concrete. A box was crumpled against the side of the building. Had Dane simply dropped it? How had the contents been broken beyond recognition?

She couldn't even tell what those bits of glass and metal had once been. Cameras?

Was Dane an amateur photographer?

Somehow she doubted that.

She hunched down to study the remnants more closely. And she noticed what else was on the sidewalk, spattered across the concrete: blood.

A gasp slipped through her lips. Someone had been hurt. "Dane?" she called out again.

She peered around the entrance to the warehouse. Despite being remodeled into living space, it was still a little unkempt. The landscaping hadn't been trimmed for a while. Overgrown shrubs crowded the sidewalk and entrance. Emilia looked through the branches to see if Dane was lying on the ground beneath them.

She didn't see a body.

But something glinted in the faint light from the street lamp. She recognized the shape of a gun. No. Dane hadn't simply dropped that box. An attack had taken place here, an armed attack.

And someone had been hurt enough to bleed all over the concrete.

Where was Dane?

A noise caught Emilia's attention, the familiar creak of hardwood. Someone was inside the dark apartment. She reached for that gun and turned with it just as a shadow fell across her and the sidewalk.

Lars had taught her how to shoot, but she hadn't liked it. The heaviness of the gun. The recoil when she'd pulled the trigger. The concern that her bullet might go astray and hit someone innocent.

She didn't care about that now. After what she'd been through, she knew she could pull that trigger. So she cocked the gun.

She could kill.

Dane stared down the barrel of the gun—his gun— to the face of the person who'd trained the weapon on him. The pale blue eyes were intent, more intent than he'd ever seen them. Emilia Ecklund was stronger than anyone knew.

"Don't shoot," he told her. "It's me."

Her breath escaped in a gasp, and she sprang up. Her arms flung around his neck, she launched herself at him.

As her soft body pressed against him, his breath escaped in a gasp, too—of pain. He grunted.

And she pulled back. "You're hurt!" Her palms ran all over him. "Are you bleeding? Were you shot?"

He shook his head, and his vision blurred as the darkness threatened to claim him again. He'd lost consciousness earlier. And he wasn't sure how long he'd been out. But he'd awakened to darkness. It had taken all of his strength to stagger inside the apartment and splash some water on his face.

He felt like he needed to do that again as he swayed slightly. Emilia slipped beneath his arm and steadied him. Or maybe she unsteadied him, as her warmth penetrated his thin T-shirt and heated his skin. His body began to throb but not where he'd been injured.

"We need to call an ambulance," she said.

"No," he said. "I haven't been shot." He'd been shot at, but the bullet hadn't hit him because he had ducked and hurled himself at his attackers.

Somehow he had rallied enough to fight them off. And remain conscious until they'd run away, jumping into some kind of vehicle and speeding off, tires squealing.

"But you're hurt," she said. Now she skimmed her fingers over his chest, over his ribs.

It didn't hurt this time when she touched him—so gently. But he grunted again as his body tensed.

"At least let me drive you to the hospital," she said. "You need to have X-rays." Her fingers touched his face now, sliding along his temple. "And a CT scan, too."

"Nothing's broken," he said. He'd had enough broken bones in his lifetime that he would have known if he had another. "I don't need medical treatment." But he needed to splash some more water on his face, so that he could focus. So that he could think…

What the hell had just happened? Why had those guys come after him?

He steered Emilia toward the apartment. And this time when he stepped inside, he locked the door. He didn't want anyone sneaking up on him again, especially with her here.

"What happened?" she asked the question he'd been asking himself.

He shrugged. "As I was bringing out the last box, I got jumped."

"Who was it?"

"I don't know." He hadn't gotten a good look at any of them.

"We need to call the police," she said. And with her hand not holding the gun, she reached inside her big purse.

But he caught her wrist before she could pull out her phone. "I don't know if that's a good idea," he said.

"You were attacked!"

"And if we call the police everyone will find out about it," he said. "Nikki Payne's brother—half brother…" He wasn't sure what the hell former FBI agent Nicholas Payne, formerly Rus, was to the Paynes. Now that he'd taken their last name, he probably was one.

"Nick's back in charge of River City PD while the new chief's on his honeymoon," Dane explained. "If we call the police, he'll find out and might tell the others."

"But there could be evidence here," she said, "that will lead to whoever did this to you."

That was another reason he was hesitant. He wasn't sure just how far her brother would go to scare him away from her. Manny had warned him. Should he have heeded that warning?

Outside the door, glass and metal crunched as someone approached. Taking no chances this time, especially not with her safety, Dane reached for the gun Emilia held, and he pointed the barrel at the door.

If anyone forced their way through it, Dane would put a bullet in him. And he wouldn't miss.

Lars jumped aside just as the bullet whizzed past his head. "Son of a bitch!" he exclaimed.

A scream rang out, echoing his curse. Emilia clutched Dane's arm, but she wasn't strong enough to pull it and the gun barrel down.

Fortunately Dane must have recognized him at the last moment. Or maybe he'd meant to hit him but had gotten sloppy.

"Why the hell are you shooting at me?" Of course he had struck the man earlier, so he probably had it coming.

Dane pointed toward the door Lars had just kicked

open, the jamb splintered. "Why the hell did you break down my door?"

Lars gestured outside. "I saw the mess and the blood." And Emilia's little yellow SUV parked at the curb.

He hadn't been surprised she was here. Nikki had told him she was. That was why he'd come. But then he'd seen the signs of a struggle...

He stepped closer and reached for his sister. "Are you okay?" he asked, that fear for her safety gripping him again. His heart was beating frantically still, even faster after that gunshot.

"I'm fine," she assured him. "Dane was the one who was attacked. Not me."

He turned to his friend now and noticed the blood that had dried on his temple. "You were jumped?"

"Like you don't know," Dane replied, his voice gruff with suspicion and resentment. "When Manny told me you were talking about killing me, I thought you were just kidding about it."

Now shock gripped Lars. "You think I did this?"

"You threatened to do it," Dane said. "And I know you don't make empty threats."

No. He didn't. But he'd only been kidding. Sort of...

Emilia reached out for Lars now and shoved him back. "How could you! He's your friend."

"That's debatable," Lars said.

She had been right earlier when she'd called him a hypocrite, though. He couldn't argue that it was wrong to date a friend's sister, not when he was going to marry one.

But Nikki wasn't like Emilia. He couldn't point that out again, though. That had made her mad earlier, and she was even angrier now.

"You really think I did this?" he asked.

She gestured at the broken jamb. "When it comes to me, we both know you get insanely overprotective."

"Obviously I have reason to be."

She flinched as if he'd struck her. She probably thought he was referring to her weeks in captivity. And she'd beaten herself up enough about that.

"I'm talking about Dane," he clarified. "He's only going to hurt you. Or get you hurt."

Dane flinched now as if Lars had struck him again. And maybe he had, with the truth.

He appealed to his friend. "You have to see that you're not good for her. This has to prove that to you."

"Is that why you did it?" Dane asked, his suspicion persisting.

And maybe he had reason to be suspicious of Lars. If Dane put Emilia in danger, he would kill him. But before he could say any more, he heard the whine of sirens in the distance.

"You called the police?" he asked.

Dane shook his head. "Someone must have heard the shots."

"Shots?" Dane had fired only one at him. There must have been more shots fired earlier. "Just what the hell happened here? What's going on with you?"

And why hadn't Dane called the police? Because he'd thought Lars was behind the attack?

He knew him better than that, knew that he might rough him up but he wouldn't kill him. Hell, if not for Dane, he wouldn't even be alive. He owed the man his life. His life.

Not his sister.

She had already been through too much. And Lars would do whatever necessary to protect her. He just wasn't sure what she needed protecting from.

Chapter 10

"You really have no idea who attacked you tonight?"

Tonight? It had been late that afternoon, but Dane didn't point that out to the young officer questioning him. He didn't want to explain why a shot had just recently been fired, that he'd nearly killed his friend.

But was Lars his friend? Was he really as innocent as he'd claimed? Or had he only acted that way for his sister's benefit?

They were both gone now. Lars had insisted on Emilia leaving before the police arrived. She'd driven off—with Lars following her—just before the patrol car had pulled up behind Dane's truck.

Dane shook his head. "No idea, Officer. As I told you, I was stepping outside with a box of electronics and I got jumped. They put something over my head. So I couldn't see anything."

"But you fought them off?" The young officer arched his brows with skepticism. "You couldn't see them but you overpowered them?"

"I have a gun," Dane reminded him.

The officer was actually holding that weapon now.

"And a permit to carry it," he added. He'd also showed that to the cop.

"Did you shoot one of them?"

He hadn't had time to draw his weapon then. And when he'd hurled himself at his attackers, it must have slipped out of his holster and fallen into the bushes. He didn't explain that to the cop, either.

"No."

"There's blood on the sidewalk," the officer said. He'd called a crime scene unit out to go over the scene of the attack.

Too bad someone had heard the shot. This was all taking too much time. And Emilia…

She wasn't alone. Her brother had been right behind her. And Nikki was at her house with Blue. They were safe.

What about him?

He touched his fingertips to his temple. "That's probably mine." His head must have hit the sidewalk. That must have been how he'd lost consciousness.

"What do you do, Mr. Sutton?" the officer asked, all suspicion and skepticism.

"I'm a bodyguard for the Payne Protection Agency."

The officer's mouth dropped open, and he stared at Dane. "Which brother do you work for?"

"Cooper Payne."

"The former Marine?"

Dane nodded. "We went through boot camp together and served in the same unit."

And the skepticism was gone. "Oh, that's how you fought them off."

Dane wasn't sure he'd overpowered them or if he'd just been more desperate than they were. He'd wanted to get to Emilia, wanted to make sure she was safe. That desperation had lent him strength.

Dane shrugged. "I don't know."

"They were probably just kids," the officer said as he held Dane's weapon out to him. "We've had a problem with gangs in this area. That's undoubtedly why most of the units in these rehabbed warehouses aren't being rented. It's not the safest area."

Dane had been in far more dangerous places than this. He just shrugged again. "Like I said, I have no idea who attacked me."

"Cooper Payne—wasn't he part of some specialized unit that carried out secret ops?"

Dane tensed. Few people knew what his unit had done. Few people were supposed to know. Maybe that was how he'd gotten good at keeping secrets: his life had depended on him doing it. Those were the few secrets Manny had actually been able to keep.

"That's what his brother Parker said about him," the officer continued. "That Cooper's a decorated hero."

"That's true." Dane had medals, too. They were in the bottom of one of those boxes in the back of his truck. He didn't need medals to remind him of what he'd done.

"Do you think what your unit did over there or maybe the cases you've worked for Payne Protection could have anything to do with this attack?"

He hadn't, but now he wondered. Sure, the missions

had been carried out overseas. That didn't mean nobody could have followed them back to the States. If they'd survived...

They had left few survivors.

Dane shrugged. "I have no idea. You're probably right about it being gang-related."

The officer stood up straighter, as if proud that Dane agreed with him. "We'll step up patrols in this area."

That wouldn't matter to Dane. He wasn't staying in this area. He was moving in with Emilia. But after the officer and crime scene techs left, he hesitated to leave, too. What if that officer and Lars were right?

What if whoever had jumped him had really been after him? Then moving in with Emilia would put her in more danger than she already was.

What if they'd attacked him in order to keep him away from her...

And he had let her leave alone.

Well, she'd left with Lars, and her brother wasn't likely to let anything happen to her. She was safe with him and Nikki. Safer than she was with him. He would probably do her a bigger favor if he stayed away from her.

Where was he? Emilia found herself wondering for the second time that night what had happened to Dane.

She had been right to worry earlier. She shuddered as she thought about the blood she'd found on the sidewalk. Had that been his or had it dripped from whoever he had fought off?

Lars? Had he attacked his friend? He was certainly angry enough with Dane.

A pang of guilt struck her heart. She hadn't wanted to come between them. But Lars couldn't know the truth.

She'd had to work to convince him and Nikki to leave her alone.

As she'd pointed out, she wasn't the one who'd been attacked. It hadn't happened here. Of course, they weren't aware of everything that had happened here.

She shivered as she remembered all the nights she'd lain awake listening to that crying. And then the footsteps…

Someone had been inside with her and Blue. Why? What had he wanted?

Just to drive her crazy?

"Damn it," she murmured.

At least Blue was asleep. Or was he…?

She could hear crying. Faint crying… And Blue, when he cried now, cried loudly. Angrily.

It wasn't coming from him. It was coming from outside the door.

While they hadn't changed the locks because Dane had wanted to catch the intruder in the act of sneaking in, he had added slide bolts to both doors for when she was alone. The minute Lars and Nikki had left, she'd slid them. And of course, she'd made certain all the windows were locked, as well.

Nobody could get inside. Nobody could get to her and Blue now.

She didn't need Dane, which was a good thing because he must have changed his mind about moving in to protect her. That was fine, though. She would probably be safer without him.

But just as that thought entered her head, she heard a creak. First on the front porch. Then against the door. As she stared at it, the knob turned.

Someone was trying to get inside. It wasn't Dane. He

knew about the slide bolts. He would know that she'd have them on, so he would have knocked.

And then there was that crying…

It was louder now. Closer.

Like right on the other side of that door.

Her intruder had come back. The door began to rattle in the jamb. And the screws holding the slide bolt to the jamb began to move slightly. Would it hold?

Would it keep out the intruder?

She wished now that she had let Lars get her a gun. Or she had kept Dane's. Where was he?

Had he arrived only to be stopped by the intruder? That must have been whoever had attacked him earlier, determined to get to her.

"Who's there?" she called out. "Who is it?"

She hoped for Dane to answer. Or even Lars or Nikki. She wouldn't have been surprised if they'd changed their mind about leaving and had come back to check on her.

But nobody answered her. The door only began to rattle harder in the frame, testing the bolt. Who the hell was out there?

And how soon before the person got inside—with her and Blue?

Hearing the fear in her voice as she called out through the closed door, he smiled. She sounded like she had all those other nights she'd heard the crying. She sounded scared and vulnerable. The original plan would have worked—had it not been for her calling that man to her rescue.

Dane Sutton must have installed some kind of dead bolt to the jamb. Because the lock had turned with the copied key from the ring he'd lifted from her big purse at the coffee shop. He'd been so close to her that day.

But he'd been close other days and nights, as well. He could have taken her out any of those times. But killing her hadn't been part of the plan.

Then.

But Dane Sutton hadn't left them much choice. How had he overpowered all of those gang members he'd hired? How had one man overpowered four?

He glanced nervously around. Dane Sutton wasn't here. Not yet.

He suspected he was coming, though. So he didn't have much time. He needed to get inside—he needed to get to Emilia Ecklund now.

While she had no one to protect her…

He wanted to just kick open the door like he'd watched her brother kick open the door to Dane Sutton's apartment earlier that evening. Except that wasn't part of the plan—the new one they'd had to concoct when Dane Sutton had interfered with the first one.

He hurried around to the back door. As he'd suspected, that one had an extra lock, too. He rattled the knob and the door in the jamb. He quickly realized it wouldn't be any easier to open than the front one.

So he stepped over to one of the windows. They were all locked. He already knew that. If only there had been enough time to carry out the plan before Emilia had gone inside the house….

But that curly-haired woman had been outside as well, the one who'd been with her at the chapel. Like Dane Sutton, she was a bodyguard. So he'd had to wait until she and Emilia's brother had driven off. And hopefully those damn kids had gone back to finish the job he'd paid them to do: completely eliminate Dane Sutton.

Anger and frustration surged through him with such force that he fisted his hand inside the leather glove and propelled his fist through the window to the half bathroom. The glass broke and tore the glove and his skin beneath the leather.

He cursed at the pain.

Emilia would pay for that, just like she would finally pay for all the other pain she'd caused.

This wasn't the original plan. But it would work.

It had to.

She must have heard the glass breaking because her scream rang out from inside the house. She was probably running toward the baby to protect him. But she would only put him in more danger.

That was why she needed to be eliminated. Now.

Ignoring the pain in his hand, he knocked aside the rest of the jagged glass and pulled himself over the sill. He was inside and that was all that mattered.

Now he could deal with Emilia Ecklund, once he found wherever she'd gone to hide with her son. But she wasn't hiding. She was standing in the doorway, a big knife clenched in her hands.

"Who are you!" she demanded to know again.

Along with the gloves, he wore a hood and a mask. She wouldn't be able to recognize him. But even if she caught a glimpse of him, it wouldn't matter.

"I called the police," she threatened.

She might have. But he suspected she'd called Dane Sutton again instead. Hopefully those damn kids had finished him off by now.

And now he could finish off Emilia.

Chapter 11

"Get out of here!" Emilia shrieked at the masked intruder. "The police are coming."

They would be coming if she had called 911, but she hadn't. She'd run into the kitchen to get her purse, which she'd left on the counter when she'd heard the glass break in the half bath off the kitchen. Instead of her cell, she'd grabbed the knife.

It would protect her and Blue more than a phone call. The police could take long minutes to arrive. And the intruder was already here, already inside with her.

Instead of heading for the window he'd broken, the intruder moved toward her. He had no weapon that she could see. Just his size. He was big. Not as big as Dane or her brother. But bigger than she was.

She lifted the knife and backed toward the door. Maybe he only wanted to move past her—to head outside that way. But she couldn't take that chance. She couldn't let him get anywhere near the stairwell and up to where her son slept.

Or at least she hoped he slept. She could hear that crying more loudly now. It wasn't coming from above them, but from within this room. She suspected he had a recorder—or a phone—in his pocket playing that awful, poignant cry.

"What do you want?" she asked. "Why are you doing this to me?"

He said nothing. She must know him or why was he wearing the hood and mask.

She lifted the knife higher and held it out between them. "Get out of here!" she screamed again. "Or I will stab you."

Instead of backing away from the blade that gleamed in the bathroom light, the man stepped closer. And as she swung the knife toward him, he closed his hands around her wrists. He was stronger than she was. He squeezed until her grasp weakened and the knife slipped from her fingers.

She kicked and cried out, trying to fight him off. But he was too powerful. He held her wrist in the tight grasp of one of his gloved hands. Then he reached for the knife with the other. And he lifted the blade toward her wrist.

"Noooo!" she screamed. "Noooo!"

He intended to kill her. Slowly.

Painfully.

The minute Dane opened the door of his truck he heard the scream. The fear and desperation in it rent the night air and his heart. Leaving his truck door open, he ran for the front door of the house. He'd drawn his gun, so with the hand not holding the Glock, he reached for the knob. It turned, but the door held tight.

She'd thrown the slide bolt he'd installed. So how had someone gotten inside with her?

She couldn't be alone and that terrified. He stepped back and lifted his leg, kicking the wood until the jamb splintered and the door flew open, banging against the wall behind it. Then he rushed through the house.

The living room was empty. So was the kitchen although the back door stood open. Unlike the front, the bolt hadn't been slid home to secure it.

"Emilia!" he called out. Her purse sat on the counter. Her keys and cell phone had spilled out of it next to an overturned knife block.

His heart beating fast and hard, he called out again. "Emilia!"

In response he heard a whimper. He also heard a cry— that came from above and sounded loud and healthy. The whimper was what tore at his heart. It was full of pain. He followed the slight noise toward another open door— this one off the kitchen.

Emilia lay on the floor, her pale hair covering her face. Blood smeared the white tiles around her.

"Oh, my God," he gasped as he dropped to his knees beside her.

She reached out and blood dripped from her wrist and streaked down her arm. How deep was the cut? Had it hit an artery?

He grasped her arm to study the wound. But she pulled away from him.

"Get him!" she said.

"Blue?" he asked. She must have heard the baby crying, too.

"The man," she said. "He just ran out."

That was why the back door stood open. Someone

had just left. Shards of glass lay on the tiles in front of the window. That must have been how he'd gotten inside.

Dane cursed. He should have come sooner. But he'd thought Lars and Nikki would stay with her. Lars and Nikki didn't know she was in danger, but he knew and had left her unprotected. He wouldn't do that again. He shook his head. "We need to call an ambulance for you. You could bleed out."

She sat up and grabbed the towel that had been hanging off the side of the pedestal sink. She pressed that to her wrist. "It's a shallow cut," she said. "I jerked away. The knife didn't hit any arteries."

But blood was spreading through the white terry cloth of the towel, turning it crimson.

He shook his head. "You're hurt—"

"I'm fine," she said. "Go—find him—before he gets away again."

He hesitated for a moment. But she was right. The only way to keep her safe was to stop whoever was trying to hurt her. "Go upstairs and lock yourself into the bedroom with Blue," he said. "I'll be right back."

He turned toward the door, but Emilia softly called his name. Had she changed her mind? Did she want an ambulance?

"Be careful," she warned him, her pale blue eyes full of fear and concern.

He wasn't certain which was the greater threat: the man with the knife or her.

"So you warned him…"

Manny clutched the dart instead of throwing it at the board on the barroom wall. He might need it to protect himself. Not that a dart would do much to ward off an attack from Lars Ecklund.

"Hey, man," Cole Bentler greeted their friend. "Good to see you could join us for a drink. Thought you were too whipped to hang out with us guys now, though."

If a woman could whip a man, it would be Nikki Payne. In fact, she'd knocked Lars on his ass a couple of times.

"I'm not here for a drink," Lars said.

Manny groaned. He was in trouble. But hell, he wasn't Dane. He wasn't a vault when it came to keeping secrets. He turned toward his mammoth friend. "You didn't tell me not to say anything to him."

In fact he'd probably wanted Manny to pass along the threat. Or else he would have said something to Cole instead. Cole was like Dane; they were good at keeping stuff quiet. Cole Bentler had a whole secret life he never talked about, but that was probably because he didn't want to think about everything he'd given up.

Manny was more like Dane. He'd never had anything but the Corps and his friends. And he didn't want to lose any of them.

Cole chuckled. "You should have known better than to say anything to Manny if you really didn't want it to get back to Dane. What the hell's going on with you two anyway? He jealous that you proposed to someone else?"

That was how close Lars and Dane were—closer than the rest of them. That had to be why Lars felt so betrayed over Dane dating his sister.

Lars snorted. "Don't be a smart-ass, Bentler."

No. That was usually Dane's job. He was the one who tossed out the hilarious one-liners with a straight face. That sick sense of humor had kept them from losing it during their especially tense missions.

It was tense now, too, though.

"Where is Dane?" Manny asked. They needed him.

"What?" Lars asked. "Do you think I tried to kill him again?"

"Again?" Cole asked, his voice cracking as all the amusement left his face. He pushed a slightly shaking hand through his dark blond hair. "What the hell's wrong with you—you really tried to kill your best friend?"

"No," Lars said. "But he thinks I did."

"What happened?" Cole asked.

"Someone attacked him earlier as he was leaving his apartment."

Manny squeezed his hand into a fist, and the dart jabbed into his palm. He cursed and dropped it. "I was with him then. I helped him finish packing."

"Thanks," Lars resentfully remarked.

"Are you sure he's really moving in with your sister?" Cole asked. "You sure he isn't just messing with you like he always does?"

Manny hadn't even considered that. But then he'd seen the way Dane looked at Emilia Ecklund. He'd seemed fascinated with the blonde beauty.

"I mean—this is Dane," Cole continued. "We're not sure he even has a heart."

A muscle twitched along Lars's tightly clenched jaw. Cole wasn't helping the situation. Nobody would want a heartless man involved with his sister.

"What happened earlier?" Manny asked. It must have occurred right after he'd left.

"Someone jumped him and beat the crap out of him," Lars said.

"Was it you?" Manny asked.

Lars cursed him. But he didn't specifically deny doing it.

Cole must have noticed that, too, because he silently studied his friend before remarking, "Sounds like that blanket party we threw you..."

"You guys didn't beat the crap out of me."

"How bad is he hurt?" Manny asked. Guilt churned up the one beer he'd had earlier, and he felt sick. He shouldn't have left the warehouse earlier. But he hadn't believed Dane was really in danger. He hadn't thought Lars would actually hurt him.

"He's Dane," Lars said with pride. "He fought them off. He's fine. Just going to have some bruises."

"Them?" Cole repeated.

Lars nodded. "I called Nick Payne at the police department. He said the crime tech found at least four sets of footprints besides Dane's."

Manny chuckled. He almost felt sorry for them. "If they really wanted to take out Dane, they needed more than four guys."

"Yeah, they've learned that now," Lars said.

"Who's they?" Cole asked. "Who the hell could be after him?"

Lars caught them both staring at him and shook his head. "It wasn't me."

Manny believed him. "If not you, then who?"

"We're not working any cases right now," Cole said. "Except for some short protection assignments, we've not been involved in anything major since rescuing your sister from that slimy adoption lawyer."

"And he's dead," Manny said.

He wasn't surprised that Lars had killed the man who'd abducted his sister and stolen her baby. Of course, he'd done it to save Nikki's life. But even if she hadn't been in danger, Manny wouldn't have been surprised if Myron Webber had wound up dead.

He hoped Dane wasn't just messing with Lars's sister. He hoped he really cared about her—like Lars cared about Nikki Payne.

But it wouldn't matter how Dane felt about her if he didn't survive.

In a deep whisper, Cole asked, "Could someone have found out where we are?"

"What?" Lars asked. "Who are you talking about?"

"From over there," Cole replied. "Maybe there were survivors or vengeful family members…"

"They would have had to find out who we are first," Manny said. "And those missions were top secret."

Those were secrets even Manny wouldn't divulge to anyone. If he did, it could cost them all their lives.

Lars uttered a ragged sigh. "It's possible," he said. "I'm going to marry a woman who can hack any computer database anywhere."

And the government had security breaches all the time. That beer churned even more in Manny's twisting gut. No matter the assurances they'd been given, it was possible. Someone could have found out what they'd done, the missions they'd carried out to defeat the enemy.

The enemy might want revenge.

"If that's what happened," Cole said, "then Dane isn't the only one in danger. Every one of us is in danger."

"And not just us," Lars said, "but the people we care about are in danger, too."

Like Nikki and Lars's sister…

Once again Manny was glad that he had no one in his life. He had no one to lose.

But his friends…

Where was Dane? Was he safe?

Chapter 12

Where was Dane?

Was he safe?

He had been gone so long that Emilia was filled with fear. She shouldn't have sent him after the man with the knife. But Dane had a gun. He could take care of himself. Better than she could take care of herself. She glanced down at the bandage she'd wound around her wrist before she'd hurried upstairs to Blue. The blood that had seeped through the white gauze had turned dark and dried. Her wound had stopped bleeding.

She was lucky that the knife hadn't hit an artery.

She'd thought she could defend herself with the weapon, but it had nearly taken her life. She'd been crazy to try to confront her intruder.

But she'd also been angry. Instead of the crying driving her crazy as her assailant must have intended, it had driven her to anger. She had wanted to hurt him, like he'd been hurting her.

Instead she'd nearly lost her life. She only had to glance down at the bloodied bandage to remember what had happened. If the man had plunged the knife into her heart, she would have been dead for certain.

Why had he chosen to slash her wrist instead?

Had he wanted it to look like suicide, like she'd done that to herself?

Her heart rate slowed with dread as she realized that might have been exactly how he'd wanted it to look: self-inflicted. She had been acting erratically. The crying had robbed her of sleep, leaving her shaky and distraught. And the calls canceling those wedding services made her look incompetent.

Someone had been setting her up for suicide. She shivered as she considered it. Hopefully Dane had found him and could prove that she had been attacked. She hadn't injured herself. She wouldn't.

She had too much to live for. She had her son. And he was everything.

The knob turned then rattled. She stepped between the crib and door. She had to protect Blue. She wouldn't stop unless the man plunged the knife in her heart this time.

"Emilia…" a deep voice murmured. "It's me…"

"Dane!"

He was back.

She rushed toward the door, unlocked and opened it to his handsome face. A bruise had swelled on his jaw—from Lars's fist—and on his temple from the attack by the thugs. She saw no new injuries. "Are you all right?"

He nodded and reached out, turning her wrist over so

that he could see where the blood had seeped through. "It looks like it stopped bleeding."

"I told you it was a shallow wound." Because she'd fought. And because Dane had arrived when he had. If he hadn't come to her...

She shuddered as she considered what might have happened. "Did you find him?" she asked.

He didn't look at her. Instead he studied that wound.

Her heart lurched as she realized what he was thinking. What someone had probably wanted him to think.

"You didn't find him," she mused.

He shook his head. "I didn't see anyone."

"Did you find the knife?" she asked.

He shook his head again.

"You believe me," she said. He had believed her before, even when she'd doubted herself. He was the one who'd suggested that her keys had been copied and that the crying she'd heard was a recording.

She knew that was true now. She'd seen that knob turn after her door had been unlocked. She'd seen the intruder in her home, had heard the crying playing from his pocket.

But Dane hadn't been here. He hadn't seen what she had.

"Don't you believe me?" she asked. "You don't think I would try to do this to myself?"

He blew out a breath he must have been holding and shrugged. "I don't know what to believe anymore, Emilia."

"The window—he broke the window," she said. "And he took the knife when he left."

"You could have cut yourself on the glass," he said, suggesting another alternative to the truth.

He didn't believe her.

Tears began to pool in her eyes. And she shook her head. "No..." Frustration burned inside her.

Dane had believed her—until now. That was almost as hard to handle as when she'd doubted herself. But before she could give in to the tears that threatened, Blue began to cry.

Blue's wail sounded like the scream she'd let out when the intruder had attacked her. Her son must have felt her frustration and anxiety.

He was the only one who sensed her helplessness now.

She couldn't count on Dane to trust her. In fact he might help her intruder. He might help to prove her incompetent. And then she would lose her son.

Again.

After assuring himself she was all right in the room with Blue, Dane had come back down to investigate the crime scene. The sight of her blood spilled across the stark white bathroom tiles had his stomach lurching.

If he'd stayed away like he'd been considering...

Or if he'd come just a little later...

He might have found her in worse shape than he had.

Sure, she could have cut herself on that glass. But he'd seen the wound. It had been clean and shallow. That wouldn't have been the case had she gauged herself on the broken glass. And if she had smashed the window from the inside, why would so much glass have been scattered across the bathroom tiles rather than outside the window?

Some of those shards had black fibers stuck to the edges—like someone wearing gloves had broken the window.

He shouldn't have doubted her. But maybe that had

been the vestiges of his head injury. His mind was clearer now, though. As he stepped inside the room and saw her holding her son, everything became crystal clear.

She was beautiful but never more so than when she looked at her son. Her face radiated joy and love. No. She would never risk losing him again.

"I believe you," he said.

Startled, she jumped a little. She must not have heard him enter the room. Her lips parted on a soft gasp, and she murmured, "You do?"

"Yes."

Her breath shuddered out now on a ragged sigh of relief. "I was so afraid…"

Anger surged through him. He couldn't imagine how frightened she'd been—with the person breaking in and then trying to slit her wrist. Rage surged through him as he realized the terror she'd endured.

"I'm sorry I didn't get here sooner," he said.

"I thought you'd changed your mind about moving in here," she said.

He couldn't deny that he had considered it.

And she must have realized that because she said, "I don't blame you. Those men must have attacked you because of me."

He wasn't so sure about that. He had made some enemies of his own, who could have just found him.

"And Lars is so angry with you…"

Her brother would be even angrier if Dane didn't tell him what was going on with his sister. But if he told him, would Lars believe her?

He'd already suggested she was suffering from PTSD. So many soldiers had come back from war only to tragically kill themselves at home. So Lars might not come to the same conclusions that Dane had.

"Should we call the police?" she asked.

"On your brother?" The smart-ass comment slipped out, but he was glad that it had when her lips curved a little.

"Did you mention him to the officer you talked to earlier?" she asked.

He shook his head. "Officer Kelly had already determined the attack was gang-related." And it might have been. But Dane wasn't so sure about that or about anyone tracking him down for revenge over those old missions.

He'd messed up the intruder's plan tonight. It stood to reason the guy wanted him out of the way.

She pressed a kiss to her son's forehead before laying the sleeping baby back down in the crib. It was late. No wonder the baby was tired. His sleep had already been interrupted twice.

She looked tired, too, with those dark circles beneath her pale eyes. Dane wasn't tired, though. He was too wired now—from the fight earlier. And from looking at her.

"Why didn't you call the police earlier?" he asked. Or him? She hadn't called him, either. He'd checked his phone.

"There was no time," she said. "I was just going for my cell when I heard the window break."

"So instead of grabbing a phone, you grabbed a knife from the block?" he deduced. Her purse had been lying open on the counter, next to the overturned knife block.

She nodded. But instead of looking proud, she looked embarrassed, her pale skin flushing with color. "That was stupid. He took it from me so easily."

"It was brave," he commended her. Emilia was far tougher than anyone—even she—knew she was.

"It was stupid," she insisted. "And you must think calling the cops would be stupid, too, or you would have done it already."

He shrugged. "I don't…"

"You don't think anyone else would believe me," she said. And from the dejected look on her beautiful face and the way her shoulders slumped, neither did she.

"It might be exactly what he wants." A report on file for something that could look like a suicide attempt.

"For me to look as crazy as he's trying to drive me," Emilia finished for him. "What are we going to do? How are we going to stop him?"

Nobody was going to stop them. They had come too far to give up now. Not when they were so close.

He turned toward his partner and said, "It's not as bad as it looks."

His partner said nothing, wouldn't even look at him.

So he admitted, "I know that it looks bad, though."

How much had Dane Sutton figured out? Anything? Or maybe tonight would give him doubts.

"It looks bad for Emilia Ecklund," he insisted. "The wound on her wrist looks self-inflicted. If they call the police, they'll think she did it to herself."

But then he glanced down at the knife he held. He'd forgotten to drop it. Would the police believe she'd hidden it? Or used another weapon?

"Damn Dane Sutton."

If he hadn't showed up when he had…

He'd ruined everything.

When that door had flown open, he'd barely had time

to escape before Dane had seen him. Taking the knife hadn't just been an instinctive reaction. It had been self-preservation in case Dane chased him.

But he'd had time to escape.

Barely.

Grasping the knife even tighter, he plunged it into the cantaloupe sitting atop the granite counter. Emilia's blood oozed onto the pale orange flesh of the melon. He wished it was Dane Sutton's heart instead.

The man kept ruining the plan.

"It's fine," he assured his partner. "An officer might think she hid it to conceal what she'd done." It would be a good thing if they called the cops.

He glanced at his partner and realized the original plan had been taking too long. Way too long.

"It's time to end this," he said. Before they got caught…

It was time to finish Emilia Ecklund once and for all. Driving her crazy hadn't worked. But that wasn't the only way to get rid of her.

Chapter 13

Dane had left again, without answering Emilia's question about what they were going to do. Where had he gone?

They had agreed they couldn't call the police. As she pulled Blue's door closed and stepped into the hall, she glanced down at her wrist. It wouldn't look good for her. It would look like she'd tried to hurt herself. Even her brother might think that. Only Dane believed her. Or did he?

He was gone.

Then she heard footsteps on the stairs. Before she could reach for Blue's door again to lock them both safely inside, a voice called out, "It's me."

And her breath shuddered out in relief. "You came back."

"I didn't leave," he said as he stepped onto the second

floor, a box cradled in his hands. "I just went to get my stuff from the back of the truck."

"You're still moving in?"

"That's the plan," he said. "We're going to follow that. It's how we're going to stop him."

She had her answer now.

"It'll stop him from trying to get in again," she said. "But then we might never figure out who he is."

"You didn't recognize him?"

"He had a hood pulled tight around his face. But it wasn't his face," she replied with a shudder at the horror of that grotesque Halloween mask. "It was a zombie mask. I couldn't tell the color of his hair or even his eyes."

"But you know it was a guy?"

She nodded. "He was strong." Stronger even than Nikki, who was physically the strongest woman Emilia knew. "And he was big."

"How big?"

"Big," she said, and her voice cracked as that fear coursed through her. If Dane hadn't arrived when he had...

He looked intense now. Angry even. Setting his box on the floor, he stepped closer and reached for her wrist again. He stroked his fingertip over the swollen flesh around the bandage. "You're going to have bruises."

"Good," she said with a surge of relief.

"What?"

"Then everyone will know I didn't do that to myself." But she suddenly cared less what everyone else thought and cared only about Dane. He hadn't seen that swollen skin before he'd believed her.

He'd trusted her.

So maybe she wasn't crazy for trusting him. She tugged her wrist from his grasp and lifted her arms to slide them around his neck. Then she pressed her body against his in a hug.

"Thank you," she said. She'd meant the embrace to express her gratitude. But other sensations raced through her, as her skin tingled and heated. She looked up and found him staring at her.

His caramel eyes had turned dark like rich chocolate. And there was a heat in them she'd never seen before.

He lowered his head and pressed his mouth to hers. And she felt the passion in him. He kissed her deeply, sliding his tongue into her mouth, playing with hers.

Then he lifted her, as easily as she lifted Blue, and carried her down the hall toward her bedroom. She wasn't surprised he knew where it was. As a bodyguard, he probably needed to know the complete layout of every place where he intended to protect someone.

Without even flipping on the light, he found her bed and laid her on it as gently as she put Blue to bed. Then he stepped back from it.

She could hear his breathing, could see it in the rapid rise and fall of his heavily muscled chest. "Dane…"

"I—I'll sleep on the couch," he said, his voice gruff.

So he'd just carried her to her bed to put her in it— alone?

She didn't want to be alone for so many reasons. But most of all, she wanted Dane. She reached out and grabbed his shirt, pulling him toward the bed—toward her. "The couch is too far away," she protested. "How is that protecting me?"

"That's how I'm protecting you," he said, "by walking away. And it's taking everything in me."

He wanted her, too.

"Then stay," she implored him. "Stay with me."

"Neither of us will get any sleep if I do," he said.

Curling her fingers into his shirt, she tugged him closer. "I'm not tired."

His teeth flashed in the darkness as he grinned. "Liar."

"Well, I don't want to sleep." After everything that had happened, she wouldn't be able to if she tried. She was afraid even to close her eyes because she would see that hooded man in the mask again. She would see the blade of the knife gleaming as it slashed across her wrist. She shivered.

And Dane groaned. He settled onto the bed next to her, wrapping his arm around her shoulders. "I know..." he murmured. "I understand. You're worried about having nightmares."

Her breath escaped in a gasp as she realized he worried about them, too. Probably because of everything he'd seen—everything he had endured. Even tonight, that must have been terrifying for him, having all those guys jump him and being unable to see any of them.

"Of course you would understand," she said. "You must have them, too."

His shoulder shifted against her as he shrugged. "Not that I remember."

That was good. When she had the nightmares, even after she jerked awake, she felt like she was still in them. But that was because of the crying. That wasn't real.

This probably wasn't real, either. But she needed it—she needed Dane. She turned toward him and ran her fingers down his chest, which continued to rise and fall with harsh breaths. "How are your ribs?"

He shrugged again.

"And your head?"

"I'm fine," he said.

He didn't sound fine. So she reached up and pressed a kiss to Dane's temple.

"Emilia…" He said her name on a groan. And his arm tightened around her shoulders. Then he turned toward her, and his mouth found hers.

He kissed her again—deeply—like he had before. His tongue slid between her lips.

She kissed him back as she curled her fingers in his shirt again, tugging it up. She wanted it off him. She wanted nothing between them but skin.

He pulled back. She saw metal flash as he took off his holster, putting it and the gun on the bedside table. Then he peeled off his shirt, and muscles rippled in his chest and abdomen. His jeans followed, pushed down his thick thighs and sculpted calves along with his underwear. His erection sprang free.

Emilia's breath escaped in a gasp. He was big everywhere. So big. And muscular.

"Are you sure about this?" he asked.

She ran her fingertips over all those muscles then she skimmed her mouth over them, too.

And his breathing grew more ragged. "Emilia…" He tangled his fingers in her hair and gently moved her head back up—to his. Then he kissed her passionately.

As he kissed her, he moved his hands up and down her body. He stroked the sides of her breasts down to the dip of her waist and the curve of her hips.

She shrugged off her sweater. But before she could take off the rest of her clothes, he undressed her, kissing every inch of skin he exposed.

She shivered as goose bumps rose on that skin. But

she wasn't cold. She was hot, heat flashing through her. Her stomach clenched with the passion gripping her. "Dane…"

He kissed the curve of each breast before closing his lips around a nipple. His tongue stroked over the tightened tip.

She moaned and shifted on the bed. "Dane…"

He turned his attention to the other breast.

She clutched at his shoulders and skimmed her nails down his back. But he was already moving his mouth down her body. He made love to her with his lips and his tongue, teasing the most sensitive part of her.

Tension gripped her, tightening every muscle. He slid his tongue inside her as he rubbed his thumbs over her nipples. The tension shattered as she came.

"Dane!"

He turned away from her. But she was greedy for more, so she reached for him, closing her hand around his throbbing erection. He wanted her, too. With a groan, he turned back with a condom packet in his fingers.

He was still protecting her as he rolled on the condom. Then he moved between her legs, easing inside her. He filled her—completely—and then some, stretching her.

She arched to take as much of him as she could. Then she lifted her legs and locked them around his lean waist. They moved together, finding a frantic rhythm that had the tension winding inside her again.

Then the pleasure exploded inside her. She shuddered as the sensations raced through her. Dane's hard muscled body tensed and he emitted a low groan, finding his release, too.

She had never known such pleasure or satisfaction. Dane slipped away for a few moments. But then he was back, sliding his arm around her shoulders again. She settled her head on his chest. And despite her reservations, she closed her eyes.

She didn't see the masked man like she'd feared she would. She saw Dane's handsome face instead, saw his eyes turning from caramel to dark chocolate with desire. She was still scared, though.

She was scared that she was falling for Dane Sutton.

Her breath whispered warmly across Dane's chest as she slept in his arms. He had never spent the night with anyone like this. After sex, he always put on his clothes and left.

But he couldn't leave Emilia and not just because he had appointed himself her personal bodyguard. He didn't want to walk away from her. Even slipping out of the bed to clean up had been hard. He'd wanted to stay inside her—as part of her—all night.

And he'd never been part of anything before. Not part of a family at least, unless his unit counted. And now there was the Payne Protection Agency. He was part of that damn family cult, but probably only until the others found out he'd been keeping secrets from them.

With Lars about to become Cooper's brother-in-law, he would probably be able to convince their boss to fire him. He was already pissed at Dane. How much angrier would he be when he learned the truth?

Probably out-of-his-mind irate. That was why Dane needed to find out who was terrorizing Emilia. Then he could redirect Lars's anger to the person who deserved his wrath.

That person already had incurred Dane's wrath. Whoever the man in the mask was—he'd spent weeks gaslighting Emilia, making her think she was losing her mind.

And tonight…

Tonight he could have killed her. Had that been his intention? Or had he only wanted it to look like she'd tried to kill herself?

Anger coursed through Dane, tensing his muscles. He must have moved enough that Emilia awoke with a start. She clutched at him before relaxing against him again.

"Sorry I fell asleep." Her face felt warm against his chest, as if it was flushed.

"I'm glad you did," he said. She needed sleep. She'd been deprived of it for too long. He stroked his hand down her bare back. "Close your eyes…unless you're afraid…"

"Of what I might see?" she asked. And she tensed briefly.

"He can't hurt you," he promised. "I'm here. I won't leave you alone again." That scream he'd heard as he'd gotten out of his truck echoed inside his head. The terror in her voice had had his pulse quickening with fear—for her.

"I guess we're not lying anymore about being involved," she said.

He tensed as the truth of her words hit him like a blow. He—who had always avoided relationships—was involved. He could tell himself that he was only concerned with keeping her safe. But he hadn't had to sleep with her to do that. He hadn't had to kiss her and touch her…

And lose himself inside her.

She must have felt his tension because she murmured, "I'm sorry. I didn't mean that we're really involved like that. I know that sex doesn't mean anything. I know that now."

How did she know that?

Despite her passion and her having had a baby, he had sensed that she was still quite innocent. He doubted she'd had many lovers.

"The baby's father," he surmised. "He's the one who taught you that?"

She nodded, her face moving over his shoulder. Her skin was so silky.

His body tensed again—with desire—and a sudden realization. "He must be the one behind this," Dane said.

"No!" she sharply retorted. "Absolutely not."

The vehemence in her voice sent a jab of pain through his heart. She'd jumped so quickly to the guy's defense that she must still have feelings for him. Was she in love with him yet?

But just because she cared about him didn't make the man innocent.

"I'll be the judge of that when I talk to him," Dane said. He couldn't wait to talk to the son of a bitch. He clenched the hand not stroking her back into a fist.

She lifted her head from his chest, and her usually sweet voice was sharp when she protested, "No, you can't talk to him!"

He touched the bandage on her wrist. The material was hard with her dried blood. "We can't *not* talk to him. We need to find out who attacked you."

"He won't know."

Dane snorted. "I think it's him."

"That's ridiculous," she said. "Why?"

"He's the one who stands to gain the most if you're declared incompetent."

"What will he gain?"

"Your son."

She shook her head, and her pale hair tumbled around her bare shoulders and brushed across his chest. "He can't."

"Of course he can," Dane said. "He's his father. If he can prove you're unstable, he can get full custody."

"He can't." She expelled a shaky sigh. "Because he doesn't even know about Blue."

Dane felt another pang in his heart—this time of fear. Emilia hadn't told the father about his son. And she'd asked him to keep secrets from his best friend. Had he been a fool to trust her?

What was she keeping from *him*?

"Man," Cole Bentler said as he studied his friend's face. "Those guys did some number on you." He touched his fingers to Dane's swollen jaw.

Dane flinched. "That was Lars."

"He swears he wasn't the one who jumped you," Cole defended their other friend. "He says the River City PD crime techs figure four guys did that to you."

Dane touched his jaw. "No. This was Lars. He hit me when he found out I was seeing his sister."

"Well, that took us all by surprise," Cole said.

Of course Dane never said much about himself or anyone else. Nobody could keep a secret like he could. That was probably why Cole himself had told him more than he should have.

Dane knew about Shawna. And Cole never talked about *her*. It hurt too much.

Dane nodded. "She took me by surprise, too."

And for the first time since they'd met in boot camp,

Cole saw fear in Dane's dark eyes. His friend was really falling for Lars's sister.

"I thought you were just acting like you were involved," Cole admitted, "just to get under Lars's skin."

"I don't have a death wish," Dane replied.

No. He didn't. He'd always been the most careful one of them on their missions. He'd also said that he would never be taken alive, either.

"Then how did this happen?" he asked, and he gestured at the house behind them, the house where Emilia Ecklund lived with her son and with Dane now.

Had he really moved in with a woman after refusing to share a place with any of them? Not that Cole had had to share a place. He had money, more money than the rest of them knew about, but he'd agreed to room with Manny. He would have preferred Dane, who didn't talk incessantly.

But he wished he could get him talking now.

Dane just shrugged. But for once he looked like he wanted to talk, as if his swollen jaw was clenched to hold in the words he wanted to say.

"What's up?" Cole asked. "You can trust me."

Dane nodded in agreement. "I am trusting you," he said. "I'm trusting you to keep an eye on her—on *them*—for me."

"An eye on them?" he asked. Was Dane worried about her son? About leaving her alone with her son? Or was there someone else in the picture? "Don't you trust her?"

A muscle twitched along Dane's jaw. Usually he was more stoic, harder to read. But Cole understood, maybe because he'd been in that position himself. He'd fallen for a woman he shouldn't have trusted. He was afraid his friend had done the same.

"It's not about that," Dane said. "It's about last night—about my getting jumped. She could be in danger, too."

Cole nodded. "Yes, we all agreed that could be the case—that someone's coming after us and might come after the people we love, too."

"Did you warn your family?" Dane asked.

Cole shook his head. "I don't have any contact with them." So nobody would think he loved them. He only wished that were true.

"What about you?" he asked.

Dane snorted. "I don't have any family."

"No, who's going to protect you?" And Cole wasn't talking about just a physical attack.

Who was going to protect Dane from the emotional pain of getting his heart broken?

Bruises healed. Hell, even gunshot wounds did. But a broken heart? That sometimes never mended.

Chapter 14

Someone was following her. Fortunately Dane had warned her that he'd assigned the duty to Cole Bentler. Or she would have been scared. He'd told Cole that he was worried for Emilia and Blue after the attack on him at the warehouse. So he hadn't broken his promise to never tell anyone that they weren't really involved.

But Emilia was disappointed that he was staying away from her after promising he would never leave her alone. She had thought he'd meant that he'd be with her always. But she should have known that wasn't possible.

For one he was trying to find Bradley Zeinstra.

For another, she suspected he just wanted to keep his distance from her. While he'd held her the rest of the night, he hadn't really been with her. He'd stopped talking and had appeared withdrawn.

And he hadn't made love to her again. Her body ached

for his, an emptiness yawning inside her that she'd never felt before. She needed him.

But he didn't need her. Dane Sutton needed no one.

He wasn't the only one Emilia needed. She carried her son into the chapel along with her purse and his diaper bag. And when she stepped into her office, she hesitated before placing him in the crib next to her desk.

He was napping. Car rides always put him to sleep, but he was sleeping exceptionally soundly after all the disruptions he'd had last night.

But she was afraid that if she put him down she might never be able to hold him again. Dane believed Blue was the reason for everything she'd been through, that someone wanted to take him away.

That couldn't be Bradley, who didn't even know about him. Who had never even gotten to hold his son.

Her shoulders slumped with guilt, and the baby suddenly felt very heavy. She settled him into his crib and stared down at him through eyes blurred with tears.

She had made so many mistakes. More mistakes than she'd even realized. Sure, Bradley Zeinstra had been a jerk to her, but he'd deserved to know he was going to be a father. She should have told him.

She needed to tell him now before Dane found him and blindsided him with fatherhood. But she hadn't talked to him for over a year. He would have graduated from college. Like her, he'd only had a semester left. With his engineering degree from the University of Minnesota, he could have moved anywhere for work. He might not even be in the country any longer.

Would he have kept the same cell number? She wasn't even certain she had it any longer. She'd been so angry over the way he'd robbed her of her innocence and stopped taking her calls that she had considered deleting it.

Had she?

She pulled her cell from her purse and began to flip through the contacts. There he was. Not as an original contact but as a recovered one.

She probably had deleted him and then changed her mind. Because he hadn't used protection, she'd known there was a possibility she could get pregnant. Of course she hadn't thought it was the right time. And she'd trusted him. She'd believed he'd cared about her.

He'd only cared about one thing. Sex. And that was all it had been.

It hadn't felt like last night. She hadn't experienced anything like last night before—the passion, the power...

Dane.

She had reluctantly told him Bradley's name. Since it was on Blue's birth certificate, he would have found it out easily enough anyway. Hopefully, he hadn't found Bradley yet.

She drew in a deep breath, bracing herself, then pressed the screen to call Bradley Zeinstra. Music played while the subscriber was located. She expected to get a voice mail recording.

Instead he answered, "Emily?"

She winced over his using the wrong name. Initially, she'd thought he called her Emily as a nickname or endearment. Then she'd realized he just didn't care enough to get it right. "Emilia," she corrected him.

"You're lucky I don't call you what I think you really are," he bitterly replied.

A jolt of alarm struck her heart. "Why are you angry with me?" She'd thought he would have been happy when she'd stopped trying to contact him. Of course it hadn't taken her long to stop when he hadn't returned her calls or texts.

He snorted. "How can you ask me that? You know you should have told me when you found out you were pregnant."

"You know? Who told you?" Had Dane already found him? That was faster than she'd thought he would.

"What the hell's wrong with you, Emilia?" he asked. "Are you crazy?"

She glanced down at her bandaged wrist. She hadn't done that. And she had the bruises around the wound to prove that she'd fought. She wouldn't have been able to bruise herself if she'd been holding the knife, as well. No, she had not done that.

And she hadn't called Brad until now. "No. I'm not."

"You told me—when you called," he said.

"But I haven't…" Called him before. Had she?

She switched him to speaker and pulled up her call log. Scrolling through the numbers, she found his—two weeks ago. Another middle-of-the night call.

"That's why I'm here," he said.

"Here?" He was here. "In River City?"

He snorted again. "Where the hell else would I be? I had to put my life on hold to make the trip out here from California."

So that was where he was living now.

"Why would you do that?" she asked.

"I want to see my son."

His words surprised her. She hadn't told Brad about her pregnancy because she'd figured he would deny paternity anyway. He'd made it clear he wanted nothing to do with her after that night. Why would he want contact with the child they'd made?

"But why?" she asked.

"Because he's mine!" he said.

Now the possessiveness in his voice had her stomach lurching with dread and fear. She'd thought Dane was wrong. But it suddenly seemed very possible—probable even—that Brad was behind everything that had been happening. Emilia wasn't losing her mind.

But she might lose her son.

"What the hell is going on?" Nikki had asked Cole Bentler when she'd caught him outside, watching the chapel. But he hadn't answered that. He had claimed it wasn't him she'd felt watching the place the day before, though.

So if her creepy feeling was right, like Mom's premonitions always were, then someone else had been stalking Emilia and her son.

When Nikki stepped into Emilia's office minutes after talking to Cole, she found her pale and shaky, staring down at her cell phone. And she asked her the same thing, "What the hell's going on?"

Emilia jumped as if she hadn't heard her enter. Her pale blue eyes widened with fear, but she quickly blinked it away. Then she reached for her wrist, which was bandaged.

And a wave of nausea crashed over Nikki. She felt so sick her knees threatened to fold. "You didn't…"

"No!" Emilia said with such indignation that Nikki believed her. Almost.

"But you've been acting so strangely…"

"I am not suicidal," Emilia insisted.

Nikki narrowed her eyes and studied her fiancé's sister. Her face was flushed now—with anger. "Then what happened? And you damn well better not lie to me!"

Hearing her own words, Nikki froze with dread. Damn, she sounded like her mother. Most of the time Penny Payne was the sweetest woman—except when someone lied to her. Then she got pissed.

Once Nikki had learned Penny's husband had fathered a son with another woman, she'd understood her mother's need for honesty. Nikki was finding in herself the same intolerance to dishonesty that she'd seen her mother display.

Emilia stared at her for several long moments before shaking her head.

"Not telling me is the same as lying," Nikki said and flinched as she heard the echo of her mother's words again. Now she understood why her brothers had given her a wooden plaque for her birthday that said: *Sometimes when I open my mouth my mother comes out.*

A sigh slipped through Emilia's lips, one that fortunately sounded like a sigh of resignation. "Okay, but you can't tell Lars."

Nikki made no such promise. She wasn't going to keep anything from her fiancé. Well, anything more...

She hadn't shared all her fears about his sister with Lars because he was already so worried about Emilia. Once he saw her bandaged wrist...

He would probably have the poor girl committed. And Emilia didn't look crazy. In fact she seemed more focused than Nikki had ever seen her before.

"What's been going on with you?" she asked. "Tell me everything."

A torrent of words poured from Emilia along with a

few tears that spilled from her beautiful eyes. Hearing what the girl had gone through, Nikki felt tears sting her own eyes. But she blinked them back and focused on Emilia.

The young woman stopped and stared at her. "Do you believe me?"

Nikki picked up the cell phone from the desk. She wished she'd investigated it earlier when the caterer and bartender had told her about Emilia making those late-night calls. She should have known Emilia loved her mother too much to risk messing up her special day. "Your keys went missing for a while," she said. "What about your phone?"

Emilia nodded. "I lost it around the house a few times. Just thought I was distracted."

Like Nikki had thought. But now she realized what she should have before. "Someone cloned your phone."

Emilia gasped. "What? How is that possible?"

"Put duplicate SIM cards in each." She sighed. "It's actually pretty easy." She'd done it to her brothers' before, when she'd suspected they were withholding information. Like Emilia had been.

"Damn it," she said, angry over what someone had put her would-be sister-in-law through. "You should have told us earlier what was going on."

Emilia shook her head. "I already put you and Lars through enough."

Nikki pulled the girl into a hug. "That's because we love you and want to be there for you." She touched Emilia's wrist. "You could have been killed."

"Dane rescued me," Emilia said. "He arrived just in time."

"Where the hell is he now?" Nikki asked.

"He's trying to find the person he thinks is responsible for all of this," Emilia said, and all the color drained from her face again, leaving her almost deathly pale but for the dark circles beneath her eyes.

"And who does he think that is?" And why the hell hadn't he had Nikki help him investigate? Nikki had solved more of the mysteries for the Payne Protection Agency than all her brothers combined. She'd also been the one who'd found Emilia when everyone else had given her up for dead.

"Dane thinks it's Blue's father."

"Dane thinks that," Nikki said, repeating her words, "but what do *you* think?"

"I thought Dane was wrong," Emilia admitted before uttering a ragged sigh, "until I just talked to Bradley. He's in River City."

Every protective instinct kicking in, Nikki stepped closer to Emilia and to the baby asleep in the crib next to her. "Well, you're not going to see him."

"I have to."

"You're not going alone." She felt sick, knowing what she should have done. She should have told her fiancé her concerns and she should have already called him here to learn what had been going on with his sister.

Emilia shivered but shook her head. "No... I can't believe it's Bradley."

"You can't take any chances," Nikki said. "So Lars will go with you. We need to tell him what's going on with you."

Emilia shook her head. "No way. Not unless you want your wedding venue to be a prison yard. If he goes with me, he'll kill Brad for sure. And he'll wind up in prison."

Nikki opened her mouth, but she couldn't argue.

Emilia knew her brother too well. Lars probably would kill the guy even if he hadn't been the one terrorizing her. He would kill him for using his sister and casting her aside. "You're right."

"I'm going with her," a deep voice murmured.

She tensed. But it wasn't Lars—thankfully—who'd joined them in Emilia's office. It was Dane. But he appeared more intense than Nikki had ever seen him. Even with him going instead of Lars, she didn't like Blue's dad's chances for survival.

"You should have stayed back at the chapel with Nikki and Cole," Dane said as he pulled his truck into the parking lot of the Lakeside Inn.

He should have stopped Emilia from coming along with him. But she sat in the passenger's seat, her hands tightly clenched in her lap. Why couldn't he refuse her anything—even for her own protection?

"I have to be here," she said.

She wouldn't have had to. Once Dane had traced Bradley Zeinstra's credit card to this hotel, he should have just confronted the man alone. But he'd stopped by to talk to Emilia first, to make sure she was safe.

She had been safe, but she'd also been determined to talk to her baby's father. So if he hadn't brought her, she would have called Bradley back and found him herself.

It was better that they come together, better for Dane to protect her. And to gauge what her feelings were for her old boyfriend. He wasn't sure why it was so important for him to know, but the desire burned inside him, like the desire he felt for her.

He wanted to touch her again. Wanted to kiss her. But

he held himself back from reaching for her. He was already too involved—with her and with her son.

Hell, he'd been too involved since the minute Lars had showed him her picture. If only she wasn't so damned beautiful…

It wasn't just her beauty that drew him. There was a sweetness about her he'd never known before.

She inhaled an unsteady breath. "Are we going in?"

He'd rather leave her in the truck, but he didn't have backup. There was no one to watch out for her. Cole had been called away for an actual bodyguard assignment and so had Manny.

Dane had turned down the job when Cooper had called him. He'd admitted he had a more important case he'd taken on himself.

Emilia was the most important.

That was why he couldn't leave her alone and unprotected. He wouldn't let anything happen to her.

He sighed. "Yeah, we're going in…" Before he opened the truck door, he patted his holster. His gun was there and ready to fire.

Bradley Zeinstra wouldn't hurt her ever again.

They didn't need to stop at the front desk and ask for the room number. Dane already had it. Hell, they didn't even have to go inside the inn. Brad had rented one of the separate cabins that were closer to Lake Michigan.

Emilia glanced at the sparkling surface of the lake. "He told me he was in the city."

But the lake was a good twenty-minute drive from the urban metropolis of River City.

Dane shrugged.

"But then I should have known better than to believe anything he said," Emilia added.

Now there was bitterness in her sweet voice. Dane couldn't tell if there was anything else, if she had any unresolved feelings for the man.

He'd given her a child, the son she loved so much. They shared a connection that Dane would never have with her. Something churned inside him, but it took him a second to identify the sick feeling as jealousy. He hadn't felt it in years, not since he was a kid envying his friends who had parents who obviously loved them.

Dane had accepted then that he wouldn't be loved. That he wasn't loveable. It was fine then. And it would be now.

As they drew closer to the blue cabin marked with the number 5, Emilia reached out and clutched his arm. She had to be nervous about seeing Bradley again.

But then she screamed as a figure emerged from the cabin and ran toward them. The guy was dressed in black, with a hood drawn tightly around his masked face.

"That's him!" she yelled as the guy ran past them.

Bradley? Dane had no time to ask before he chased after the black-clothed man. This was how she had described the intruder, the one who'd tried to slash her wrist.

It had to be Zeinstra. But whoever it was, Dane intended to catch and stop him. He drew his gun. But before he could squeeze the trigger, he heard another scream.

It came from behind him, from where he'd left Emilia frozen in fear near that cabin. The scream was full of fear and horror.

Despite his best intentions, Dane had left her alone and unprotected. And apparently this guy, who had disappeared while Dane had turned back, wasn't working alone.

His partner must have grabbed Emilia. Giving up the chase, Dane ran back toward the cabin. He only hoped that this time, he wasn't too late to save her.

Chapter 15

A hand was pressed over Emilia's mouth to hold back another scream. It was her hand trembling against her lips as she tried to contain her horror. Seeing the masked man again had been terrifying enough.

But seeing what he'd done...

Brad sat on the ground, his back pressed up against the wall he must have slid down leaving a trail of crimson to stain the white beadboard. His head was slumped against his shoulder, his eyes open and blank as he stared up at her.

But it was the handle of the knife protruding from his chest that affected her the most. It was the teal-blue handle from the set in her kitchen. It was the knife that had cut her wrist, and now it was buried to the teal hilt in Brad's chest. Blood gurgled from the wound and spread across his once white T-shirt.

Another scream threatened as the horror overwhelmed her. It burned in the back of her throat. And when strong hands closed over her shoulders, it escaped through her lips and her trembling fingers.

Had the man returned? Did he intend to kill her now like he'd killed Brad?

She lashed out, swinging her arms. But those strong hands gripped her firmly. And she recognized that touch.

"Dane…" She gasped his name with relief. The masked man hadn't killed him.

He turned her in his arms, spinning her to face him. "What's wrong?" he asked, as he cupped her tear-dampened cheek. "Are you okay?"

No. She wasn't. She wasn't sure she would ever be okay again.

"Did you stop him?" she asked.

He shook his head. "No, he got away." He stared down into her face, his eyes dark with concern. "Are you okay?" he asked again. "Why did you scream?"

She stepped aside, so he could see the body slumped against the wall.

"Who is that?" he asked. "Do you know?"

"That's Bradley," she explained. "That's Blue's dad. Was…"

That *was* Blue's dad. Bradley Zeinstra was dead.

Over a year ago, when he hadn't returned her calls and texts and she'd realized he'd only been using her, she had wished him dead. Once. Guilt flashed through her now over how childishly she'd reacted. Sure, he'd been an ass. But she'd been too naive.

She wasn't naive anymore.

And Bradley Zeinstra wasn't anything anymore.

"If that's Zeinstra..." Dane murmured. "Then who was I chasing?"

"I don't know," she murmured.

She'd been right. Bradley hadn't been the one terrorizing her. But she wished now that it had been him—because then it would be over. Instead it felt like this nightmare would never end.

Dane had been right. The man in the mask had had a partner. But it looked like he'd eliminated his partner instead of Emilia. Her scream hung yet in the air.

And so did the distant wail of a siren. The police must have been called. He wasn't surprised another hotel patron or staff member would have dialed 911. Someone couldn't have helped but overhear Emilia's screams.

And if the screams had caused them to look out their windows, they had probably seen him and Emilia. She was definitely remarkable enough for witnesses to be able to accurately describe her. So they couldn't leave the scene, even though Dane's every instinct told him they should run.

But if they ran, they would look even guiltier than they already did. According to Emilia, Zeinstra claimed he'd had a call from her that had brought him to the city.

An officer might believe she'd lured him here to kill him. And that Dane was her accomplice.

Dane glanced toward the open door, tempted to rush her to his truck and flee the scene. But there were probably surveillance cameras that would catch his plate number as they left the lot.

He released a shaky breath. "This doesn't look good."

"What do you mean?" Emilia asked.

He gestured toward the body. He recognized the hilt

of the knife: it matched the ones in the block on her counter. That must have been the knife the intruder had used on her the night before.

So her prints and her blood would be all over it— mixed with Zeinstra's.

As she glanced at her old boyfriend, the color drained from her face, and she began to tremble with shock. "I can't believe he's dead."

And he heard the regret in her voice. She must still have feelings for the man.

Dane had been a fool to sleep with her the night before. She'd turned to him out of fear and gratitude. This was the man she'd loved—the father of her child.

Of course Dane knew he was unlovable. His real mother hadn't loved him enough to keep him. And the parents who'd adopted him hadn't been able to bring themselves to love him at all. And they'd sworn they'd tried. They just hadn't felt it.

He didn't expect Emilia to feel it, either.

She glanced up from the dead body of her ex-lover, tilting her head as she must have heard the sirens, too. "You called the police?"

He shook his head. It might have looked better for them if he had. But he hadn't had time.

Her lips parted on a gasp as she realized what he'd meant. How it would look for them to be found standing over a dead body.

And her voice tremulous with fear, she repeated his words, "This doesn't look good…"

"So you work for the Payne Protection Agency?" Nicholas Payne asked.

The name was new to him; he'd just started using it

a few months ago. He'd wanted his son to carry on the name. He'd wanted the same name as his family.

Dane Sutton's name was one he'd heard a few times now. He'd seen it on a few police reports, as well. He'd even met the guy a couple of times.

Dane nodded. "Yes. I work for Cooper Payne."

For his team, Cooper had hired all ex-Marines. With his buzz-cut hair and muscular build, Dane Sutton had clearly been a Marine—a formidable one.

"Cooper is my brother," Nick said with no hesitation. It was no longer hard for him to claim his family, like it had once been when he'd first come to River City. Maybe that was because they'd all freely claimed him as their own.

"You look just like him," Dane said.

Nick and Cooper were almost the same age, too.

Dane's brow furrowed in confusion. "But I thought all Cooper's brothers were bodyguards."

"I am a bodyguard, too," Nick said. "I work for Logan. Or I will once I formally resign from the FBI. I'm an agent."

"Someone called the FBI?" Dane asked.

Nick shook his head. "I was assigned to the River City PD. Right now I'm acting as police chief since the new police chief is on his honeymoon."

Dane nodded. "Woodrow Lynch. I was at his wedding."

Nick nodded. "I thought I saw you there—with her." He nodded to where a female police officer talked to a trembling Emilia Ecklund.

"We weren't together…then."

"But you're together now?"

Dane nodded.

"Then I guess I'll be arresting you both." He stood up and gestured at the female officer. "Read her the Miranda."

"No," Dane protested as he stepped toward Emilia, as if to protect her.

Was he her boyfriend or her bodyguard?

"We just found him like this," Dane said. "We didn't do this. Talk to Nikki—your sister. She knows. We were with her before we came here."

That was the problem. Nick was related to too damn many people. He couldn't risk being accused of favoritism. He needed to err on the side of caution so he didn't let a murderer walk just because of who he or she knew.

He reached out and clasped his hand around Dane Sutton's arm. The guy was huge, nearly as big as his friend who'd proposed to Nick's sister. If he tried to resist, Nick wasn't confident he would be able to subdue the guy without shooting him.

He didn't want to shoot him, though. For one, he wasn't sure a bullet would stop him. He was that damn big. For another reason, he didn't want to get off on the wrong foot with the man about to become his new brother-in-law.

Lars Ecklund wasn't going to be happy that Nick had arrested his sister, though. So it probably wouldn't matter if Nick shot his best friend, as well.

"I have to do this by the book," Nick explained. "There can be no hint of impropriety here." He'd spent months cleaning up the River City PD. He wasn't going to risk looking corrupt himself.

Nor was he going to risk a suspect getting away with murder—no matter who the hell she was related to.

Chapter 16

Emilia had already been read her rights. She'd been booked and photographed for a mug shot—all under the suspicion of murder, even though no charges had actually been pressed.

Yet.

She knew that the murder weapon would come back with her prints and with her DNA on it. She was going to go to prison for a murder she hadn't committed.

She didn't need to be read the riot act, too.

"Stop lecturing," she implored Lars. He hadn't even waited until they'd left the police station.

He yelled at her in the crowded lobby. "I can't believe you didn't come to me. Didn't you learn anything from what happened last time?"

She flinched.

"You nearly lost your son and your life," he reminded her.

And she murmured, "I know…"

She would never forget what had happened no matter how much she wished she could. But that was the past. Right now she was worried about the future.

She was worried about her son.

He was with Nikki. He was safe.

But he'd started out the first few weeks of his life without his mother. Now he was about to lose her again, maybe for the rest of Emilia's life.

"So why didn't you tell me about the crying and the phone?"

Nikki must have filled him in on everything Emilia had shared with her. She doubted he'd talked to Dane.

Dane stood behind him in the lobby. Lars hadn't even acknowledged his presence. All his anger was directed at her right now. And she was about to buckle beneath the guilt and pressure of it. All she wanted was to go home to her son. To hold him as long as she could.

No. That wasn't all she wanted. She wanted Dane, too.

But she'd already caused him enough trouble. She'd cost him his friendship with her brother. Maybe his job. And now possibly his freedom if he was arrested as an accomplice to the murder she hadn't committed.

"I'm sorry," she murmured. The words weren't for her brother. They were for Dane. But like Lars was ignoring him, he was ignoring her. He wouldn't even look at her.

He probably hated her for all the trouble she'd caused him. And she couldn't blame him.

And she couldn't help but love him.

Dane closed his eyes. But it didn't matter. He could still see her face, pale with fear and weariness. And he could hear her brother ranting and raving.

He needed to just walk away. Lars knew everything

now. He would make sure nothing happened to her. But Lars was hurting her. She'd actually flinched over some of the things he'd said. Nobody knew Lars better than Dane. The guy was impulsive and reacted with emotion rather than logic.

But he needed a little sensitivity now. He wasn't helping Emilia at all. He was only making her feel worse. And Dane, who never lost control, lost his temper.

"Shut up!" he yelled. And all conversation in the busy police department lobby ceased. "Shut the hell up!"

Lars turned toward him. "Don't you dare talk to me," the bigger man warned. "You're not my friend anymore— you proved that!"

"I don't give a crap about your friendship," Dane said. And at the moment, he didn't. He only cared about Emilia.

He'd promised to protect her. He hadn't realized he might need to do that against her own damn brother. He stepped between the siblings and took Emilia's hand in his. Her fingers were trembling. And her slight body shook, too—probably with exhaustion and shock.

"Don't touch her!" Lars growled in warning. "Don't you dare touch her!"

Lars had no idea exactly how much Dane wanted to touch her again, like he had the night before. But it didn't matter what he wanted right now. He only cared about what she wanted.

"Are you sick of listening to his big mouth?"

Her lips curved into a slight smile, and she nodded.

"Then I'll get you out of here," he offered.

But before he could lead her to the exit, a big hand clamped over his shoulder. "She's not going anywhere with you," Lars threatened.

"She's not a child," Dane said. "She gets to choose where she goes and with whom—not you."

Dane kind of choked on the words as he uttered them. He doubted she would choose him. No one else had. Or if they had, they'd regretted the choice.

Lars's throat moved as if he were spluttering with anger.

Emilia squeezed Dane's hand with suddenly steady fingers. Then she told her brother, "I'm leaving with Dane."

"No!" Lars bellowed. "He won't keep you safe!"

"He has," Emilia insisted.

Lars gestured at her wrist. "You were attacked and now arrested. He's been no help to you. He's hurt you."

Dane shook his head. "I wouldn't do that. You're the one who's hurt her, yelling at her after all she's been through." That was why he hadn't been able to walk away, why he couldn't leave her with her brother. Lars didn't understand all she'd been through.

Lars's face flushed. He should have been embarrassed over how he'd treated his sister. Instead he must have been angry—because he swung out.

His hand held in hers, Dane couldn't deflect the blow. It caught him on the chin. He must have been tired because he staggered back a step before regaining his balance.

Like he had stepped between the siblings, Emilia stepped between them now. She shoved Lars back. "Stop it!" she yelled at him. "You're an idiot. Dane saved my life. You should be thanking him. Not hitting him."

"Em—" Lars reached out for her.

But she stepped back to Dane's side and slid her arm around him, as if he needed her help now. "Stay away from me!" she told her brother. "Stay away!"

Despite his chin throbbing from Lars's blow, Dane felt sorry for his friend. His heart hurt with the thought of her telling him the same thing, to stay away from her. He suspected eventually she might tell him that, if he didn't do all the things he'd promised.

If he didn't protect her…

From the man terrorizing her and from a murder charge.

"You are an idiot," his ever-supportive fiancée told him. Nikki Payne was incapable of being anything but direct. And right. She was always right.

While she was the first to claim that, Lars couldn't argue with her. His head throbbed as if he'd taken a blow. Emilia's words had hit him hard, almost as hard as the tears he'd seen in her eyes when he'd railed at her.

"I couldn't stop myself," he admitted. "The words just kept spewing out…"

"You yelled at her," Nikki said.

"I was so scared," Lars admitted.

He'd come so close to losing Emilia again—forever this time. That bandage around her wrist had been stained with dried blood. But what if the knife had hit an artery?

She could have bled out in her bathroom. She could be dead. That was so much worse than being arrested.

But she'd been arrested, too. He could lose her to prison, as well. He might have already lost her to his own stupidity and temper.

She wasn't the only Ecklund who'd been arrested today. Cuffs had been snapped around his wrists before Emilia had even walked away with Dane. His *friend* had done him a favor, though. He'd told the officer arresting Lars that he didn't want to press charges. But there had been too damn many witnesses to the assault.

Assault?

It had just been a little tap. Really. Dane must have been tired, or he wouldn't have even stumbled back. Unless he'd done it for the benefit of those witnesses...

Fortunately Lars hadn't had to make bail. His future brother-in-law had released him on his own recognizances, just as Emilia and Dane had been released. They hadn't even been charged like he'd been.

He'd only gone down to the police department to pick her up. But he'd made everything worse.

Small but strong arms wrapped around him. He sat on a stool near the computer desk in Nikki's office/gun safe/home gym. If he hadn't been sitting, she wouldn't have been able to reach his neck where she pressed a kiss to the tense muscles.

"You are an idiot," she said. "But you are also the most loving and loyal man I've ever known."

"I shouted at her," he miserably admitted, his voice cracking with emotion.

"You were scared," she said. "My brothers have yelled at me so many times."

Because Nikki had scared them so many times. The woman constantly put herself in danger.

But Emilia...

She wasn't like Nikki. She wasn't invincible. She was vulnerable. And Dane had taken advantage of that vulnerability. He'd stepped in to play her white knight. But Lars knew he was no such thing. Someday Emilia would learn the same, and then her heart would be broken.

"She yelled back," Lars said, which had surprised him. Emilia had never yelled at him before—until that other day when he'd struck Dane. "She jumped to his defense."

"She loves him."

Lars groaned. "He's going to break her heart."

"Why?" Nikki asked.

"Because he's Dane," Lars said. "He doesn't care about people."

"He's your best friend," she said.

"But—but—"

"He put his life on the line for you how many times?" she asked.

Lars groaned again—for another reason. Guilt.

"You told me he's saved your life before," Nikki reminded him. "And he's risked his to help you and now to help her."

Lars had already felt bad. Now he felt worse.

"He's always been a good friend to you," Nikki said. "He wouldn't be if he didn't care."

"I am an idiot," Lars said with a heavy sigh. He'd alienated his sister and his best friend.

"Yes," Nikki agreed. "And now we won't be able to convince Emilia to let us help her. She won't stay here where *we* can protect her."

He groaned again as misery and frustration gripped him. He'd screwed up so badly.

"So we're going to have to trust Dane to do it," Nikki said.

Lars wasn't sure he would ever be able to trust his best friend again. "He should have told me what was going on. She should have told me."

Nikki squeezed her arms around him. "They were both worried you'd do what you just did—overreact."

"She was nearly killed," Lars said. "And she's now a murder suspect. I don't think I overreacted at all." But he could have handled himself better, could have held his temper. He was just so scared. And if he were honest with himself, he wasn't just scared for Emilia. He was scared for Dane, too. He was afraid that he was going to lose his sister *and* his best friend.

Forever.

Chapter 17

"I am so sorry," Emilia said as she held the ice pack to Dane's swelling chin.

"Stop apologizing," Dane said. "You're not the one who hit me."

"No," she said. "But my idiot brother did." Emilia's only satisfaction at the moment was knowing that Nikki was probably giving him the lecture he had given her. Unfortunately, they had both deserved it.

"He's my idiot friend," Dane said.

"Was," she corrected him. "I doubt you're friends any longer." And that was her fault, too. "I'm sorry."

"Stop apologizing," he said again. He took the ice pack from her hand and tossed it onto the counter. It landed next to the knife block that was missing one knife.

The knife buried in Bradley's chest.

"Lars shouldn't have made you feel bad," he said.

She shook her head. "It wasn't Lars…"

"Zeinstra?"

Seeing his body hadn't made her feel anything but horror. She'd felt bad that he was dead. But she hadn't felt any sense of loss or regret. She couldn't believe that she had ever been attracted to him. He had really been just a boy.

He hadn't been a man. Like Dane.

She shook her head again then sighed. "I'm sorry he's dead. But…"

"You're not upset about it?"

"Brad used me," she said. "He never cared about me. And I was a fool to think I cared about him when I didn't even know him."

Did she know Dane any better? How could she when his own best friend claimed he didn't even know him?

"He was a bigger idiot than your brother," Dane said.

She sighed. "I can't be mad at him, though. He gave me Blue."

The baby was upstairs, asleep in his crib. She'd barely seen him that day, what with finding Bradley and then being questioned in his murder. Maybe she needed to get used to not seeing him. She'd been worried about him being taken away from her again. But she would probably be taken away from him.

And taken to prison…

As if he'd read her mind, Dane pulled her into his arms and held her. "We'll figure this out," he promised. "You won't go to prison."

"If I do," she said, "I probably won't go alone." He could be arrested, too—like he had been today—when the acting chief had slapped cuffs on his wrists.

Because of her injury, she hadn't been cuffed. But

she'd been put into the back of a police car and driven to the police department like Dane had. Separately.

They'd been questioned separately, too, as if being tested to see if their stories would match.

"I'm not worried about that," Dane said. "I've been in worse places than prison."

She'd probably been, too, when she thought of that cold, abandoned warehouse where she had nearly bled to death after giving birth. She shivered as she remembered the cold that had penetrated her flesh and bones.

Dane pulled her closer. "You're cold. And it's late. You need to get some rest."

Before she could head toward the stairwell, he lifted and carried her. Without his help, she wasn't sure she would have made it on her own to the bedroom—to the bed where he laid her. She was that exhausted.

But then he began to undress her and a new energy surged through her with desire. Her skin heated and tingled. "Dane…"

"I'm sorry," he said. "But I can't *not* be with you."

He made love to her gently—with a tenderness of which she would have never believed him capable. He kissed her softly and skimmed his lips over every inch of her.

Emilia had never felt so cared for. But she didn't deserve his gentleness, not after everything she'd put him through, everything she had cost him.

She owed him for his protection. For his sacrifice. So she pushed him off the bed until they were both standing beside it—although her legs trembled. And she undressed him. First she removed his holster and settled it onto the table next to the bed. Then she tugged up his shirt and pulled it over his head, baring his muscular chest and washboard abs.

Her fingers trembled as she unbuttoned his jeans.

And he sucked in a breath.

Then she lowered his zipper and his breath escaped in a ragged sigh.

"Emilia…"

She dropped to her knees on the hardwood floor, and she made love to him with her mouth. She moved her lips up and down the length of him, taking him deep into her throat.

He groaned, and his fingers clutched in her hair. "Emilia…"

She flicked her tongue over the head of his erection. He tugged her away from him, found a condom and sheathed himself. Then he lifted her. Muscles bunched in his arms as he held her up. Then, still standing, he eased inside her. She wound her arms around his broad shoulders and locked her legs around his waist.

While he moved inside her, he lowered his head and kissed her. Then he lowered his head more and flicked his tongue across the taut tip of her nipple.

She moaned as sensations spiraled through her. Tension built inside her. And she rode him, seeking release as the tension became unbearable.

He thrust his hips, moving deeper inside her. And deeper and deeper.

She didn't know where he ended and she began. She'd never known she could feel like this—so full—so complete and yet crazy with desire, too.

All her fears and exhaustion dropped away, leaving only desire. Then the tension broke as pleasure overwhelmed her. Her body shuddered as she came.

Dane tensed, the muscles in his neck standing out like cords. With a deep groan, he came, too. His big body shuddered as his passion overwhelmed him.

She overwhelmed him. And the things she made him feel, things he'd never felt before. He took his time in the bathroom, cleaning up. So she was asleep when he came back into the bedroom.

He could have walked away, or he could have at least gone down to the couch to sleep. But just like at the police department, he couldn't walk away from her.

And now that he was with her, he couldn't leave. Eventually he would have to once they'd caught whoever was after her. She wouldn't need his protection then. She wouldn't need him.

That was good, though.

Because his protection was all he really had to offer her.

Maybe he was losing it because he heard that faint crying. Was the son of a bitch in the house again?

He'd had the front door and broken jamb replaced and had personally changed the locks on both. The intruder wasn't going to come back—not now when he knew Dane was staying there—when Dane had nearly caught him. Twice now.

So the crying wasn't some sick recording. It must have been Blue.

Emilia murmured in her sleep and began to awaken. But he leaned over and whispered, "Shh… I got this. Go back to sleep."

Moments later, he wondered what the hell he was doing when he lifted the baby from his crib. The kid blinked and stared up at him, his blue eyes bleary with sleep.

Dane expected him to cry louder. But Blue was too taken aback by his presence. He should have been getting used to him. Dane was getting used to him, to his slight weight and his startling blue eyes.

He wasn't used to changing diapers. But the baby was damp. So he had no choice. Fortunately—for Blue—he had disposable diapers. There were no pins. Just tape.

Dane managed to change the diaper and find a new sleeper thing for the baby. Getting his tiny legs into the garment was a new challenge, but he managed.

The struggle must have fully awakened the baby, though, because he didn't seem at all tired now.

"Do you need a bottle?" Dane asked. He could probably figure out how to make one. The kid wasn't crying though, so Dane didn't think he was hungry.

"No bottle," Dane murmured. He sat on the rocker in the corner of the nursery and clasped the baby against his chest. The kid was warm and smelled good now that he'd been changed. He shifted around until he settled against Dane's shoulder, which was exactly where his mother slept.

"That's what you need, isn't it?" Dane mused. "Your mother…"

Dane was afraid Blue wasn't the only one who needed Emilia, though.

"I'll make sure you don't lose your momma," he promised.

He should have been alarmed at the number of promises he'd been tossing around lately. But these weren't empty promises. He had every intention of keeping them, even if it cost him his life.

* * *

He wished he still had the knife. He so wanted to plunge it into another heart—into Dane Sutton's heart.

He had done a little more research into Emilia's self-appointed bodyguard.

A former war hero.

A boy who had been given up for adoption.

How could he help a woman who'd nearly done the same thing his mother had? Couldn't he see that she didn't deserve to have her son?

Bradley Zeinstra hadn't deserved him, either.

What a fool. Killing him had been doing the world a favor. And it should have gotten Emilia put behind bars.

Even though she'd been arrested, she hadn't stayed in jail. Why had they released her?

It didn't matter now, though.

Without Zeinstra to claim custody of her child, the baby would go to Emilia's next of kin, to her Neanderthal brother and his fiancée. And they wouldn't give him up like Zeinstra had agreed to do.

Too bad that idiot had gotten greedy. He'd wanted more money. But that wasn't all he'd wanted. He'd wanted a relationship with his kid, wanted to stay part of his life.

When he'd been told that wasn't possible, Zeinstra had claimed that he'd changed his mind. He'd even threatened to come clean to Emilia about the plan.

So Zeinstra had had to die, even though his death hadn't been part of the plan. And now the plan had to change.

Again.

If they couldn't get the baby the original way, they would have to just take him. They probably should have done that weeks ago—when they had first gotten inside the house. When they'd been able to see him…

But only see him…

They hadn't dared to touch him, to disturb him and wake him up. They hadn't wanted Emilia to catch them. They hadn't wanted to kill.

Then.

Now it was clear that was the only way.

Bradley Zeinstra had had to die.

But he wasn't the only one.

With Dane Sutton living there, it wouldn't be as easy to take the baby. But Dane Sutton wouldn't be a problem much longer.

Because he would be taken out the same way Bradley Zeinstra had been—with a knife through his heart.

Chapter 18

"I guess I should be relieved you didn't slap the cuffs on me this time," Dane mused, but he rubbed his wrists anyway, remembering how the steel had felt against his skin. How it had hurt to have his arms shackled behind his back.

Yeah, it was good Nick Payne hadn't put the cuffs on him again. But it wasn't good that he'd picked him up from Emilia's.

Fortunately, Cole and Manny had arrived before he'd been hauled off in the back of another police car. They would protect Emilia and the baby.

He'd fallen asleep with Blue in his arms. Emilia had awakened him early that morning with a kiss. For a moment Dane had let himself imagine what it would be like to wake up that way every morning—with Emilia's lips brushing softly, tenderly across his.

But that wouldn't happen. She was just grateful for his protection. She didn't love him. And he...

He didn't know how to love. She and Blue deserved more than he could give them. For now they needed what he could give them—protection.

But he couldn't keep them from danger if he wasn't with them. And he still didn't know why Nick Payne had had him picked up. He'd already made it clear he wasn't going to press charges against Lars for sucker punching him in the lobby. So he wasn't here about that.

The acting chief stared at him across his desk in his corner office with the glass walls. If Dane were still a suspect, wouldn't he have been brought into an interrogation room with no windows but for the two-way mirror? Wouldn't he have been handcuffed to the table, so he couldn't try to escape?

He returned Nick's stare. The guy looked so much like Cooper they could have been twins like Logan and Parker Payne were. If Dane had the story straight, they were only half siblings. Penny Payne wasn't Nick's mother although she acted like it.

Apparently, she acted like everyone's mother—everyone's but his, which was a good thing. Nobody had ever acted like his mother, and he was fine with that. He didn't need anyone. Never had. Never would.

Nick Payne's unreadable face cracked with a slight grin, and he chuckled. "You and I are a lot alike."

"Really?" Dane doubted that. Nick was part of a huge, loving family.

"I didn't know I had any family until a few years ago," he said.

And Dane started. Had the guy read his mind? How could he have possibly known what he was thinking?

"I was also a Marine," Nick said.

Dane shrugged. "So you had me brought in so we could become friends?"

"I've never been a smart-ass, though," Nick said.

Dane could not say the same. But his snarky humor was his way of handling things. He'd never needed it more than now.

"I'm not always smart," he admitted. He'd risked his life so many times. But then he didn't have much to lose.

"Is that why you got involved with your best friend's sister?" Nick asked.

Anger surging through Dane, he fisted his hands. He didn't care who the hell Nicholas Payne was. If he said anything about Emilia…

As if he could see the fists through his desk, Nick motioned with his hands for Dane to settle down. "I'm not passing judgment," he assured him. "That's yet another thing we have in common."

"What?"

"I fell for my best friend's sister, too," he said with a grin. "And I fell hard."

Panic chased away Dane's anger, and his hands shook a little. "No, no, that's not the case."

He hadn't fallen in love with Emilia. Not at all.

"What is the case?" Nick asked.

"It's not love," Dane insisted. "I don't know anything about love."

"Neither did I," Nick said. "Until I met the Payne family. Then I realized what love is. And that I had already loved Annalise for a long time."

Dane shivered. "I thought you picked me up to interrogate me," he said. "Not counsel me on my love life."

Nick snorted. "Yeah, you are a smart-ass."

He shrugged and leaned back in his chair, as if they were just having a casual conversation.

Dane guessed it was anything but, because he surmised he was still a suspect in Zeinstra's murder.

"I've known Annalise a long time," Nick said. "All her life. I know she's a good and honest person."

Dane tensed. Maybe *he* wasn't the suspect.

"How well do you really know Emilia Ecklund?" Nick asked.

"She's my best friend's sister," Dane reminded him.

"A best friend you didn't meet until boot camp," Nick said.

Dane's tension increased. Acting Chief Payne had thoroughly investigated him. "Just because I haven't known him as long as…"

"I grew up next door to Gage and Annalise," Nick remarked. "When did you meet Emilia?"

Irritation frayed Dane's nerves. "I'm sure you already know." But he answered anyway, so Nick would remember what she'd been through. "When her brother and your sister rescued her from weeks of captivity."

Nick nodded. "She endured a lot."

"Yes," Dane said. "Unfortunately her ordeal hasn't ended."

Nick narrowed his blue eyes as if skeptical. "That's what she says."

"That's what I say, too," Dane said.

"So you've heard the tape of crying she claims she's heard?" he asked. "You saw the intruder slit her wrist the other night?"

Dane's stomach muscles tightened with dread. "No, but I saw the man running away from Zeinstra's rented cabin. He was dressed like she said he'd been dressed the night he attacked her at her house, with the zombie mask and the hood."

If only he'd caught the son of a bitch, there would have been no need for either him or Emilia to be questioned.

It would all be over…

She wouldn't need him anymore then. He could move back to his studio in the old warehouse. He could leave her and the baby and get back to his life. Why did that life suddenly feel very empty?

"She didn't call the police the night her home was broken into," Nick mused. "Wouldn't she have done that if she'd truly been frightened?"

She had been frightened that no one would believe her. Apparently she'd had good reason to fear that.

"The guy got in before she could call," Dane said. "And then I showed up."

"But you didn't see him."

"I saw him yesterday," he said. "I was chasing after him when I heard her scream."

Nick nodded. "That's right. So he got away. And when you went back to her, you found Bradley Zeinstra with a knife in his heart."

"Yes. He'd been stabbed."

"Did you see it happen?" Nick asked.

Dane's head began to pound with confusion. This was the interrogation. Nick had asked him these questions the day before, though. Was he double-checking his story or Emilia's?

"No," Dane said. "The knife was already sticking out of his chest when Emilia found him."

"You were with her?"

Dane's breath caught for a moment. He wasn't the suspect. Emilia was. "I heard her scream when she found him."

"So you weren't with her."

He uttered a heavy sigh before slowly admitting, "No."

"So you really have no way of knowing how that knife got in Bradley Zeinstra's chest."

"The guy in the mask," Dane said, the irritation fraying his nerves so that his voice got sharp. "He's the one who stabbed him."

"With a knife from Emilia Ecklund's kitchen."

"Yes," Dane said. "She told you that. The guy took it after he cut her wrist with it."

Nick nodded. But he appeared even more skeptical now.

"She's telling the truth," Dane said.

"How do you know?" Nick asked him. "You didn't see who stabbed Zeinstra. She entered that cabin alone."

"And found him dead."

Nick tilted his head. "Or killed him."

"No!" Dane stood up now. He'd heard more than enough. "If I'm not under arrest, I'm leaving."

"You're not under arrest," Nick said as he stood up, too. He was tall like his brothers. But Dane was a bit taller, a bit broader. "I believe you."

"Good!"

"I'm just not so sure you should believe her."

"How can you question her after everything's she's been through?" Dane asked.

"Sometimes bad experiences can change a person," Nick said. "But you don't even know what kind of person she was before she was taken hostage."

"Lars—"

"Lars is her brother," Nick said. "And she wasn't completely honest with him, either. She didn't tell him she was pregnant. She met with that lawyer instead of Cooper. She might not be the person Lars thinks she is."

Dane shook his head. "You don't know Emilia."

"Unfortunately, neither do you," Nick persisted.

Dane wanted to argue with him, but he couldn't. He hadn't known Emilia long enough to know her well. He only knew what her devoted brother had told him. And maybe Lars loved her too much to see the truth about her.

Maybe Dane loved her too much to see the truth, as well. The thought shocked him.

It wasn't true. None of it could be true.

Emilia couldn't be a killer. And Dane couldn't be in love with her.

Where the hell was Dane?

He had been gone a long time, so long that Cole had bailed on Manny, leaving him alone to protect Emilia and her baby. Cole claimed he'd been called into the office. But Manny wondered if he'd actually gone to check on Dane.

Dane would be furious with him.

"Where is he?" Emilia asked.

"Cole?" Manny asked as he paced the length of the living room. He could clearly see the street through all the windows. But no police car pulled up to drop off Dane.

Her brow furrowed for a moment. She must not have even realized Cole had left. Or perhaps she didn't even know his name. Dane had introduced them before he'd left. He'd intended to go to Payne Protection and meet up with Nikki to do some computer searches for possible suspects. But before he'd been able to get in his truck, the police car had pulled up.

"Dane," she replied. "His truck is out there. I thought he left…" Her voice cracked a little with fear and emotion. Didn't she feel safe without Dane?

Of course Dane was a damn good bodyguard. He had no qualms about risking his life for anyone and everyone else. So she knew that and was worried about Dane. He was safe where he was now. Probably safer than he'd be anywhere else.

"He's at the police station," Manny replied. "They picked him up as he was leaving."

The color drained from her face. "Was he arrested?"

Manny shrugged. "I don't think so. They didn't put handcuffs on him or anything."

"He's been gone a long time," Emilia finished for him. And now her face flushed with color. "I need to go down to the police department."

"Why?" he asked.

"To bail him out if he's been arrested."

Manny shook his head. "He wanted you to stay put."

"Who else would bail him out?" Emilia asked. "Lars isn't talking to him."

"Cole left." In the Payne SUV, leaving Manny stranded there.

"So he didn't care about Dane's orders to stay put," she said. "And neither do I." She headed from the room then only to return moments later with her baby and a purse and diaper bag slung over her shoulder.

He shook his head. "You can't leave."

"You can't stop me," she said as she headed toward the front door.

This was why he was single. And why he would remain so. Women were a pain in the ass. They were too damn stubborn and too much trouble.

If something happened to this one, though, he'd lose two friends—Lars and Dane. Or they'd lose him, killing him like Lars had threatened to kill Dane. He uttered a ragged sigh. "I'll drive..."

As he helped her and the baby into her small SUV, he kept one hand on his holster. He had that feeling—that had the skin tingling between his shoulder blades—like someone was watching him.

It was probably Lars. Knowing his sister was in danger, he wasn't likely to stay away from her. Yeah, it was probably Lars. So he had to make sure his friend knew Manny was doing a good job as a bodyguard. He secured the baby in the back and Emilia in the passenger's seat before sliding behind the steering wheel.

As he pulled away from her house, he glanced into the rearview mirror. He was a good bodyguard, so good that he wouldn't miss a tail. But it would be harder to stop one on the city streets, so instead of turning toward the city, he turned the other way. To draw out whoever was following him, he needed less-traveled roads. It didn't take him long before he noticed the white van. A big conversion model.

Where had Lars found that?

He slowed as it drew closer. And a grin tugged at his lips. He was going to make it clear to Lars that he'd been busted. But then that van slammed into the rear bumper of the SUV. It wasn't Lars following him.

His heart pounding fast with fear, Manny pressed hard on the accelerator. The SUV was a little one, with a small engine. It didn't jump forward with the speed of one of the Payne Protection Agency's SUVs. The little yellow vehicle gained some speed but not enough. He couldn't make it go fast enough to escape the van. It kept ramming into them, metal crunching and plastic snapping.

The last thing Manny heard before the little yellow SUV left the road and began to roll was both the baby and Emilia screaming in terror.

Emilia's vision blurred. She blinked, but it wouldn't clear. She lifted her hand to push back the hair tangled across her face, hoping that would help her see. But her fingers touched something wet and sticky. And she realized she was bleeding.

She didn't care about herself, though. She fought against the seat belt holding her up on her side, so that she could turn toward the back. Blue was secured in his car seat, his eyes wide with shock.

"Are you okay, baby?" she asked, her blood chilled that he was so quiet.

Just moments before he'd been screaming—with her—as the van had pushed them off the side of the road. Her little SUV had rolled until trees stopped it. It lay on the driver's side.

"Jordan?" she called out to her brother's friend.

Like Blue, the dark-haired man was still, wedged against the driver's door that was jammed against the ground. His eyes were closed. Was Jordan Mannes unconscious or dead?

"Manny!" she called out, using the nickname his friends had given him. "Manny!"

He didn't stir, but Blue began to cry again, probably at the fear in her voice. She was afraid. For Manny...

And for them. Who had driven them off the road?

And where was he?

She didn't have long to wonder because she heard someone banging against the undercarriage of the SUV.

It was someone coming to help? But then glass shattered, raining down inside the SUV. She doubted a rescuer would be so careless with their safety.

Blue screamed now. And when Emilia turned back to him, she saw gloved hands reaching through the broken window, reaching for the baby.

She struggled against the belt binding her to the seat, as she tried to turn fully around and fight off those hands reaching for her son. But she was trapped.

And helpless.

As helpless as she'd been the last time Blue had been taken away from her. She'd gotten him back then; she didn't think she would get that lucky again.

Chapter 19

"Emilia!" Dane called out her name as he stepped into the house.

It was empty. He'd felt it even before he called for her. If she'd been here, he would have gotten that tingly, hot feeling he got whenever she was close to him.

Her vehicle wasn't parked at the curb like it had been when he'd left. And Payne Protection's black SUV was gone, too. Only his truck was parked out front where he'd left it.

He pressed the button on his cell again. He didn't call her. He called Manny. But as it had the last couple of times, it went to voice mail.

He cursed and scrolled down the call log. Then he called her number. It, too, went to voice mail. Even though he knew she wasn't there, he searched the house, seeing if she'd left a note on the kitchen counter or in her bedroom.

But he didn't walk through the house alone. Nicholas Payne hounded his every step. The guy had insisted on personally giving Dane a ride back.

"Where is she?" Nick asked.

And Dane realized why the acting chief had insisted on bringing him back to his vehicle and her house. He'd wanted to talk to Emilia again.

"I don't know," he admitted.

"She's not picking up her phone?"

"No."

"Guess we were both wrong about her," Nick murmured as he pulled out his cell.

"What do you mean?"

"I didn't think she'd run," Nick said. He cursed now. "I should have realized she must have been getting desperate enough to do that."

Dane shook his head. "No. She wouldn't run."

"You think she would stay?" Nick asked. "And risk losing her son again?"

And Dane's blood chilled. No. She wouldn't risk losing Blue.

"But my friends were here—Cole and Manny—they were watching her."

His cell rang, and when he saw it was Cole, he breathed a sigh of relief. "Where the hell are you?" he asked as he accepted the call.

"I'm sorry," Cole said. "I shouldn't have taken off and left Manny alone with her. But…"

"What?" Dane asked. "What's going on?"

"I—I got a call from home," he said. "I had to make sure everything was okay."

"You flew out west?" Dane asked. With bigger issues on his mind, he couldn't remember exactly where Cole was from but it wasn't Michigan.

"No, no, I had to make some more calls—check out some things online."

And he hadn't wanted to do it where Manny could overhear. He hadn't trusted their loudmouth friend.

Now he knew why Cole had left.

"So where are they?" he asked. "Did he tell you?"

"What do you mean?"

"I'm back at the house, but they're gone."

"I don't know," Cole said. "I haven't talked to them. I tried calling Manny's cell before yours, but he didn't pick up."

So he wasn't picking up for anyone, not just Dane. He wasn't sure if he should be relieved or more concerned.

Nick had stepped into the other room. But Dane could hear his call anyway. He'd put out an APB on Emilia Ecklund.

He should have been upset. But he was relieved that at least she would be found. But would it be soon enough?

When the acting chief rejoined him in the kitchen, Dane said, "You didn't need to do that. I'm sure she just talked Manny into bringing her to the wedding chapel." Before hanging up on Cole, he'd asked him to check it out.

He didn't think she was there, though, because he had an uneasy feeling. It wasn't just the doubts Nick Payne had put in his head. He didn't believe Emilia was running—at least not from a murder charge.

He was worried that she was running from a murderer, though.

"No!" Emilia yelled as the gloved hands grabbed at the infant car seat.

It was buckled tightly into the seat, though, and wouldn't be easily extracted. But then the SUV rocked on its side, and the arms extended farther through that window, reaching for the straps holding down the seat.

"No! Leave my son alone!" she yelled again in protest.

Whoever was reaching for Blue ignored her completely. If he was a Good Samaritan who'd stopped to help, he would have said something to her, would have assured her that he was just trying to rescue them.

But that wasn't the case. He'd driven them off the road instead. And unfortunately the road in this wooded area wasn't well-traveled. She couldn't count on anyone stopping to help. This man was intent on taking the baby. So intent she wasn't sure how she could stop him.

She stabbed at the seat belt clasp, trying to free it. But it must have gotten jammed in the crash. She couldn't get the button to give way. With a trembling hand, she pushed the shoulder strap over her head. At least she could move a little more, but she still couldn't get into the back seat. She couldn't shove those hands away from Blue.

So she turned back to Manny. None of the screaming had awakened him. She was worried that he wasn't just unconscious. Had someone else died because of whoever was after her? But the person wasn't after her. Just like Dane had suspected, the killer was after Blue.

She wasn't going to lose her son again, though. And definitely not to a killer.

"Manny!" she yelled. But not even an eyelash flickered. Dread tightened her stomach. She couldn't help him and he couldn't help her.

Then she noticed the glint of metal beneath his arm from the gun poking out of his holster. Fortunately for her Manny must have been left-handed for the gun was on his right and within her reach. She grabbed for it, flipped off the safety and turned the barrel toward the back seat. She had to be careful, though. If she fired and hit the metal of the SUV, the bullet could ricochet back inside the vehicle.

It could hit her son.

He was screaming, too, his tiny fists clenched while his face turned a deep crimson. He had his uncle's temper. His uncle's fight.

But Emilia felt Lars's strength, which she'd always envied, surging through her now. She wasn't just scared. She was angry.

So she concentrated on that window opening, training the barrel there—toward those arms. And she pulled the trigger. She couldn't see who she was firing at, but she didn't care. She just wanted to stop him from taking her son.

Nick had just stepped onto the porch of Emilia Ecklund's rented bungalow when he heard the gunfire. It came from a distance. But he'd heard so many shootings that the sound was unmistakable to him.

It must have been to Dane Sutton, too, because he slammed the door behind him and ran down the porch steps toward his vehicle.

"Where are you going?" Nick asked as he ran after the big bodyguard.

"You heard that," Dane said. "Someone's shooting." His hand shook as he grabbed the handle and pulled open the driver's door.

Instead of insisting on driving, Nick hurried around to the passenger's side and climbed into the truck, too. "We don't know that has anything to do with Emilia."

"I hope like hell it doesn't," Dane agreed.

But he didn't believe his wish would be realized. Maybe he had that same thing Nick and Penny Payne-Lynch had, that *feeling* when something bad was about to happen. Even though he wasn't her child, Nick had her strange sixth sense about danger.

"It could be gang-related," Nick said.

"This isn't my neighborhood," Dane said.

If it was, Lars wouldn't have let his sister live there alone. Nick knew his future brother-in-law well enough to know that. He also knew him well enough to know that he had good friends he could trust.

Nick trusted Dane. Maybe he should have trusted him about Emilia. Maybe she really wasn't the danger. Maybe she was in danger.

At the end of the street, Dane hesitated. "I don't know which way to turn…"

"We came into the neighborhood that way," Nick said, pointing toward the right. And they had passed nothing suspicious-looking.

So Dane cranked the wheel toward the left, pulling out in front of a car that braked with a screech of tires burning against the asphalt.

Nick cursed. "Don't get us killed."

"It was on my side," Dane remarked, as if he didn't care what happened to him.

Nick had once not cared that much about his own safety, either. But now he knew he had people who loved him, who needed him as much as he needed them.

"That's on my side, too." Dane pointed toward a van parked on the side of the road. The front of it was smashed. So it wasn't the only vehicle involved in the crash. As Dane pulled up behind the van, Nick noticed the tire tracks trampling the weeds on the shoulder. Another vehicle had veered off the road.

Why would there be gunshots fired at an accident scene? Unless it was a case of road rage. As a lawman Nick had investigated a few of those.

Nick reached for his weapon, drawing the gun as he reached for the door handle. "You can stay here," he said. "This probably has nothing to do with Emilia."

But Dane was already out of the truck and heading down the steep embankment toward that crash. "I think that's Emilia's vehicle." He shouted and pointed his drawn weapon. "And that's the guy—the guy from the inn!"

He fired. But the guy, dressed entirely in black, disappeared into the woods. Dane didn't follow him. He headed instead toward the SUV. As he drew closer to it, his steps slowed, almost like he dreaded what he might find.

Nick hesitated himself, torn between checking out the crash site and chasing after that mysterious suspect in black. Had Dane and Emilia been telling the truth?

Was someone after her?

Bypassing the crash, he headed toward the woods. Before he got more than a few steps into the trees, another shot rang out from the mangled yellow metal of the SUV. Someone had fired at Dane.

He shouldn't have let him approach it alone. Now he might have lost him…

Chapter 20

Lars's legs shook as he ran through the doors and into the hospital lobby. A security guard ran up, his hands shaking as he reached for his weapon. "Sir, sir!"

"It's okay," a deep voice said. A dark-haired Payne stepped between Lars and the guard. Lars was so upset that he wasn't immediately certain which Payne it was. All Nikki's damn brothers looked alike.

"But he's armed, Chief Payne."

Nick. It was Nick. Nikki's favorite brother. Lars's least favorite, since the man had brought in his sister on suspicion of murder. He swallowed a groan.

"He has a permit," Nick said. "He's licensed to carry."

"But, sir, you know why weapons aren't allowed in the hospital."

Apparently, the place had gotten shot up before. And knowing the Paynes, they had probably been involved somehow.

Lars reached for his weapon, which had the young security guard reaching for his again. But Lars had his by the barrel, and handed it to the kid.

"Where's my sister?" His voice cracked as he added, "And my best friend." Dane had been shot.

If he didn't make it...

Nick glanced around him. "Where's Nikki?"

She'd gotten the call that they were at the hospital. Not Lars. His sister hadn't called him, and neither had Dane.

Lars jerked his hand toward the door. "Nikki's parking the car." She'd wanted him to wait for her, but he'd jumped out before she'd even slowed the car to drive toward the parking garage.

"What about Blue?" he asked, and now his voice shook. "Is my nephew all right?"

Nick grabbed his arm and squeezed it. In consolation?

"Just tell me!" Lars implored him.

Then Nikki was there, wrapping her arms around him. "He's fine," Nikki said. "I told you that."

Had she? She'd been talking in the car. But he wasn't sure he'd heard everything or anything she'd said after one of her brothers had called from the hospital.

"Emilia and Dane are at the hospital."

"Why?" he'd demanded to know. Then he'd turned on her. "You said he would protect her. You said I didn't have to worry!"

"He was shot," she'd said. "Dane was shot..."

After that he'd heard nothing else she'd said—with his pulse pounding so frantically it had echoed throughout his skull. His damn thick skull...

He didn't deserve her now, as she offered him her love and support and strength. Nikki was the strongest woman he'd ever known. So he leaned on her now as his legs threatened to fold beneath him. "You're sure?" he asked her.

"The baby's fine," Nick answered for her. "I got him out of the wreckage before the firemen even arrived with the Jaws of Life."

"Jaws of Life? What the hell happened? Did they need the Jaws of Life to get Emilia out? And what about Dane—is that how they crashed—because he was shot?"

"Dane wasn't driving," Nick replied. "Manny was driving. The Jaws of Life was needed to get him out."

Manny, too? He leaned forward as he gasped for breath.

Nikki glared at her brother. "Where's Emilia?" she asked. "Lars needs to see his sister and his nephew."

And his friend. Dane might no longer consider him a friend, though.

And what about Manny? Was he all right?

"This way," Nick said. And he led them through the ER waiting room toward a door leading to the back.

She hadn't been admitted. So that was good. But why had she been brought here anyway?

"What are her injuries?" he asked.

"She has a cut on her head," Nick replied. "They were going to check her for a concussion." And they must have taken her to radiology because there was no one lying on the gurney when Nick pulled back the curtain to the area in which he must have left Lars's sister.

"Where's Blue?"

"He's here," a deep voice murmured. And the curtain next to Emilia's was pulled aside.

Manny lay on the gurney in that area, one arm awkwardly supporting the sleeping baby. A bandage stained with blood was wrapped around his head.

Lars asked his friend, "Are you okay?"

"Yeah, yeah, I'm fine," Manny assured him with a sigh of relief when Nikki took the baby from him. "Just had to get a few stitches…"

"You have a concussion," Nick said, as if he needed to remind the man. Then he turned toward Lars. "They're going to keep him overnight."

"So much for patient privacy laws," Manny grumbled, which was ironic coming from a man who struggled to keep anything secret.

"What happened?" Lars asked.

Manny shook his head then groaned. "Got ran off the road, man. I thought it was you."

Indignation had Lars bristling. "You thought I would run you off the road?" With his sister in the car? With his nephew? Manny must have hit his head hard.

"I thought it was you following us," Manny explained. "Otherwise I would have shaken the tail."

Guilt struck Lars with a sharp pang in his heart. He should have been there. But he'd believed that Emilia had wanted nothing to do with him anymore, not after the way he'd treated her at the police department. He'd acted like such a jackass. He only hoped she would forgive him.

He didn't have to wait long to find out as a nurse pushed Emilia into the room. She looked so small and fragile sitting in a wheelchair. Like Manny, she had a bandage on her head.

"Does she have a concussion?" he asked the nurse.

The woman looked at him but shook her head. He didn't know if she was assuring him that his sister didn't have one or if she couldn't tell him because of the privacy laws.

Hoping Emilia would talk to him, he dropped to his knees in front of her. "Are you okay?"

She stared up at him, and tears pooled in her pale blue eyes. She wasn't all right.

Was she still furious with him? Emilia was the kind of woman who cried when she got angry or sad or happy. He couldn't tell what her tears meant.

"Do you have a concussion?" he asked.

"No," she replied.

He stared at her. Except for the bandage on her head and the old one on her wrist, she didn't appear to have any other injuries. "Then you're all right?"

She shook her head. "Nooo…"

"What's wrong?" Was she still angry with him? "I'm sorry, sweetheart." He probably should have started with the apology. "I know I've been acting like an ass. I never should have yelled at you."

Her voice cracked, "Dane…"

"Or Dane," he agreed. "I never should have yelled at him. He's been trying to keep you safe." And instead of doing that, Lars had made things worse.

One of his fiancée's hands gripped his shoulder while she balanced his nephew on her other arm.

"I know," Emilia murmured. "But I shot him."

"What?" Lars asked, shock gripping him. "You shot him?"

The tears in her eyes spilled over and trailed down her pale face. "I—I didn't mean to," she said. "I was shooting at the guy who ran us off the road."

Lars turned toward Manny now. "What the hell happened?"

Manny shrugged. "I don't know. After we got run off

the road, I was unconscious. I couldn't help her. So she took my gun. She protected her son."

"Did you get him?" Nikki asked. "Did you shoot the guy who's been terrorizing you?"

"He got away," Nick answered for her. "I had started pursuing him when I heard another shot."

"That was when I shot Dane," Emilia said. "I thought he was the guy—that he came back for Blue." The tears continued to flow.

Lars patted her knees as gently as he had when she'd been a little girl who'd fallen and gotten hurt. He wished he had a doll to give her like he used to. But she didn't need dolls anymore. She had Blue. "That's good then. You were smart to grab the gun, smart to protect your son."

"But I shot Dane." Her voice cracked now with regret and horror.

"Because of that, I'll need to take her down to the department," Nick said. "I'm going to need to book her."

"On what charges?"

Discharging a firearm? Assault with a dangerous weapon? Or manslaughter? Had Dane survived? Or was his best friend gone forever?

"No!" Dane protested as Nick Payne pulled out a pair of handcuffs. "You are not going to arrest her!"

Lars stood protectively between his sister and his future-brother-in-law, so he was clearly not going to allow Nick to slap the cuffs on Emilia, either. He turned toward Dane and breathed a sigh of relief. "You're alive!"

Dane nodded and touched his hand to the bandage on his arm. "The bullet only grazed me." It had actually passed through and hurt like hell. But he knew how badly Emilia felt. She'd been hysterical at the crash site.

And tears continued to stream down her face now.

"I'm fine," he assured everyone. "And I'm sure as hell not going to press any charges."

"That's not up to you," Nick Payne informed him just like the officer had the day before when he'd booked Lars for assaulting him.

"This can't still be about Zeinstra," Dane said. "You saw the guy, too, as he was running away from the crash."

Nick shrugged. "I didn't get a good look at him. And we don't know why he was running. It could have been because she was shooting at him like she shot you."

"She didn't run us off the road," Manny jumped to her defense. "That van did. I couldn't see who was driving, but it was a big guy dressed all in black."

Like the one she'd said had broken into the house and slit her wrist. It had to be him. But who the hell was he?

"The van was there when we drove up," Dane remembered. "Did you find out who it was registered to?"

Nick nodded.

"And?"

"It was stolen from a dry cleaner's this morning," Nick said. "It's been impounded, and the crime techs will scour it for prints."

"He was wearing gloves again," Emilia said. "You're not going to find anything."

She sounded miserable. Dane couldn't blame her. He was frustrated, too. Mostly with Nick Payne. "Put the cuffs away," he advised the lawman. "I am not going to press any charges."

"She shot you."

"By accident," Dane said.

"Come on, Nick," Nikki addressed her brother. "You know she was just protecting her son."

That was the problem. The acting chief believed she would do anything to protect her son, even kill the baby's father. But, albeit reluctantly, he snapped the cuffs back onto his belt.

"I won't be making any arrests today," he assured them.

"That's too bad," Dane said. "You should have caught the guy. That should have been the arrest made today."

"You got shot," Nick reminded him of why he'd been distracted from chasing after the masked guy.

Dane couldn't criticize him too much. He'd chosen not to pursue the assailant, as well, when Emilia had screamed. Frustration gnawed at him more than the throbbing pain in his arm. "The guy keeps getting away."

"Not anymore," Nikki said. "We'll all work together from now on." She patted the baby's back. "We'll protect Blue and Emilia."

With all of them working together, Dane wasn't needed anymore. He could move out of Emilia's house. He could probably even tell everyone he'd only been pretending to be involved with her, so that he could protect her. He doubted she would hold him to that secret anymore.

But he also knew that he wasn't just pretending anymore—if he ever really had been.

Emilia breathed a sigh of relief as the door closed. She was home with Blue. And everyone else had finally left, everyone but Dane. Since he'd stepped in to stop Nicholas Payne from arresting her at the hospital, he hadn't said another word.

She couldn't blame him, though. He had to be furious with her.

"I'm sorry," she said. But she knew how inadequate an apology was for shooting him.

He glanced at her as if surprised that she'd spoken to him. With everyone else in her house—Nikki and Lars and Manny and Cole and Cooper and Nick Payne—discussing what had been going on, she'd been quiet except for answering their questions. But she hadn't had many answers to give them.

She had no idea why someone was after Blue.

They'd asked her about Bradley's parents, but she hadn't been able to help there, either. She'd never met them. Brad hadn't talked about them at all. He'd only talked about himself—about how athletic he was, how smart.

None of it made sense. So she'd had nothing to contribute to the meeting.

Neither had Dane, though.

He was probably tired. She should encourage him to go to bed. But she was worried that he might just go.

"Are you mad at me?" she asked.

"For what?" he asked.

"I shot you," she said.

"You thought I was that guy."

"I shouldn't have," she said. "He was wearing those black leather gloves, but after I started firing at him, it was like I couldn't stop. I just wanted him to leave me alone."

"Do you want *me* to leave?" Dane asked.

"That isn't why I shot you," she said, appalled that he would think that. "I really thought you were him coming back. He was so determined to get Blue."

He glanced out the front window to where a Payne Protection SUV was parked at the curb behind his truck. "Nobody's going to get Blue now."

She released a breath of relief. He was right. She and Blue had more than one bodyguard now. They had them all.

"You don't need me anymore," Dane said. "Not now that everyone knows what's been going on."

She couldn't tell if he was disappointed or relieved.

"Do you want to go?" she asked as her body tensed with fear. She wasn't afraid that she and Blue would be in danger if he left. She was afraid that she might never see Dane again.

He shrugged. But then he asked her, "Do I have any reason to stay?"

They hadn't told the others everything. But then no one had specifically asked if they were really involved or if they'd only been pretending to be in order to catch her assailant. If they'd asked, she wouldn't have known what to say.

She wasn't pretending anymore.

But maybe that was all Dane had ever been doing, even when they were making love. She wanted to make love with him again. She needed to feel him inside her, needed him to fill the emptiness.

And most of all, she wanted his arms around her when she slept. She wasn't sure that she could even sleep without him. She could imagine all the horrific memories that would flit through her mind if she closed her eyes.

The van hitting the SUV. The SUV rolling over and over. Blue screaming. Those arms reaching out for him…

And squeezing the trigger of that gun.

She reached out then and skimmed her fingers over the bandage on his arm. "I really am sorry."

"I know," he said. "But you did the right thing."

He didn't say it, but she heard the word he left unsaid. *Then.*

She hadn't always done the right thing. Not when she fell for Bradley Zeinstra's swarthy charm. Not when she called Myron Webber…

So how could she trust that she was doing the right thing now—falling for Dane Sutton? How could she know that he wasn't just another mistake?

Chapter 21

Dane sat alone in the empty offices of the Payne Protection Agency. This was where he'd intended to go that morning. But everything had fallen apart—from Nick having him brought in for questioning to Emilia shooting him in the arm.

He'd left her. It hadn't been easy, not with her touching his arm and staring up at him with those pale blue eyes of hers. He'd wanted to lower his head and brush his mouth across hers. But he'd known that if he kissed her, he wouldn't leave. He would sweep her up in his arms and carry her upstairs, like he had those other nights he'd kissed her.

Or she had kissed him.

She didn't kiss him then, though. And she'd pulled her hand away from him.

"I know I've made a lot of mistakes," she'd said.

And he'd realized then that he had just been another one of them. So he'd nodded in agreement. He was a mistake. Everyone eventually realized that about him.

"I understand," he'd told her.

She'd shaken her head. "No. You don't. You haven't made the mistakes I have. The mistakes I make nearly get people killed." Her skin paled. Maybe she was thinking of Zeinstra. Or Myron Webber. "Hell, they do get people killed."

"Emilia, none of this is your fault."

She'd shaken her head again, tumbling her hair around her shoulders. "I wish that were true." She'd stared at him almost longingly. "I wish."

He'd stepped closer to her then, as drawn as he always was to her vulnerability and delicate beauty. "What, Emilia? What do you wish?"

"I wish I was stronger," she'd said. "Like Nikki. I wish I didn't need armed bodyguards in order to protect myself and my son."

"You had no one today," he'd reminded her. "Manny was unconscious. Cole and I were gone. And you protected yourself and your son."

Her chin had lifted with pride. "You're right," she said. "Maybe I don't need anyone."

He'd taken that as his cue to leave. He wasn't sure even now if she'd really wanted him to go. But she hadn't asked him to stay. She hadn't given him any reason to stay.

She didn't love him. She probably never would.

It was better that he left her before he got in any deeper. But despite all her bodyguards, he wanted to be the one to make sure she would be safe. He wanted to be the one to solve all her problems.

So he'd come to the office—as he'd originally intended—to pull the old case file on Myron Webber. Sure, he was dead, but someone might have cared enough about the sleazy lawyer to want to avenge his death. Or maybe he'd had a secret partner—like the guy in black—who wanted to continue what he'd started.

Stealing Blue...

Dane wasn't any computer expert like Nikki. He wasn't sure he could hack into the police department files like she did. But he could at least pull up the information Payne Protection had discovered about Myron Webber.

None of it was good. He'd stolen other babies besides Blue. Other women besides Emilia had been his victims. There were more people likely to celebrate his death than want to avenge it. And he could find no hint of a secret partner.

But then he remembered the man from the morgue.

The coroner had been working with Webber. He'd been helping to deliver some of those babies. And in order to flush out Lars, he'd claimed to have a body in the morgue that could have been Emilia's.

Lars hadn't gone to identify that body, though. Dane had. He shuddered even now as he remembered the pale blond hair spilling out from beneath that sheet.

He'd thought it was her. And when he'd discovered it wasn't, he'd been so relieved. But he hadn't been convinced she was still alive, though. He had been convinced the coroner was in collusion with the slimy adoption lawyer. And he'd asked Nick Payne to investigate him. How had that investigation gone?

Was the coroner in jail? Or was he out for vengeance? That would make sense for why Dane had been attacked. It hadn't been just to keep him away from Emilia. It had been for revenge, as well.

He reached for his cell to call Nick but then noticed the time on the small screen. It was nearly 3:00 a.m. Too late or too early to call anyone. The last thing he wanted to do was piss off the lawman right now. Nick still had his suspicions about Emilia.

But Nick was wrong.

Sure, she'd made some mistakes like she'd said. Himself included. But she was a good person. She would never intentionally hurt anyone.

The pang that had struck his heart when he'd walked out of her house wasn't her fault. He was the one who'd started thinking what they had was real—when he knew better. The only real relationship he'd ever had was friendship.

He'd probably lost those now. He was pretty sure that Lars still hated him. And Manny—he'd nearly gotten killed doing a favor for Dane. He probably didn't want to be his friend any longer, either. And everyone had been angry that he'd kept Emilia's secret from them, that he'd risked her life by thinking he could protect her alone.

He had been stupid. Maybe he deserved to be alone.

When he heard the rattle of the doorknob, he knew he wasn't alone anymore. Someone else was inside the building. At 3:00 a.m.?

There was only one reason for someone to come inside then—for him. They'd learned last time that four guys weren't enough to take him out.

How many were there now?

He reached for his gun and checked the clip. Hopefully, he would have enough bullets. Or at least he would have to make sure every one of them counted.

* * *

Nikki drew her gun as she walked into the dark house. Emilia and Blue were alone inside now since Dane had left a couple hours ago. But were they alone?

Nikki had been carefully watching the house from the SUV across the street. So she'd noticed the faint glow of a light moving through the rooms. Someone with a flashlight?

Had someone broken in on her watch?

She would never forgive herself if something happened to Emilia and Blue. And neither would Lars. Hers would be the shortest engagement ever because it would end days after it had begun.

But she wasn't worried about herself right now. Or even about Lars. She was worried about Emilia and Blue.

Careful to keep her steps light—like Garek Kozminski the former cat burglar had taught her—she moved silently through the house. She'd thought she had seen the light moving behind the blinds at the kitchen window.

It made sense that someone might have slipped in through the back door. She had been watching the front. She wouldn't have missed someone.

But Cole Bentler had the back. He'd left earlier, leaving Manny alone with Emilia and Blue. Maybe he'd slipped away again.

Something was going on with him.

The last thing Lars needed was another friend keeping secrets—like Dane had kept Emilia's secret from him. He had been so upset.

Nikki passed the kitchen counter where the knife block sat. One of those knives had been used on Emilia and on the father of her baby. But now another one was missing.

She sucked in a breath as she realized where it was—the point of it pressed against her back—at the bottom of her rib cage. If it pushed through her flesh, it would hit some organs.

Nikki knew more about computers and guns than human anatomy, though. Her kidneys and liver were back there somewhere. But she might have a better shot of surviving getting stabbed in the back than taking a knife in the heart like poor Bradley Zeinstra.

But then a soft voice tremulously threatened, "Put down the gun or I will impale you."

And she laughed.

"Nikki!" The knife fell to the floor with a clank. "I'm so sorry. I didn't know that it was you!"

Nikki turned around and hugged the young woman. "I'm so proud of you!"

"Why?" Emilia asked, appalled. "I almost stabbed you!"

"That's good," Nikki said. "You were defending yourself."

Emilia shook her head. "You're all crazy—all you bodyguards."

Nikki's heart swelled with pride. She was finally the bodyguard she'd wanted to be for so many years. She'd begged her brothers to let her be one of them. But they'd never agreed, until recently. Until she'd taken on the assignment of protecting Blue.

That assignment should have ended several weeks ago, though. The baby and his mother should no longer need protection. And maybe they wouldn't.

"It's good you're defending yourself," Nikki explained. "You grabbed the knife."

"I almost didn't," Emilia admitted. "The last time I

grabbed one, the guy took it away from me." And used it on her.

Nikki flinched as she caught a glimpse of the white bandage wound around Emilia's wrist. They could have lost her then. "You should have a gun," she said.

Emilia shook her head again. "No."

Before Nikki could ask why she was so adamant, Blue began to cry. From being his nanny for a few weeks, Nikki knew his cries. This wasn't an "I'm wet" cry. Or hungry. Or even lonely. This was a cry of fear.

His mother must have recognized it, too, because she ran for the stairs. Emilia was taller than Nikki, her legs longer. She couldn't overtake her. She couldn't protect her, either, if she were running straight into a trap in the nursery.

"It must have been just a bad dream," Emilia murmured as she settled a sleeping Blue back into his crib. He'd been so scared, though, trembling with fear over whatever nightmare had awakened him.

Nikki released the breath she must have been holding in a ragged sigh. "I thought there might be someone inside the house. That's why I came inside."

Emilia tensed. "I didn't hear anyone until I found you in the kitchen."

"I saw a light," Nikki explained. "Like someone had a flashlight."

Emilia held up her cell phone. "I was using the light on it to walk around."

"Why aren't you in bed?" Nikki asked, and she stepped closer, peering at Emilia in the faint glow of the nursery night light.

Suddenly self-conscious, Emilia lifted a hand to her

face. She knew she had big dark circles beneath her eyes. She looked like she felt—like hell.

Emilia shrugged. "I couldn't sleep." And it had been too hard to lie in her bed without Dane, without his strong arm wrapped tightly and protectively around her.

But she'd shot that arm. So she didn't blame him for wanting to leave.

"Are you having nightmares?" Nikki asked.

Emilia would have had to be able to sleep to actually dream. She shook her head.

"It's understandable if you had them," Nikki assured her. "After everything you've been through."

Like she'd told Dane, that was all her fault—because of her mistakes. He hadn't argued with her.

"And if you're afraid, that makes sense, too," Nikki said. "You have every reason to be afraid."

Emilia smiled and gestured at her and the gun. "Blue and I have the most protection anyone could have right now. I know we're safe."

"Yes," Nikki agreed. "You are. So you should go to sleep."

"I can't," she said. Nikki wasn't just her bodyguard or her future sister-in-law. She'd proved herself to be a friend, as well. So Emilia confessed, "It's because of Dane."

"You're worried about him," Nikki said with a nod of agreement. "He shouldn't have gone off alone, not after that attack at his place a few nights ago."

Emilia's stomach lurched. She hadn't thought about that, hadn't considered that his leaving would actually put him in danger. He should have stayed—for so many reasons—but most of all for his own protection.

She reached out and grasped Nikki's arm. "Do you know where he is? Do you know if he's safe?"

"I've been watching you and the house," Nikki said. "I saw him leave, but I have no idea where he was going."

And Emilia had been too proud and stupid to ask him to stay. What if she'd just made the biggest mistake of her life? What if she never got the chance to see him again?

She would never get the chance to tell him how she'd just realized she felt about him…

Chapter 22

As Lars stared down the barrel of the gun, he raised his hands in the air. "It's me," he said. "Don't shoot."

But Dane didn't lower the gun.

Lars couldn't blame him for wanting to shoot him, though, not after how he'd been treating him. "Or do you want one free shot?"

Dane's lips curved into a slight grin. And he cocked the gun.

Lars's pulse leaped with a momentary flash of fear that his friend—his ex-friend—might actually shoot him.

But instead of pulling the trigger, Dane uncocked it and tucked the Glock back into his holster. "Don't sneak up on me like that again."

"You're one to talk about sneaking," Lars said. "You've been sneaking around with my sister."

Dane groaned. Probably because Lars sounded like a broken record about it.

But now he knew he needed to stop. He just had to have his say first. "You should have told me what was going on with her."

"She asked me not to," Dane said.

And suddenly Lars understood everything. Dane was notorious for keeping secrets. He'd kept all of Lars's, even when the other guys had pressed him for the truth. "I'm sorry," he said. "I should have known."

"You realized something was going on with her," Dane reminded him. "That's why you asked me to watch out for her."

"But why didn't she come to me?" Lars asked, and his heart ached that once again his sister had turned to someone else for help instead of him.

"She didn't want to worry you," Dane explained. "You'd just moved in with Nikki, just gotten engaged. She didn't want to impinge on your happiness."

That sounded like Emilia, selfless and sensitive. But he was worried there was more to it than that. He'd acted like such an ass with her.

"Is that really the only reason?" he persisted.

Dane sighed. "She didn't think you would believe her," he admitted. "Hell, she wasn't sure what to believe. She thought she might be losing her mind."

Anguish pierced him at the thought of the terror his sister had endured. Alone. She was so young to have gone through so much. "Thank you for being there for her," he said. "For protecting her."

Dane never accepted gratitude, so Lars wasn't surprised when he shrugged it off and said, "I didn't do that great a job of it."

"She's alive," Lars said. "And she has Blue. That's a great job." He narrowed his eyes and studied his friend's face. His bruises were darker now. Unfortunately they weren't all from the men who'd attacked him outside his apartment. "That's all you were doing, isn't it?"

"What?" Dane asked.

"It was just a job," Lars said. "You pretending to be involved, that was just the cover to explain you moving in with her?" Just like Nikki had posed as a nanny months ago to protect Blue.

He'd been such an idiot.

"I should have known you wouldn't get involved with my sister," Lars said. "Hell, you won't get involved with anyone, let alone a woman with a kid."

He, better than anyone, knew about Dane's aversion to family. Dane had almost quit Payne Protection because it was too much family.

"Will you please accept my apology?" he implored his friend. He had to know they were all right, that they could go back to being the best friends they'd been since boot camp.

But Dane shook his head. "I can't."

"Why not?" Lars asked. "Don't all the years we've been friends mean anything to you?"

He had once told Emilia how he couldn't read Dane, about how he couldn't tell if the man really cared about anything or anyone. After that, she would have been a fool if she'd fallen for him. While she'd made some mistakes, she wasn't a fool.

"I won't accept your apology," Dane said, "because I don't deserve it."

Lars tensed as he realized what his friend meant.

Dane braced himself for the blow he was certain was coming—that he had coming. He'd just admitted to Lars that it hadn't all been a cover. He had crossed the line with Emilia, more than once.

But when Lars finally bellowed, it was with laughter. Instead of losing his temper, had he lost his mind?

"Do you understand what I'm telling you?" Dane asked.

Manny was the one with the concussion. Not Lars. But he must have lost his comprehension.

"I get it," Lars said. "It wasn't an act."

"Yeah…"

So why wasn't Lars hitting him again?

"None of it was an act," Lars continued. "You really do care about her."

Dane tensed. "No, that's not what I meant."

"So you don't care about her at all?" Lars asked, and the amusement was gone. "You were just using her?"

"Of course not." If anything she'd used him.

And once she hadn't needed his protection anymore, she'd basically told him to leave, to get out of her house and out of her life.

She didn't need him. She didn't care about him.

He shouldn't have expected that she would.

"I wanted to keep her safe," he explained. "That's why I agreed—"

"So it was her idea?"

"No." It had been his. Had he used it as an excuse to get close to her? "Because she didn't want anyone to know what was going on."

A muscle twitched along Lars's tightly clenched jaw. "She didn't want *me* to know."

"Or Nikki."

"Because she knew Nikki would tell me," Lars said. But instead of sounding upset, he sounded resigned now.

Maybe that was why he hadn't swung at Dane again.

"I should have told you," Dane admitted. But then he wouldn't have had an excuse to move in with her, to be that close to her. So close that nothing had separated them but skin...

So close that he'd become a part of her. And she would forever be a part of him.

"I'd beat you up," Lars said. "But I can see you're already beating yourself up enough for the both of us."

"I thought I could catch the son of a bitch in the act," Dane admitted. "I thought I could get him as he was breaking in or something. But he keeps slipping away from me."

Just like Emilia had slipped away.

"I don't think it's him you're upset about," Lars said.

"Of course I am," Dane said. "You're the one who must have lost your damn mind. First you're laughing, now you're talking crazy. I want that son of a bitch caught!"

Lars's blond brows arched high over eyes that widened with shock.

Shock that Dane couldn't understand.

"He terrorized her for weeks," he reminded Lars.

Hadn't the guy been paying attention earlier?

"He broke in and cut her wrist," he said. "Hell, he just ran her and Blue and Manny off the road. What the hell's the matter with you?"

Lars shook his head. "Nothing. I'm just not used to seeing you like this."

"Like what?"

"Emotional," Lars said.

He uttered a pithy curse. "Emotional? What the hell are you talking about?"

Lars chuckled again. "I never thought I'd see you like this."

"Like what?"

"Scared," Lars said. "All those dangerous missions we went on—I never saw a hint of fear in you. You didn't care about yourself. You didn't care about anything. But now you do."

"You don't know what you're talking about," Dane murmured, as he began to sweat, a trickle running between his shoulder blades. "You're talking crazy. I'm not scared."

Not for himself. Sure, he was scared for Emilia and for Blue. He wanted them to be safe.

"What reason would I have to be afraid?" he asked. "Sure, four guys jumped me a few nights ago. And I was shot. But it's not like any of that hasn't happened to me before."

Lars grinned. "Something has happened to you that hasn't before. That's why you're scared."

"You're crazy."

"And you're in love," Lars declared. "You've fallen for my sister."

Dane shook his head. "No…" It wasn't possible. He wasn't capable. "No."

But Lars wasn't listening. He just kept laughing at him.

He hadn't been able to sleep. Hell, he hadn't even tried. Too much adrenaline had been rushing through his body yet.

He'd come so close.

So close to getting the baby.

So close to getting shot.

So close to getting caught.

He shuddered as he remembered Nicholas Payne pursuing him to the edge of the woods. If that other shot hadn't rang out…

He wasn't sure he would have escaped the younger man. He wouldn't have escaped Dane Sutton at the inn, either, if the woman's scream hadn't distracted him.

She'd helped him—without even realizing it—both days. But she'd also nearly shot him. And that hysterical screaming...

She was crazy. She didn't deserve to be a mother. She didn't deserve Daniel. That was the baby's name, not that horrific nickname she used. Blue.

That was something one called a pet. Or a stuffed animal or a car. It was a color. Not a name.

No. She didn't deserve the baby.

And he didn't deserve to get caught.

Nicholas Payne had already questioned him once. But he hadn't been able to press charges that time. He wouldn't be able to press them now, either.

Unless he caught him in the act.

That was what would happen if he tried to grab the baby again. Daniel had too many bodyguards.

So once again the plan would need to change. Fortunately Bradley Zeinstra hadn't had time to cash the last check he'd written him. So there was extra money now, enough to hire even more help.

There wasn't enough money or muscle to take out all those bodyguards. No. He couldn't get Daniel. So he'd have to find a way to compel Emilia Ecklund to bring her son to him.

Perhaps as some sort of exchange. While she and Daniel had a lot of security, everyone else she cared about did not. She'd nearly given up her son once. She would again—with the right incentive.

If someone else she cared about was about to lose his life.

Chapter 23

Her heart beating fast and hard, Emilia asked, "Are you sure he's all right?"

"I just told you," Nikki said, "he's at Payne Protection with Lars."

And that was why she was concerned. "They shouldn't be alone together."

Nikki sighed. "Probably not. But they won't be alone long. Once Manny gets here to relieve me I'm going to join them."

"That's good." If anyone could stop Lars from committing murder, it was his fiancée. "Don't let them kill each other."

"They're fine," Nikki assured her. "They're working together on a lead."

And her heart raced again. "A lead?"

Could they actually have a suspect?

"It could be nothing," Nikki cautioned. "So don't get your hopes up."

She wouldn't make that mistake again. She'd gotten her hopes up that Dane might actually be capable of falling in love with her. But she should have known better.

"I'm going to join them at the office to get some records for them." Nikki was infamous for computer hacking. For years, that was all her brothers had let her do.

"I want to go with you," Emilia said.

Nikki shook her head, tumbling auburn curls around her delicately featured face. "No way."

"But I can help."

"We had the meeting—" she glanced to where light was glowing behind the blinds, with night having slipped into dawn "—last night. And you had no idea who could be behind any of this."

She still had no idea. That was why she wanted to go along, to learn who the suspect was. And to see Dane. She really wanted to see Dane.

"I need to know what's going on," Emilia persisted. She had been wondering too long about the man in that horrible zombie mask and about Dane.

"It's too dangerous," Nikki said. "You know what happened the last time you left this house."

Thinking of those gloved hands fumbling with Blue's car seat had Emilia shivering with dread. "I know. That's why Blue will stay here with every one of these Payne Protection bodyguards watching him. And just I will go with you."

"It's not safe," Nikki insisted.

"Blue will be safe." She had no doubt that Lars and Dane's friends and the Payne family would protect her son. They'd done it before—when she hadn't been able to get to him. She hadn't been able to help herself then, let alone him.

But she was stronger now. Everyone else kept pointing that out to her. She could help herself and her son. But first she had to know what was going on—who this suspect was.

"I'll be with you," Emilia reminded her. "You will protect me."

Nikki narrowed her usually big brown eyes. But then she chuckled. "I will protect you," she agreed. "By making you stay here."

Lars had affectionately referred to his bride-to-be as being stubborn and pigheaded. Until now Emilia hadn't seen that side of Nikki.

And until now, she hadn't realized she had a stubborn side of her own. "I'm going," she insisted.

She was determined, not just to help in the investigation but to see Dane again. Despite his handsome face being so unreadable, she needed to read it.

She needed to know if he had any feelings for her at all. Or if all the feelings were just hers—for him.

"Yo, it's Manny the nanny!"

Manny glanced up from the diaper he was changing to glare at Cole Bentler, who stood in the nursery doorway. He would have cussed out his so-called friend, but he didn't know how soon kids started repeating stuff.

Sure, Blue was probably too young. But he didn't want to take the chance of the kid's first word being something he'd said.

Something wildly inappropriate.

"Rub it in that I got assigned babysitting duty," Manny remarked.

"You should be happy," Cole said, "that they still trust you after you got rolled yesterday."

Manny flinched. He hadn't been the only one who'd gotten rolled. Emilia and Blue had been with him when the van had forced her little SUV off the road. His head began to pound with the memory.

Damn concussion. While his head still hurt, at least his stomach had stopped rolling like the SUV had.

Manny pointed at him and then gestured toward the window. On the street below were parked a couple of Payne Protection Agency black SUVs. Other bodyguards sat in them or paced the perimeter of the small yard. "Doesn't look like they trust me all that much."

Cole shrugged. "Yeah, nobody's getting in here..."

"No," Manny agreed.

"That guy would be an idiot to try."

And he was smart, or they would have caught him before now. "Yeah, he won't be breaking in here." But he was desperate enough to force Emilia's vehicle off the road the day before.

He wasn't going to give up. So he'd have to go after what he wanted another way. Manny tensed. "You better call everybody."

"You just said he's not going to break in here," Cole reminded him.

"He won't," Manny agreed. "He'll go after someone else instead."

Cole's breath hitched as he must have come to the same conclusion Manny had. He pulled out his cell phone and pressed in a number. "Dane?"

His phone must have been on speaker because Dane's deep voice filled the nursery. "What's wrong?"

The baby kicked his legs and smiled, as if he recognized the voice, as if he cared about the man.

"Nothing, we hope," Manny answered for Cole.

In his usual no-nonsense way, Dane asked, "Why don't you know for certain?"

"Because Nikki just left here with Emilia," Cole replied now. "And they insisted we all stay behind to protect the baby."

Dane cursed as he realized what Manny and Cole just had. Emilia and Nikki were the ones in danger now.

Another curse echoed Dane's, in a deep, bellowing voice. Dane was with Lars. Hopefully the two of them could get to the women before anything happened to them.

"What do you want us to do?" Cole asked.

"Stay where you are," Lars replied. "You don't want to piss off my fiancée."

Manny shuddered. That was damn well the truth. He didn't want to piss off any woman, let alone a Payne. That was why he intended to never get involved with anyone.

"We'll make sure they're okay," Lars assured them. And as if the guys were in a hurry to do just that, they disconnected the call.

"They'll make sure they're all right," Cole said, as if trying to reassure himself.

Manny wasn't reassured. After the crash the day before, he knew exactly how dangerous this man was.

And how desperate...

The minute he saw his opportunity, he would act.

"Why aren't they picking up?" Dane asked as he pressed the button again for Emilia's number. She probably didn't want to talk to him. As he'd pointed out, she didn't need him anymore.

"Nikki isn't picking up, either?" he asked as he watched his friend's hand tremble slightly on his phone.

Lars shook his head.

"Where the hell were they heading this early?" Dane wondered. "The chapel?"

Lars's huge shoulders bowed slightly. "I asked Nikki to come over here."

"Why?" They would have been safer at the house. Both of them.

"To hack into the police department case file," Lars admitted. "She'll be able to find out what Nick Payne learned about that coroner."

"She could do that by talking to him," Dane said.

Lars grinned. "Probably. But she likes hacking. And she'll find whatever Nick might have missed."

If the coroner hadn't gone to prison, then Nick must have missed something.

"That's all good," Dane agreed. "But why is she bringing Emilia with her?"

"I don't know," Lars admitted.

Fear coursed through him. "And why the hell isn't she picking up her phone?"

"I don't know."

Dane cursed. "Maybe because she can't," he surmised. "Something must have happened to them."

"Or she's trying to make sure it doesn't." Lars drew in a deep breath, his chest swelling with air and with pride. "Nikki's the best damn bodyguard there is. She won't get run off the road or shot. She'll protect them."

His friend sounded confident in his fiancée's abilities. But Dane had known him too long to miss the fear in Lars's pale blue eyes. No matter what he claimed, he was worried.

That made two of them.

"We need to find them," Dane said. "We need to make sure nothing has happened."

"It hasn't," Lars insisted. But he reached for his phone again, pressing the button to call his fiancée.

And like before she didn't answer.

Dane's hand trembled as he called Emilia again. Again his call went right to voice mail. Her soft voice filled his head: *"I'm sorry. I'm not available to take your call. Please leave a message and I will get back to you as soon as possible."*

Would it be possible for Emilia to get back to him ever again?

Or had something horrible happened to her?

Sure, Blue was safe. She'd made certain of that. But why hadn't she been concerned about her own safety?

She'd talked about the mistakes she'd made. He might have made the gravest mistake of all when he'd left her. Now he might have lost her forever.

Chapter 24

"Thank you for letting me use your phone," Emilia said as she finished talking to Penny and handed the phone back to Nikki. Hers had died, and she'd left the charger at her house with Blue and his bodyguards. "I think you missed a few calls from Lars, though."

"That's fine," Nikki said as she pulled the SUV into a parking space outside the Payne Protection Agency. "We're here. We'll see him in a minute."

And Emilia would see Dane.

"How's Mom?" Nikki asked.

"Your mom is awesome," Emilia said wistfully. She envied the relationship Nikki and Penny shared.

Nikki reached across the console and squeezed Emilia's hand. "You know she's yours, too, now."

Emilia's heart warmed at the sentiment, but she laughed. "You're marrying my brother—not me."

"You're family, too," Nikki said. "You're my sister now. That makes Penny your mother, too. Why did she want to talk to you?"

Penny had texted Nikki that she wasn't able to get a hold of Emilia and she'd been worried. That was why Emilia had used Nikki's phone to call her back. "She wanted to make sure that I'm all right."

"Premonitions again?"

Emilia shivered and nodded.

"She doesn't get them about me," Nikki said. "That used to bother me because it felt like I didn't have the connection with her that everyone else does. Now I realize I'm lucky."

Emilia nodded again. "It's unnerving. And now I feel like it's going to be a self-fulfilling prophecy."

"No, it won't." Nikki squeezed her hand again. "We're all going to work together to find out who's after you. And we're going to catch him and stop him. You'll be safe. And Mom's only premonitions will be about how happy you're going to be."

Happiness had been so fleeting for Emilia. She had been happy with her son and her new job. But then the crying had started, stealing her sleep and her happiness and almost her sanity, as well.

Even after that, she'd known moments of happiness—actually of a bliss she'd never known existed—in Dane's arms. She glanced toward the building and shivered a little in anticipation of seeing him again.

Then Nikki's hand tightened on hers, almost painfully. And the other woman reached for her gun.

"What's wrong?"

"Do you hear that?"

Emilia shook her head. "What?" But even as she

asked, she realized what Nikki referred to—the distant wail of sirens. "Those sirens could be for anything," she said. "A car accident. A fire…"

Nikki shook her head. "There's an echo of gunshots."

Then Emilia felt it too, like a vibration on the air. "They're in the distance," she said.

So they couldn't have anything to do with Dane or Lars.

But Nikki didn't look convinced. Her face was tight with anxiety, her eyes wide with fear. Maybe she was like her mother in more than just appearance. Maybe she had the uncanny ability to know when bad things happened, too.

"I need to make sure they're all right," Nikki said as she reached for the door handle. Then she glanced back at Emilia. "You stay here."

"That gunfire is in the distance," Emilia pointed out. "Not in the building. They're safe."

Nikki nodded but not in agreement with Emilia. "You wouldn't be if I leave you out here. They could come back. You'll have to come with me."

Emilia had had every intention of doing just that. But Nikki was super vigilant as they headed the short distance to the lobby doors. She kept walking around Emilia, as if trying to protect her from every direction, from every threat. Emilia had thought that vigilance unnecessary until she saw the lobby door.

The shattered glass was strewn across the sidewalk leading up to that door. And drops of blood were spattered across those fragments.

She gasped.

As if trying to protect her from what she was seeing, Nikki stepped around her. A gasp slipped through her lips, too, and her grip tightened on her gun. "I'm going inside alone."

"No," Emilia said, following Nikki through the doorframe that was empty of all its shattered glass. The other glass inside the building had been shot up, too. The walls of Nikki's office lay in fragments on the commercial carpet. Desks were overturned, and blood spattered one of the solid walls, droplets running down the dark paneling.

Nikki shivered. "What the hell happened? Is this why Lars was calling me?"

Emilia began to tremble as a horrible thought occurred to her. "What if they killed each other?"

Nikki didn't deny the possibility, just murmured, "There are no bodies."

But there was blood. All those bullets hadn't missed. Someone or two had been struck. They were bleeding. Hurt. Maybe dead…

Emilia shuddered, blinking back the tears stinging her eyes. "Where are they?"

Nikki walked around the building, checking every office. The place had been destroyed. But it was empty. "Cooper is going to go ballistic," she murmured, her lips trembling as tears pooled in her eyes.

Emilia wasn't the only one frightened. They were both so on edge that when the phone rang, they screamed. The ring sounded like Emilia's. But her phone was dead.

"It's in here," Nikki said as she picked up a cell phone from the conference room table.

"It's my ringtone," Emilia said. Neither Lars nor Dane used music; theirs was just the standard ring. "How— how is that…"

"It's the cloned phone," Nikki said as she handed it to Emilia.

Her hand trembled. "What—what do I…" But she knew. She had to answer it. So she clicked the green button to accept the call and another button to put the call on speaker so Nikki could hear, too. "Hello?"

"Emilia?"

He sounded so surprised that he must not have expected her to be the one to answer the phone. But yet he'd recognized her voice.

"Who are you?" she asked.

He ignored her question. "It's good to speak to you directly."

Nikki stood before her, making a motion to draw out the call as she flipped open a small laptop she always carried in her purse, and started silently tapping the keys.

"You could have spoken to me the other night," she said, "when you broke into my house. Or when you ran us off the road yesterday."

The guy chuckled. "I had nothing to say to you then."

"And you do now?"

"Now I have something you want," he said.

Nikki's eyes widened. And she mouthed the words, "Your brother?"

Was that where Lars had gone?

"What—what's that?"

He chuckled again. "You must be at the office, or you wouldn't have found the phone," he said. "So you know what's missing. Or should I say who?"

She blinked hard, fighting those threatening tears. "What did you do?" she asked. Had he killed both Dane and Lars? "Where are they?"

"They?" He snorted. "I figured you would only be concerned about one of them."

So he'd killed the other? Who had survived and who

had died? Her heart ached for both men. Emotion overwhelmed her, choking her, so that she had to clear her voice to ask, "What do you want?"

Why was he terrorizing her?

"You know what I want," he said. "And if you want to see your boyfriend again, you'll give up your son."

So Dane was alive.

For now…

But how long would he remain alive when this crazy man realized she had no intention of giving him Blue?

Dane had to be dead.

That was the only way the men would have been able to take him—if they'd dragged his dead body out to that van. Lars had chased it as far as he could, firing shot after shot at it. He'd blown a tire, but it had kept going, the rim sparking against the asphalt once the rubber had ripped away. It had kept going. But Lars hadn't been able.

Damn gunshot wound…

His thigh was numb now. But that might have been from the belt Dane had strapped around his leg to stop the bleeding. Once he'd applied the makeshift tourniquet, Dane had turned back to the men who'd fired their way into Payne Protection.

And he'd taken on all of them alone.

A couple of them had been shot. Lars knew he'd hit at least one. And Dane had probably hit more than that before they'd gotten him.

When Lars had finally gathered his strength again to run after them, Dane had already disappeared. He'd had to be in the back of that van—which was undoubtedly another stolen one. As Lars limped back toward the brick building that was Cooper's franchise of Payne Protection, the pain returned, shooting through him.

He wasn't going to make it. Both legs folded beneath him and he dropped to the asphalt in the parking lot. He was so close—so damned close…

But knowing he couldn't make it all the way back to the building, he lifted his gun to shoot at an SUV in the lot. The trigger just clicked. He'd emptied the chamber and all his magazines. So instead of shooting the gun, he hurled it toward that vehicle. At least he'd had enough strength left to propel it through the window.

An alarm rang out and the lights flashed on and off on the SUV. He lay back on the asphalt and waited. As he'd predicted, footsteps echoed as someone ran toward him. But he wasn't sure who was coming—friend or foe.

"Lars!" Nikki dropped to her knees next to him. As she leaned over him, tears dropped from her eyes onto his face. "Are you all right? I thought you were dead!"

He shook his head, but it took effort. He could feel oblivion threatening as his beautiful fiancée's face blurred before his eyes. He reached up a hand stained with his own blood and cupped her cheek. "I love you…"

"I love you," she said, and the tears continued to flow from her face to his. Then she spoke to someone else, giving out the address. "We need an ambulance. Gunshot wound. Units are already en route?"

Lars's lids grew heavy. But as he closed his eyes, she patted his cheek. "Stay with me, sweetheart," she implored him. "Help is coming."

He would be okay. He'd just lost a lot of blood. That was all. "I'm not worried about me. Dane…"

"The man has Dane," Nikki said. "He called Emilia."

Lars shook his head. "Dane can't be alive…" It wasn't

possible. The one thing Dane had said before every one of their dangerous missions had been, *They'll never take me alive.*

If they'd taken him, he hadn't been alive.

He must have died. For everything was dark…

Dane could see nothing. Could feel…

Only the coldness, the hardness of concrete beneath his face. He moved his head, and pain radiated throughout it. He tried to lift his hand toward it, but they were bound behind his back.

Then he felt the rest of the pain shooting through his body. His shoulder throbbed, not from where Emilia had shot him. That wound was lower on his arm. He had a new gunshot wound.

Maybe two.

And so damn much pain.

He tried moving his legs. Like his wrists, his ankles were bound together, too. Whoever had grabbed him had made damn certain he couldn't escape.

He'd never felt so helpless, not even when he'd been a kid.

Was this how Emilia had felt? For weeks she'd been held captive in a space that was probably very much like this—cold and dark. She'd been kept alive for those weeks, though. There was no reason for them to keep Dane alive. Maybe they didn't even realize he'd survived. But then why tie him up? Why not just kill him at the agency?

Of course Lars had been there, too. But he was hurt. Or worse. Had he survived?

He cleared his throat, relieved to discover he had no gag in his mouth. He could speak. He could call out for help. But he called out, "Lars!"

No one answered him. That didn't mean his friend wasn't there, lying next to him in the darkness. He forced himself to move, rocking back and forth until he rolled to his side. The concrete ground against his wounded shoulder. And a groan of pain tore from his throat.

If Lars was there, that would have awakened him. If he could be awakened.

Maybe Dane's makeshift tourniquet hadn't stopped his bleeding. Maybe he'd bled out.

If Dane couldn't stop his shoulder from bleeding, he might not make it, either. There was no bandage on it, nothing to stem the flow of blood down his arm to where it soaked into the concrete.

He cursed.

This was why he'd always vowed to never be taken alive. He'd figured death was less painful than torture. But a slow death might be even worse…

Oblivion began to threaten again. He must have lost consciousness at the agency because he had no idea how he'd wound up here. He was about to lose it again.

Then he heard the rattle of a lock, and the creak of a door. His death wasn't going to be so slow after all. They must have returned to finish him off.

Chapter 25

The car alarm had drawn Nikki away. But Emilia hadn't stopped talking to the man who'd cloned her phone, who'd tried to ruin her life. He would have, had he taken Blue. If he really had Dane, then he had shattered it, anyway.

"I don't believe you have him," she said. That could have been him in the parking lot, setting off the car alarm.

"You think Dane Sutton's a superhero," the guy grumbled. "He's just a man."

"He took out the four guys you hired to attack him a few nights ago," she reminded him. "So you really expect me to believe they got him this time?" She glanced around at the shattered glass and blood spatters.

This scene was far worse than the one outside Dane's apartment. More violence had occurred here. The guy must have hired many more men to do his dirty work this time.

He was quiet for a long moment.

And Emilia realized why. "You don't know for certain. You haven't seen him. You only have their word that they didn't fail this time."

"They have him."

"Alive?" she asked as she glanced around at the destruction and the blood.

"They had orders to take him alive."

What about Lars? What had happened to Lars? Then she saw for herself. Nikki helped him into the office, her arm wrapped around his waist as the big man leaned heavily on the petite woman.

She would have never believed Lars could find a woman stronger than him. But in Nikki Payne, he had.

"I won't consider a switch," she said. And that was true. So true. "Unless I hear his voice."

Lars straightened up and glared at her through eyes that looked glazed with pain. She was relieved he was alive. But she didn't want him interfering. So she waved her hand to keep him quiet.

"So if you want my son," she said, "you better find out if your men were really able to take Dane alive. And…"

She paused and gestured at Nikki to check her computer.

Lars seemed impatient, but he held his silence.

The man waited for her, too. He hadn't broken the connection. She'd kept him on the line for a long time.

Nikki looked at her computer and gave Emilia a thumbs-up signal.

"And you better not try to pass off a recording as his

voice," she said, "like you must have with those wedding vendors."

Because so many of them had sworn it had been her voice leaving those messages. But since he'd cloned her phone, the man had had access to her outgoing voice mail message.

"I want to really talk to Dane," she said. "I will ask him questions only he will be able to answer. So don't try anything."

Like she was trying. She wanted to buy Dane time, if he were actually alive. She wanted to buy time for Nikki to track him down.

She didn't wait for the man to agree to her deal. As a kidnapper, he should understand that she needed proof of life. So with a trembling fingertip, she disconnected the call.

Tears burned her eyes, but she blinked them away. "What if he doesn't call back?"

Then that would mean that Dane was dead.

That he was lost to her forever.

Nikki's heart lurched along with her legs as Lars leaned more heavily on her. He was so big. She couldn't hold him up any longer. She turned back and gestured at the paramedics who'd stood outside the shattered lobby door.

Lars had refused to let them treat him until he'd seen his sister, especially when Nikki had admitted she was on the phone with the man who'd tried to abduct Blue.

Who claimed he had Dane...

The paramedics rushed forward and helped Lars onto the gurney they'd rolled into the office. But he didn't let go of Nikki. He clasped her hand tightly until she leaned closer to him.

"Don't let her do it," he pleaded. "Don't let her switch Blue for Dane."

"She won't," Nikki assured him. "She was just stalling him so I could track the call." She glanced at her computer screen. "The call pinged off a tower downtown." Which wasn't going to pinpoint the abductor's location alone.

She needed to narrow it down. But she needed to be with her fiancée, too. "He's lost a lot of blood," she told the paramedics.

"We'll get him to the hospital right away," the young African American paramedic assured her.

She had probably met the man before. She and her brothers had been hurt so many times over the past couple of years. "I'll ride with you," she said. "He's my fiancé."

"No," Lars protested. "You need to protect Emilia, to make sure she doesn't do anything stupid."

"I love you, too," Emilia remarked. "Can you fix his disposition and his leg?" she asked the paramedics.

The young men stared at her in awe. Emilia was that beautiful.

Nikki had never realized how strong and smart the young woman was, as well. She had survived hell before, but she'd done that for her son. Now she was fighting for Dane.

Nikki had no doubt that she would never exchange Blue for Dane. But she would fight every bit as hard for him as she had to be with Blue again.

Lars clasped Emilia's hand now. And Nikki could see that he was offering comfort now. "He's not alive, Emilia. There's no way they took Dane alive."

Emilia's breath escaped in a gasp, like her brother had struck her stomach. Hard.

"You—you saw him get shot?" she asked.

He shook his head. "I saw him shooting. He helped me before going after them, after all of them."

Emilia shivered now. "He went after them alone?"

Lars nodded weakly. "There were too many, Em. There's no way…"

Nikki gestured at the paramedics. "You need to take him." Before it was too late for Lars—the way it sounded like it was too late for Dane. So Nikki started out after the stretcher with her husband-to-be.

Emilia caught her arm and pulled her up short of the shattered door. "You don't need to go with him," she said. "Lars will be fine."

Nikki knew that. She knew her fiancé well. She knew how tough he was. She also knew that his friends were tough, too.

"You need to stay here and track down Dane," Emilia implored her.

Even though Nikki's heart ached for the young woman's desperation, she shook her head. "You heard Lars…"

"I love my brother, but he's a pessimist," Emilia said. "He gave me up for dead. You were the one who convinced him to keep looking for me."

"I knew you were alive, that you would fight to stay alive for your son," she said. "Blue is too special…" Nikki loved her future nephew so much that she might actually consider having a child of her own—someday. But first she had to make sure she would have a husband.

"He is," Emilia agreed. "And I would never consider an exchange."

Lars had been an idiot to think that she would. Nikki knew her better than that. "I know."

"But I won't give up on Dane," Emilia said, "just like you didn't give up on me."

"I'll search for him once I know Lars will be okay," Nikki promised. "You need to come with me." Because Emilia did need her protection. And Nikki wasn't certain when everyone else would arrive.

Hadn't alarms gone off to notify Cooper of the break-in? Or Mom called and told him? She always knew stuff before the rest of them did.

"No…" Emilia shook her head and drew back. "I can't go to the hospital. My cell phone won't even come in down there. And what if Dane calls…"

What if he didn't? Nikki was more worried about the effect that might have on Emilia. It was obvious she'd fallen for her brother's best friend. And no matter how much they'd been fighting lately, Dane was Lars's best friend.

Nikki couldn't treat Lars's leg wound, but she could help find his friend. She rushed after the paramedics who were loading Lars into the back of the ambulance; the lights were already flashing. Her stomach lurched at the seriousness of her fiancé's injury. She should go with him.

But instead she rushed up to the stretcher and told him, "I love you so much. And I'll get down to the hospital as soon as I can."

He reached out and cupped her face in his palm again. "Thank you."

"For what?"

"For being there for my sister more than I ever could," he said.

"I'll protect her," she promised. "And I'll find Dane." She only hoped for both Lars's and Emilia's sakes, as well as Dane's, that he was alive.

"I love you," Lars called out as the stretcher rolled all the way into the back.

"I love you!" Nikki yelled back at him. Her heart beating fast and heavy with fear for her fiancé, she forced herself to step back from ambulance. She waited until it sped from the parking lot, lights flashing, before heading back into the shot-up building.

Emilia stood near Nikki's laptop, staring at the screen. But she doubted she could see anything. Tears streamed down her face.

Nikki nudged her aside to start tapping keys. "I'll see if I can narrow down the location of your caller. And we'll call in everyone else to help in the search." She also intended to follow up on the suspect Dane had come up with, the coroner he thought had helped Myron Webber steal babies.

"Thank you!" Emilia exclaimed as she hugged the petite woman.

Nikki pulled back and cautioned her, "Don't get your hopes up. I was right about you. You may not be right about Dane. We might not be able to rescue him like we rescued you."

"We have to," Emilia said.

Nikki shook her head. "We can't if Lars is right—if he's already gone."

Emilia shook her head. "He's not dead. He can't be dead..."

He was dead. Or at least that was what he wanted his captors to think. But then a boot kicked Dane right in his bleeding shoulder. He couldn't hold in the grunt of pain, couldn't continue to play dead like he'd been trying since that door had opened.

"You're not dead!" the young man exclaimed. He kicked Dane again. "Billy's dead!" Another kick. "And Raul." Another kick. "And Jerome!"

How the hell many young thugs had come after him and Lars? Dane had emptied a few magazines, and he'd made certain most of his bullets had counted. The gang-bangers hadn't been as trained on firearms as the Marines had trained him and Lars.

Their shots had gone wild. The one that had hit Lars in the thigh had been a lucky one. Unlucky for Lars.

Was his name among the dead?

"You shouldn't have come after me," Dane said as he rolled to his side, so he could move his arms even though his wrists were bound.

When the kid kicked him again, Dane moved fast enough to catch his foot and jerk him down onto the concrete. The guy let out a cry of surprise and pain. He must have taken a bullet, too. If Dane could find where the wound was…

But his wrists were tightly bound. Catching the foot had been hard enough. Now he swung out with his legs. His bound ankles made his kick doubly strong.

The kid screamed now.

And the door rattled as someone else stepped into the room. "What the hell, Gonz?"

"Shoot him!" Gonz yelled. "Shoot him!"

A gun cocked. But it didn't fire. Instead the other kid said, "But what about our money? We don't get it if we kill him…"

"Then we'll just take it from the rich guy," Gonz said.

Dane chuckled. "That rich guy isn't someone you want to double-cross…"

Another gun cocked. But there was no hesitation. Shots fired. Dane braced himself, and just as he'd feared, he got hit. When he glanced down, he saw it was just with a shard of concrete though—not a bullet.

Gonz lay next to him, his eyes open wide with shock, a bullet in his forehead.

"Stupid kid…" he muttered.

"You warned him not to double-cross me," a deep voice murmured. "Thank you for that."

There wasn't much light spilling in from the hall. Dane couldn't see the guy's face clearly. Was it the coroner who'd helped Myron Webber?

He didn't think so. This guy was younger. His hair dark. "Who are you?" he asked.

"My name won't mean anything to you," the guy said.

So it was someone he'd never met?

"What the hell do you want with me then?" he asked.

"I am going to switch you for the baby Myron Webber promised us."

Myron had sold Emilia's baby to several couples desperate for a child of their own. They'd been victims of his scams—just like Emilia had been. That was why, even though the authorities had talked to them, no one had pressed charges against them for bypassing the proper adoption channels. They'd been hurt, too. Dane hadn't realized how desperate that disappointment would make them.

"The man was a bastard," Dane said.

"No, he was getting babies into loving, two-parent households. Emilia Ecklund's baby is being raised by a single mom," the man said, "She was going to give him up or she wouldn't have met with Myron in the first place."

"But she didn't give him up," Dane insisted.

"No, she wasn't like your mother, who left you in a bathroom," the man said. "But she's nearly as bad."

Dane tensed. "You really checked me out." Not many people knew his past that well because he hated talking about it.

"I had to know who I was dealing with," the man replied. "I can't believe you would help her."

He wasn't much help now—to her and even to himself. "She's my best friend's sister," Dane said. But that wasn't really why he'd helped her. He'd helped her because he cared about her.

"And that baby is ours," the man insisted.

Dane grunted, more in disagreement than pain. "No, he's not. Webber conned you."

"Webber knew that a child needs the security of two well-established parents," the man haughtily explained. "Not a desperate single mother."

Dane had had the two well-established parents. But he'd had less security than he would have with a single mother who'd loved him. Unfortunately nobody had ever loved Dane.

"We deserve him. She doesn't."

Dane shook his head. "She was scared and alone when she called Webber. But she had no intention of going through with it then and especially not now. She's never going to give up her son."

"You better hope you're wrong," the man said. "Because if she won't exchange her son for you, I will have no use for you." He kicked the gang member who'd fallen dead in front of him. He'd killed that kid and Gonz. The man was good with a gun and a knife. "And you'll wind up just like these guys."

With a bullet in his brain.

Dane had seen Emilia with Blue too many times. He knew there was no way she would risk losing her son again. Especially not for him.

The man was crazy to think she cared enough about Dane to barter for him. Dane had to find a way to get untied before the man realized how wrong he was, or he was certain to wind up dead.

Chapter 26

With Cooper's Payne Protection Agency now a crime scene, they'd moved to Parker Payne's new offices. Emilia had met all the Paynes at Penny's wedding and most of them before that when they visited their mother at the chapel, but she still couldn't tell any of the brothers apart in appearance. They were all blue-eyed, with black hair.

Parker must have been who cautioned them, "No shooting in my new offices. If gunmen come in here, you will have to disarm them with your hands or—" he gestured at the blond-haired Garek Kozminski "—your smart mouth."

Garek flipped him off. "Hey, I had nothing to do with Cooper's office getting shot up."

"That was my fault," Emilia said.

Parker walked over and comfortingly squeezed her

shoulder. "No, it wasn't. It was the scumbag who we will all work together to get out of your life."

"Don't talk about her brother like that," Manny said as he walked into the office carrying Blue.

She rushed over to take the baby from his arms, and the bodyguard breathed a sigh of relief. Blue snuggled against her and emitted a soft sigh, as if he'd missed her. And it had only been hours. What would happen if they were separated again for weeks or years…?

She shuddered at the thought.

"If you want to lay him down, there's a nursery off that hall," Parker said. "My wife is my office manager, so she brings the kids along to work."

All the Paynes had wonderful, strong marriages. Penny had told her how happy she was that her boys had found their soul mates. And at long last, so had Nikki.

"How is Lars?" she asked.

Nikki glanced up from the computer screen she'd been studying at the conference room table. "He's bellowing to be released already," Nikki said. "I'm not sure he even let them stitch him up."

Emilia breathed a sigh of relief now. She'd been right about Lars, that he would be fine. Now she just had to hear from Dane. Had to know he was alive…

Finally, after nearly an hour of waiting, the cloned cell phone rang. The guy could have been watching them. Maybe he'd known when she had Blue, so she could make the trade.

But she tightened her hold on her baby. She would never let him go. There had to be some other way she could help Dane. If only to give him more time.

When Nikki nodded, Emilia pressed the button to accept the call on speaker. Everyone else in the crowded conference room fell eerily silent.

"Yes?"

"Emilia?" It was Dane's deep voice rumbling in her ear.

"You're alive!"

"Yeah, yeah, but now I know how you felt—" He grunted as if someone had kicked him. And she realized he'd given out a clue.

"Emilia." It wasn't Dane's voice calling out her name this time.

She shivered. "I want to talk to Dane."

"You just have," the man replied. "You know he's alive. And if you want him to stay that way, you will make the exchange. Daniel for Mr. Sutton."

"Daniel?"

"I refuse to call the boy the ridiculous nickname you gave him," he explained.

She wanted to shout, *Blue, his name is Blue.* But Dane's grunt of pain echoed inside her head. She didn't want him hurt again. "Where—where do you want to exchange Dane for—" she forced herself to say it even though she nearly choked "—Daniel?"

Nikki stared up at her, her dark eyes wide with shock and disappointment. Did she think Emilia would actually risk her son's life? Never.

But she didn't want to end Dane's. And she was afraid that if she refused, the man would kill him with her listening. And that would kill her, too.

"See…"

Another grunt echoed throughout the phone.

"I told you she would do it," the man said, and he was obviously speaking to Dane. "She doesn't deserve Daniel."

Tears stung her eyes, and she blinked them back. She could feel everyone in the office staring at her, wondering if she'd lost her mind. She hadn't lost her mind.

She had lost her heart.

"Where?" she asked, her voice sharp with impatience now.

The man named a busy downtown park within the hour. "And don't try anything stupid," he said. "Don't let your brother try anything stupid, either. Or your boyfriend won't make it."

"I want to talk to him again," she said.

There was another grunt, then Dane said, "Don't do it, Emilia! Don't do this for me. I don't love you. I was only using you—like Brad."

There was the crack of plastic. Then the sound of a blow, of something hitting flesh and bone. But Dane uttered no grunt of pain. Was he beyond feeling? Was he dead?

The phone rattled with the man's heavy breathing. "Don't listen to the hero," he said. "He is just trying to protect the boy."

Of course Dane would be the hero. That didn't mean he was lying. She didn't think he loved her. She didn't expect him to when she had been nothing but trouble for him.

"I know," she said. "You better know that you will not get the baby if Dane Sutton is dead."

"I will see you and Daniel in the park," the man replied. And he clicked off the cell without confirming if Dane was even still alive.

She glanced at Nikki. "Did I keep him on the phone long enough?"

Nikki shook her head. "Not enough to narrow the search."

"But Dane gave us a clue," Emilia reminded them, "when he said he knows how I felt. He must be being held in an abandoned warehouse."

Nikki nodded now. "Yeah, I got that. And the signal pinged off towers in that old industrial area of the town."

"That's good," she said, her heart lifting with relief. "We can find him."

"There are a lot of warehouses down there," Nikki said. "The only reason we found you was because we followed someone there. We can't follow someone to Dane."

"You can follow them," she said. "The kidnappers."

"Are you serious about exchanging the baby for Dane?" one of the Paynes asked.

"Hell, no!" a deep voice growled in response as Lars staggered into the room on a too-short pair of crutches. "You're not doing it!"

Nikki jumped up and rushed to her fiancé. "You idiot! How dare you check yourself out!"

"Had to," he said. "Or my sister is going to do something idiotic!"

"Must run in the family," Emilia murmured as she cradled her son close. His tiny body had tensed, probably because he'd felt his uncle's anger and her fear. "I would never exchange Blue. But they don't know that."

"What are you thinking?" Parker Payne asked the question.

"I want to make the switch," she said.

"What?" Lars exclaimed. "You just said—"

She held up her hand to stem her brother's argument. "I intend to go to the meeting," she said. "But I won't bring Blue. I'll bring a doll instead."

"And they'll kill you when they find out you've duped them," Lars said. "It's not going to happen."

"No, it's not," she agreed. "I will be perfectly safe because I will have so many Payne Protection bodyguards discreetly protecting me."

"And what about Dane?" Lars asked.

"He's alive," she said. "You gave him up for dead. But he's alive."

"Are you sure?" he asked.

Nikki nodded. "We all heard his voice. He was alive."

Lars tensed. "Was?"

"He stopped talking."

Emilia shook her head. She refused to accept that she'd heard Dane get murdered. It wasn't possible. He had to be alive. "I told them I'd have to talk to him again. They can't exchange him if they don't bring him."

Lars tilted his head and looked at her sadly. "They're not going to bring Dane to that park," he said. "And you can't go, either."

Nikki stepped in front of her fiancé, standing between him and Emilia. "She's right, you know. We can all protect her."

"But Dane won't be there."

"Probably not," Nikki agreed. "Once we figure out who has Dane, we can trace his steps back to him."

"It's one of the parents," Emilia said. "It's one of the couples—or at least the father—who bought Blue from Myron Webber."

Nikki hurried back around the conference table to her laptop. "Of course!"

"Cross-reference the name Daniel," Emilia suggested. "It's either his first name or the first name of someone the man lost—like a father or a brother or father-in-law."

Emilia's skin heated as she felt everyone staring at her in shock. "What?"

"You're so smart," Cooper said. "I think I hired the wrong Ecklund. You want to quit the wedding planning business and work for me?"

She shuddered at the thought. "No. I love working with your mom."

"We're not all bad," Parker said.

They were all wonderful.

"We'll see how today goes," she offered.

"I don't like this," Lars said. "I don't want you putting yourself in danger."

"Why not?" she asked. "Every one of you has put his or herself in danger for me. I owe you all the same." And no one more than Dane.

Lars hobbled closer and settled his big hand over Blue's small head. "He's why," he said. "He needs you."

"He's not going to lose me," she said.

Nikki looked up from her computer. "We kept her safe before, Lars. We'll keep her safe again."

Emilia's heart lurched with fear. They were actually going to let her do this. She was a wedding planner. Not a bodyguard. Was she prepared to meet a killer?

To save Dane, she would take the risk. She just hoped she was able to save him. And that she survived, too.

Like Lars had said, her son needed her.

Dane jumped and shivered, shaking off the ice water that had been doused over his head.

"There you are," the man said. "You were out for a while."

"You son of a bitch!" Dane cursed him.

The man chuckled.

"She was lying to you," Dane insisted. "Emilia would never give up her son." Certainly not for him. But she might risk her damn life to try to help him, probably out of some sense of obligation.

"Then she will give up her life," the man remarked, as if Emilia's life didn't matter at all.

Of course he had no idea how amazing she was, how beautiful inside and out. How generous and loving...

Dane had only said what he had on the phone about using her, so that she would get angry with him, so that she wouldn't sacrifice herself or her son for him. He didn't want her giving up anything for him.

He wasn't going to let her. But if he couldn't stop Emilia, maybe he could stop them from meeting her. "It's a setup, you know," he said. "She won't meet you alone."

"Her brother was shot," the man reminded him. "From what Gonz's friends have said, I doubt he survived."

What if Lars hadn't made it? Emilia would be devastated that she'd lost her brother.

Dane could have told him about the others, the Paynes, who adopted everyone they met as family. He hadn't liked that before, but he was grateful for it now. They would protect Emilia as best they could.

They might not see this refined-looking man and his timid wife as a threat. The woman hadn't spoken at all. She stood in the hallway, her head bowed as if she didn't have the energy to lift it.

Was she sick? Abused?

Dane wouldn't put it past this man to hurt his wife. He was a killer. He'd killed Zeinstra. And he would probably kill Emilia if she actually met him.

Dane couldn't take the chance that she might. He had to escape.

But the man motioned at some other men who walked into the room. "Make sure he doesn't try anything," he said. "I want him alive in case she does want to speak to him again. But once she does, I want him dead. He's caused me too many problems. Kill him slowly and painfully."

One of the gang members grinned. "For sure, Mr. Montgomery."

This was why Dane had always sworn never to be taken alive. He would have been better off dead than having Emilia risk her life for his—when he was going to die anyway.

But he was Dane. He was a Marine. He was a Payne Protection bodyguard. He wasn't going to give up without one hell of a fight.

If only he could free himself...

Reginald Montgomery steered his wife toward the meeting place at the edge of the park. They were close to the parking lot, to escape if this was the trap Dane Sutton had warned him it was. But if they were to get away, Cynthia would have to move faster. She walked so slowly, lethargically, but that was the side effect of the antidepressants she'd been on since...

Since they'd lost Daniel. But they hadn't lost him.

"We just have to wait a little longer, my love," he assured her.

She blinked and glanced up at him. He couldn't tell if she'd heard him or not. Or maybe she'd heard and just hadn't believed. He'd failed her too many times.

But not this time.

He glanced around the park. It was busy with joggers and young families playing with their kids. A couple of sidewalk vendors. It was always busy like this. It had been when he'd brought their other son here. That Daniel was gone. They'd lost him to the genetic defect neither had realized they had, until they'd passed the death sentence onto the only child who'd made it to full term.

Cynthia had lost so many unborn babies. And then Daniel…

Despite how sick he'd been, their little boy had loved the park. The new Daniel would love it, too. And he was perfect. Myron Webber's doctor friend had run all kinds of tests on the baby. He was healthy and strong.

He wouldn't die on them. He wouldn't leave them.

Their life would be a little more difficult now. They would have to go into hiding with him for a while. Because even though she was willingly giving him up, Emilia Ecklund would probably claim to change her mind again. She would act like she wanted him back.

That was why the first plan had been the best. Drive her crazy, then once she was declared an unfit mother, have his father seek full custody of his son. But Dane Sutton had interfered with that pain. And Bradley had kept pushing for more money. Then he'd even threatened to renege on their agreement. He had deserved Daniel even less than Emilia did.

Cynthia shifted against his left side. On his right, he held his gun beneath the coat he'd tossed over his arm to hide it. He also had a knife in a sheath on his belt. There had been something so satisfying about shoving that blade in Bradley Zeinstra's greedy, cold heart. Maybe Reginald would shove this knife in Emilia's.

So that she couldn't come after them. So that no one would try to find them.

Cynthia moved again, and he murmured, "It won't be much longer now."

Then he glanced up and saw her. With her pale hair and eyes, she looked almost like a ghost moving toward them. That was how she would leave them—once she handed over the baby she held in her arms.

Yes, he would plunge that knife in her heart just as he had the baby's father. Then Daniel's only parents would be him and Cynthia. They would be all he needed. And he was all they needed.

Chapter 27

Emilia's legs trembled beneath her as she headed down a path she had never knowingly gone before. She'd unwittingly stumbled into it before, but she had never walked purposefully into danger.

No. She had no intention of quitting the wedding planning business to become a bodyguard. If she survived this assignment, she would leave all future assignments to the professionals. She heard their voices buzzing in the transmitter Nikki had fitted in her ear.

"I don't have a clear enough visual to see if that's him," Nikki warned her.

Emilia knew that it was. She forced herself to keep walking.

"That couple?" Cole Bentler's voice asked the question doubtfully. "They don't look like killers."

"Just because they look rich doesn't mean they're not dangerous." Manny's voice was unmistakable.

"Money sometimes makes them more dangerous," another voice cautioned. It took her a moment to place it as Garek Kozminski's.

"He's armed," one of the Paynes warned her. Probably Cooper. He hadn't been as convinced as Nikki that Emilia should do this. Or maybe he'd just been trying to be loyal to Lars. Or he honestly thought she would get herself killed. "He has a gun under that coat over his arm, and he has a knife strapped to his belt."

She shuddered as she remembered what he'd done with a knife—both to her and to poor Bradley. But she forced herself to close the distance between her and that mismatched couple.

While the man looked rich and powerful in a dark suit and red power tie with the overcoat tossed over his arm, the woman looked like she'd just woken up. Her blond hair hadn't been brushed, and she wore no makeup. She had an overcoat wrapped around her, but Emilia wouldn't have been surprised if she had on pajamas or a nightgown underneath it.

"Emilia," the man greeted her. He wasn't surprised that she'd come. Then again he looked like the kind of guy who always got what he wanted.

But for Blue...

He'd wanted Blue and had been denied. Was that what had driven him to such desperation? To madness?

The woman reached up to clutch his arm, and her coat sleeve slid away from her wrist, revealing a jagged scar.

Emilia held in her gasp of shock.

Had he done that to her? Or had she done it to herself, after their son had died?

"Reginald, Cynthia," she greeted them.

The man tensed and lifted his hand beneath the jacket

over his arm. She had no doubt the gun barrel was pointing directly at her now.

"How—how do you know our names?" he asked.

"You don't think I would figure it out?" she scoffed. "You don't think everyone will?"

He shrugged then. "I don't care what anyone thinks."

Maybe he didn't care anymore, but he was the kind of man who once had, who drove expensive cars and lived in a mansion just so that he could impress others. Was that what Blue would do for him? Impress others? Or replace the son they lost?

"I want the baby," Cynthia murmured.

Reginald turned toward her, as if surprised that she'd spoken.

Emilia tightened her arms around the blanket-swaddled doll and it emitted a little cry. They'd found the very lifelike doll in the nursery in Parker Payne's office.

Cynthia whirled toward Emilia, her dark eyes wide. And wild...

Reginald had not acted alone in trying to steal Blue. Or at least he hadn't acted entirely for himself.

"You can't have the baby," Emilia said. "Not until I see Dane Sutton."

Reginald snorted. "You thought I would bring him here?"

"No." But she refused to think he was already dead. She wouldn't believe it. "You need to let me talk to him, to know that he's being released."

"Then we get the baby?" Cynthia asked hopefully.

Reginald sighed. "I could call," he said, "and let you talk to him—one last time."

"One last time?"

"But I'm not even sure those gang kids I hired waited

until we left the warehouse to kill him," he said. "They nearly had earlier, out of spite for all their friends he and your brother killed."

Emilia's pulse quickened. "Dane's strong," she said. "He can survive anything."

Reginald shook his head. "Not a bullet to the brain."

"I—I need to talk to him," she said.

"No, you need to hand that baby over to my wife," he said. "You're not going to change your mind again."

Fear rushed through Emilia's blood, pounding in her pulse, so that she couldn't focus on the commands coming from the earpiece. Were they commands, though? It sounded as if everyone was shouting over everyone else.

She'd counted on them to protect her. But she had no idea where they were. She couldn't see them. She could see only Reginald Montgomery and his crazy wife.

She stepped back. Reginald lifted his arm straight out. The coat dropped away, revealing the gun they'd all suspected he'd been holding. The barrel was pointed right at her heart.

"Don't shoot!" the woman cried. "You'll hit the baby!"

But Reginald shook his head. It was clear he'd figured it out. "There's no baby," he said. "Dane Sutton was right. She had no intention of making the exchange."

Dane had known.

Her own brother had doubted her. But Dane had known. Was that because he didn't think she cared enough about him? Or because he knew how much she loved her son?

As she stared down that barrel, she worried that she would never get to see Blue again. But if Dane was dead, as Reginald claimed, then she might see him again.

Soon.

* * *

She was just standing there. Waiting to die…

Or maybe she was frozen with fear.

Everyone else seemed to be frozen, too—suspended in motion. Or inaction.

So Dane ran toward her. Lifting the gun he had taken off one of the gangbangers, he fired at Montgomery. Or as the gangbangers had called him, Moneybags Montgomery.

He couldn't be certain his bullet would take out Reginald, though. He couldn't be certain he would kill the guy before Montgomery managed to get off a shot and hit Emilia. So he threw himself against her, knocking her to the ground, protecting her with his body.

A woman screamed. It wasn't Emilia. She was curiously quiet. Maybe too quiet.

Mrs. Montgomery screamed. "The baby! The baby!"

The doll was the only thing that made a sound beneath him. Letting out a cry as he pressed down on it—and Emilia. He tried to lever his weight off her to see if she was all right.

But then he saw the glint of metal as Reginald lifted a knife. Blood spread from the guy's shoulder. Dane had hit him with a bullet, but it hadn't done enough damage.

Just like the gang members had figured out the bullet that had torn through Dane's shoulder hadn't done enough damage. It hurt like hell, but it hadn't weakened him. Once he'd snapped the zip ties on his wrists and the one on his ankles, he'd overpowered them.

Now he needed to overpower Reginald. He caught his wrist, squeezing it. The guy was stronger than he looked. Or maybe Dane had grown weaker than he'd realized.

He struggled to hold the blade away from him and away from Emilia, who lay still beneath him.

She had to be all right.

He had to make sure she was all right.

He squeezed harder, hoping to snap the bones in Reginald's wrist. The guy let out a growl of madness and rallied his strength, pushing that blade closer to Dane's chest. To his heart...

If Emilia was dead, if Montgomery had killed her, then he'd already ripped out Dane's heart.

And thinking of that, of the pain this man had put her through, Dane squeezed hard enough that the knife began to fall free of his grasp. But then Reginald fell, too, his suddenly lifeless body dropping onto Dane.

If Dane's weight alone hadn't crushed Emilia, their combined weight might. So Dane shoved him off.

The guy dropped back onto the sidewalk, his eyes open in shock. His wife didn't even spare him a glance. She just kept screaming, "The baby! The baby!"

Dane felt sorry for her, but he didn't quite trust her, either. So he kicked away the knife and the gun her husband had brought with them before he rolled off Emilia's soft body.

The doll let out another cry.

And Mrs. Montgomery rushed forward, grabbing the doll before Dane could stop her. She clutched it in her arms and murmured, "Daniel, it's okay. Momma has you now. Momma has you..."

Dane turned from her to stare down in Emilia's beautiful face. Tears trailed away from her pale blue eyes.

"What's wrong?" he asked. "Are you hurt?" He glanced down her body, looking for blood.

It was smeared across her dress. But he figured that

was his, from where he'd hit her with his wounded shoulder. He could see no rips in the fabric—no obvious injuries. But he could have broken her ribs or struck her head against the sidewalk when he'd knocked her down.

"Emilia!" he shouted her name as he touched his fingers to her tear-dampened face. Maybe she was just in shock. "Emilia! What's wrong?"

"You're crushing her, you idiot," Lars said as he leaned on a pair of crutches and reached down a hand toward Dane.

Instead of taking his hand, Dane surged up with his fist and plowed it into Lars's jaw. Pain radiated from his knuckles to his wounded shoulder, and he cursed. He'd forgotten his friend's jaw was like granite.

Lars staggered back a little and dropped his crutches. He'd probably just been off balance to begin with. Dane doubted he would have moved him otherwise.

Or maybe he had been angry enough to do it. "Damn you! Why would you let her do this? Why would you put her in danger like this?"

"I'll tell you why…" Lars's usually booming voice grew faint.

But Dane realized it wasn't his friend who was weakening—when his vision blurred then turned black. The last thing he knew was the concrete rushing up to meet him as he fell. Hard. Just like he'd fallen for Emilia Ecklund…

Lars stroked a hand over his swollen jaw. It throbbed like his leg. Maybe he should take the painkillers he'd been prescribed. But he hadn't even filled the bottle. After how he'd been acting, he knew he deserved to feel a little pain.

He'd be lucky if Nikki didn't break their engagement.

But she stood behind him as he sat in the chair next to Dane's hospital bed. And she squeezed his shoulder.

"He's going to be all right," she reminded him of what the doctor had said. The doctor hadn't wanted to tell him anything, though. There were privacy laws. And they weren't related to him. Dane had no family, though.

The doctor had finally spoken to him because on the medical directives and legal forms the Marines had made him fill out, Dane had listed Lars as his next of kin. Since boot camp, they had been like brothers.

"Will we be all right?" Lars asked.

"You and Dane?" Nikki laughed. "Of course you will. I don't know how many times I've watched my brothers pummel each other only to hug it out moments later."

"That was probably because Penny made them do it," Lars said. She was warm and affectionate, so of course she would make her children hug each other.

Nikki laughed. "Yeah, it was."

"She's still on her honeymoon," Lars reminded her. But that was only because Nikki insisted she not come home. Her mother loved Emilia like she was her daughter, too. And she had been so worried about her. Penny didn't have to worry anymore, though.

Emilia would be safe now.

But was she okay?

He'd been surprised when she hadn't wanted to come to the hospital. They should have made her, just so she could get checked out at least. But she hadn't been hit with a bullet. Only Dane's broken body had shielded her as he'd used the last of his strength to knock her out of harm's way. Lars touched his jaw again. Well, not the last of his strength. But instead of wanting to go to the hospital with Dane, Emilia had wanted to go home to Blue.

"Since Penny isn't here," Lars said, "I don't expect Dane and I to hug anything out."

"You better *not* try to hug me," Dane murmured from the bed.

"You should get so lucky," Lars teased as relief flooded him. His friend was going to be all right.

But would *they* be all right? Would they ever regain the friendship they'd once had?

Dane glared at him. "Why did you let her do it? Why did you let her put herself in danger like that?"

Nikki snorted. "Do you really think he *let* her do that?" she asked.

Lars glanced over his shoulder at his beautiful fiancée. "No," he said. "You let her. Hell, you practically encouraged her." He should have been furious with her. But he loved her too much.

"Why the hell would you do that?" Dane asked, and he glanced at Nikki's hand as if checking to see if she still wore Lars's engagement ring.

"For you, you idiot," Nikki said. "That's why we all agreed with her plan. To buy us some time to find you."

He had found them instead.

"Of course you couldn't wait for us to rescue you," Lars said, feigning disgust. "You had to be a damn show-off as usual—rushing in to save the day."

Dane snorted now. "Somebody had to do something. You all were standing around with your hands in your pockets, going to let Emilia get shot."

Nikki had had to hold Lars down from rushing in himself. "Manny had the shot," she said just as she'd convinced Lars at the time.

Manny had sniper training.

"Then you messed it up by running in like a rookie, blowing the whole stakeout," Lars said.

"What the hell were you waiting for?"

"We didn't want to take a kill shot," Nikki said. "Because then we didn't know if we'd be able to find you in time."

Dane looked from Lars to Nikki and narrowed his eyes. "You really did all this for me?" His doubt was evident.

"Why is that so hard for you to believe?" Nikki asked.

But Lars knew. Dane never talked much about himself, but when he had, Lars had listened. His past—being given up for adoption, his adoptive parents being cold sons of bitches—had convinced Dane that nobody cared about him, that nobody could.

"You've had some tough breaks," Lars said.

Dane shrugged then flinched as he moved his wounded shoulder. "We all have."

"But you think you're unlovable," Lars said.

Dane snorted, but his face flushed with embarrassment. As hokey as it sounded, it was what he believed.

"And you're wrong," Lars said. "The guys all love you. They'd lay down their lives for you." He blinked hard and cleared his throat. Must have been some dust in the room. Damn allergies…

"And I love you," he said.

"Even when he's trying to kill you," Nikki added for him as she squeezed his shoulder. She knew he had no allergies.

Dane shook his head.

Why wouldn't he believe them?

But then he added, "You made your choice. You're marrying Nikki. Not me. So stop with the sweet talk."

Lars laughed.

"You're both idiots," Nikki said. But she wasn't surprised—not with all the brothers she had. She pressed a kiss to Lars's cheek then leaned over and pressed one to Dane's before stepping out of the room.

Maybe she was checking on something. Maybe she was just giving them some privacy.

"Don't be an idiot like I've been," Lars warned his friend. "The person who took the biggest risk for you today was Emilia."

Dane sucked in a breath, and his eyes darkened again. "You shouldn't have let her."

"There was no stopping her," Lars said, and pride filled him. "My sister is so much stronger than I ever realized."

"She is," Dane agreed.

"She's stubborn, too," Lars added.

"Can't imagine where she'd get that," Dane remarked as his lips curved into a slight grin.

"You know why she did that today?"

Dane started to shrug then stilled his shoulders. "Gratitude," he said. "Kindness…"

"Love," Lars said. "She loves you most of all."

"No…"

Dane might have accepted that he wasn't unlovable, that his friends genuinely cared for him. But would he be able to accept that Emilia could?

"Don't be an idiot," Lars warned him as he struggled out of the chair. "Don't blow the best thing that's ever happened to you."

"She is the best," Dane agreed. "And she deserves better. She and Blue both do. I'm not husband material. And I'm certainly not father material. You were right to threaten to kill me when I got involved with her. I had no business going anywhere near her."

Lars shook his head with disgust. "I used to think you were the bravest man I'd ever met," he said. "But I see now that you're just a coward."

"I'm doing this for her," Dane said. "Because I…"

"You love her," Lars finished for him. "And that's all that matters. You can learn how to be a husband and a father—as long as you want to. As long as you're brave enough to try…"

All those years he'd known Dane he'd thought his friend had had no fear. Until now…

Would his love for Emilia be enough for him to overcome that fear?

Chapter 28

The crying echoed softly in Emilia's head just as it had so many times before. She knew whose crying it was now. Daniel. The Montgomerys must have recorded it, so they would have a reminder of their loss.

But that loss had driven them out of their minds. She pressed the button on her cell phone and shut off the recording. Because the SIM cards matched, she had everything on her phone that they had on theirs. So the recording had been there the entire time. None of it had been in her head.

She hadn't been losing her mind. And she hadn't lost her son. Her arms tightened around her sleeping boy. She should probably put him in his crib, but she continued to rock him in the chair in his nursery.

She wasn't trying to soothe him. She was trying to soothe herself.

She hadn't lost her mind. Or her son.

But she had lost her heart.

To Dane Sutton.

He didn't want it, though.

Sure, he'd rescued her at the park. That was who he was, what he did. He had been a war hero even before he'd become a bodyguard. He willingly put his life on the line all the time.

He had never put his heart on the line before.

As if he felt her melancholy, Blue emitted a soft sigh. And she felt a pang of guilt. She should be happy. She had so much.

Tears stung her eyes as she thought of Mrs. Montgomery. The couple was so wealthy, with fancy houses and cars and clothes and jewelry. But they had had so little. She could still see the woman clutching that doll, rocking it lovingly in her arms. Maybe it would give her some comfort. And the mental facility to which the authorities had brought her would get her some help.

Emilia blinked away her tears and smiled down at her son. Then she carried him to his crib and settled him into his bed. She could walk away and know that he would be fine. No one would take him away ever again.

As she stepped out of the nursery, she heard the creak of a door. Then footsteps on the stairs. She fumbled around in the hallway, looking for a weapon. Pulling the lamp from the hall table, she lifted it over her head, ready to swing.

But a strong hand wrapped around her wrist, lowering her weapon.

"You've turned into quite the fighter," Dane remarked as he put the lamp back on the table. "No, I guess you always were—or you wouldn't have survived what Myron Webber had put you through."

She'd spent weeks in that warehouse, unable to escape. It had taken Dane only hours. She had no doubt who was the better fighter.

That was why she hadn't gone to the hospital with him, why she hadn't visited the past couple of days he'd spent there. She knew, even if he had feelings for her, that he would fight them. He didn't want a relationship, a family. He'd made that clear from the beginning.

That their involvement was only a cover.

She was the one who'd stupidly fallen in love.

Pride had her tugging her wrist from his grasp. If he kept touching her, she might throw herself at him. She wanted so badly to step into his arms and lay her head on his chest. Wanted him so badly…

"I'm surprised you're out of the hospital already," she said.

"I checked myself out a little early," he admitted.

She shook her head. "Just like Lars." Her brother was a macho jerk, too. But he had vowed to never act that way with her again. From now on he would give her the respect she deserved, and she believed him.

If he didn't, she and Nikki would kick his ass. Her future sister was going to teach her some self-defense moves and some ultimate fighting ones, too.

"I had to check myself out," he said. "You wouldn't come to me. So I had to come to you."

She tensed. "What?"

"Don't you want to know why I'm here?"

"To get your clothes," she said. "Your things. It's over. We don't need to pretend anymore."

He stepped closer and lifted his hand to her cheek.

"I don't think I was ever pretending," he said, and as he stared down at her, his eyes darkened from caramel to dark chocolate. "I think I started falling for you before I ever met you."

She shook her head, and his hand dropped away from her face. She must have fallen asleep in that rocking chair, like he had that night. She must be dreaming but for once the dream was sweet.

Bittersweet because she knew it wasn't real. It couldn't be real...

"No," she murmured. She didn't want to wake up.

His lips curved into a slight grin. "And I've been accused of being the one who doesn't think he can be loved."

"I love you," she said. And because it was just a dream, she could say it freely. "I love you!"

He leaned down and pressed those smiling lips to hers. His mouth moved over hers, first tenderly and then with passion. And she knew she wasn't dreaming.

Passion overwhelmed her. Her pulse pounded. Her skin tingled. She didn't have to pinch herself. She knew this was real.

But then he murmured, "I love you..."

And she struggled to believe. "Dane?"

"I do," he promised. "I love you."

He swung her up in his arms. But she reached out and clasped his bandaged shoulder. "No! Put me down. You're going to hurt yourself."

He chuckled. "I'm already hurting," he said. "I'm aching for you." He ignored her concern and carried her down the hall to her bedroom.

To their bedroom...

Since that first night he'd spent with her that was how she had come to think of it. And she struggled to sleep in that bed without him, without his arm around her, without his shoulder beneath her cheek.

He laid her down and began to take off his clothes. Desperate to be with him—just skin to skin—she dragged off her dress and dropped it onto the floor along with her bra and panties.

He sucked in a breath.

And she rushed to him. "Are you okay? Are you hurt?"

"You're killing me, Emilia," he said. His erection pressed against her, pulsating with the need she felt for him.

She dropped to her knees before him and skimmed her lips down the length of him.

His breath shuddered out and his hands clutched her hair. "Emilia…"

She persisted, wanting to show him how much she loved and appreciated him. But he must have wanted to do the same because he lifted her again. This time he followed her down onto the mattress.

His hands and lips touched her everywhere. Stroking. Kissing.

He focused on her lips, which he thoroughly kissed—nibbling gently at them as he dipped his tongue inside her mouth. She suckled on it, holding on to it as she held on to him. He chuckled but broke the kiss. Then he skimmed his lips down her jaw and her throat and over her breasts. His lips closed over a nipple, pulling it into a tight bud.

She cried out as sensation raced through her. Her core throbbed with need. "Dane…"

But he denied her release, just continued to tease her to madness. She touched him back, caressing his skin and muscles. Reaching between them, she touched his cock. It jumped against her fingertip.

And he cursed. "Emilia…"

He might have wanted to take it slow. But she needed him too much. She closed her hand over him.

He pulled back. She heard the rip of a condom packet. Then he was between her legs, nudging against her. She arched and moved, taking him inside her, pulling him deep. He moved in and out. And she rose up to meet his thrusts.

One of his arms began to tremble where he'd braced it against the mattress, and sweat beaded on his brow. He was hurting. Really hurting from the gunshots wounds to his shoulder and his arm.

"Dane…"

She pushed him back. But careful to keep him inside her, she moved with him until he was lying down and she straddled him. Then she rode him, sliding up and down and back and forth. He clutched her hips, helping her move, helping her find the rhythm that had her body tensing before pleasure slammed through it.

She let out a soft cry as ecstasy claimed her. She had never had as powerful an orgasm. But he kept moving, thrusting up his hips. One of his hands moved from her hips to her breast. He teased the nipple. And the tension wound up inside her again.

He was close to coming himself, though. Sweat beaded on his lip and his brow. And a cord stood out in his neck as he struggled for control.

But he'd brought her close again.

He pulled her head down and kissed her deeply, sliding his tongue into her mouth as he slid inside her body. She shattered—pleasure rippling through her. He tensed and groaned as he joined her in ecstasy.

She left him lying there as she headed into the bathroom for a cloth. She cleaned them both before lying down beside him and resting her head on his good shoulder.

"Are you sure I'm not dreaming?" she murmured.

But before he could answer her, she was…dreaming of a future where she spent every night in Dane Sutton's arms.

"Shh…" Dane said as he lifted the crying baby from the crib. For a moment he'd thought the sound was that damn recording. But then he'd awakened fully and realized it was Blue. He'd rushed to the nursery before Emilia could awaken. "Come on, buddy, let's let your mama sleep."

Blue immediately stopped crying and stared up at him from those pale blue Ecklund eyes. "Yeah, you'd do anything for her, too, wouldn't you?"

Blue kicked his legs. And Dane realized the baby was wet. Ignoring the pain throbbing in his shoulder, he changed him. Putting him in a pair of clean pajamas was a struggle, though. As if he thought they were playing a game, Blue kept kicking.

"You're gonna be as ornery as your uncle, aren't you?" he asked. But he grinned. Lars's orneriness had kept him alive. "You're gonna give your mama some trouble if you're as pigheaded as Lars is." He swallowed hard. "And me…"

Blue gurgled out a laugh as if Dane had just told a funny joke. Or maybe it had just been gas.

"It is funny, though," he admitted. "The thought of me trying to be a father. I'm not going to have a damn clue what I'm doing."

Getting to know the Paynes had taught him the most important thing about families.

"But I'll love you and your mama. And I'll take care of you." That was what the Paynes did. They loved each other. Sometimes a little too much.

As Dane stared down at the baby, he realized that wasn't possible. You could not love enough. But you could never love too much.

"And I'll try not to screw this up," he promised.

A soft hand slid down his back, soothing him like he'd soothed the baby. "You won't," Emilia said. "As long as you keep loving us."

"I'll never stop," he vowed. "I will love you and Blue forever." He slid his arm around her while he cradled their son in his other one. "And all the other kids we'll have."

She smiled up at him even as her eyes glistened with tears. Happy tears. "More kids?"

He nodded. "But first you have to plan our wedding. Or have you quit the chapel to work as a bodyguard?"

She shuddered. "No. I will keep working with Penny. But we'll have to wait for our wedding."

"Why?" he asked. Then he remembered. "You have to plan Nikki and Lars's wedding first."

She sighed. "There's that. But there's another reason."

He tensed. Had he already screwed up? Had he done something that would make her doubt him? "What?"

"You have to propose."

"Oh, I will do that," he said. But he wanted to do it with style and romance and a ring. "I'll surprise you."

Her smile widened and the tears slipped through her lashes. "You already have—in the best possible way. You love me."

"And you love me…" He hadn't thought it was possible. But he knew that it was true. Emilia Ecklund loved him. And someday soon she would be his bride.

"Why the hell did you bring me here?" Manny asked as he glanced nervously around the jewelry store. At least it wasn't some stuffy upscale place. It was more like an artist's studio because Stacy Kozminski-Payne was an artist with jewelry. But Manny had no interest in helping pick out an engagement ring.

"I need your opinion," Dane said.

Manny stared at the guy as he leaned over a case admiring the rings inside it. "And I'll give it to you," he said. "My opinion is that you've lost your damn mind."

Dane laughed.

"It's not funny, man," Manny insisted. "What did they do to you in that warehouse? Shock treatment? Waterboarding? What the hell changed you from the smart guy who wanted nothing to do with women and kids to…" He didn't even know how to describe this new version of Dane.

Except that he was happy. Disgustingly so…

He shook his head. "Yeah, must have been shock treatment."

Dane laughed again.

"I'm serious, man," Manny said. "You should have quit back when you'd had the chance. You shouldn't have let Cooper talk you out of it." He wasn't going to, not when he gave his resignation, which was going to be damn soon.

He wasn't taking any chances like his idiot friends. Oh, he'd risk his life again, any time. He just wasn't going to risk his heart.

"What do you think of this one?" Dane asked after Stacy handed him a ring.

She was beautiful with green eyes and hair that had strands of every color in it. But Manny forced himself to look away from her and focus on the ring. She posed no threat, though. She was married to the boss's boss.

"Why are you asking me?" Manny asked. "Why didn't you bring her brother with you to ring-shop?"

"Because he doesn't know Emilia as well as he thinks he does," Dane said.

Manny had no argument for that. The girl had proved herself way tougher than Lars had thought she was. "I barely know her at all," Manny reminded him.

Dane nodded. "True. But I know you. I know you have terrible taste, so if you think the ring is pretty, I'll know to pick another one."

Manny focused on the ring. The delicate band was nearly white and wound around a big round diamond and two smaller pale blue stones. It was pretty perfect for Emilia Ecklund.

And Dane knew it because he knew her best.

So Manny shook his head. "It's hideous."

While Stacy gasped in indignation—like he'd called her baby ugly or something—Dane chuckled. "I knew it was the one. Just like I knew she was…before I ever met her."

Manny ignored his brain-damaged friend and asked Stacy, "There aren't any more single Payne women, right? The guys don't have another sister?"

She shook her head.

"You're the only female Kozminski?"

She narrowed her eyes and nodded.

He expelled a slight breath. "Good." Dane didn't

have any sisters. He wasn't sure about Cole. But since he didn't have anything to do with his family, it wasn't like Manny would meet any of them. He didn't have to worry about staying away from friends' sisters.

He just had to worry about damsels in distress. If Cooper didn't want him to quit, he would have to promise to only assign him cases where he protected men. Maybe he'd ask for the job protecting Teddie Plummer. He'd heard Cooper mention that the guy needed a bodyguard. But it was an out-of-state assignment.

That was good, too.

Manny needed to get the hell away from his sappy, in-love friends and all their damn engagement and wedding stuff. Yeah, he'd take that job protecting Teddie Plummer. It didn't matter how much danger the guy was in, Manny would be safer protecting Ted than sticking around here. Maybe.

* * * * *

Look for Manny and Teddie's story, the next thrilling installment in the
BACHELOR BODYGUARDS *series,*
coming in 2018!

Don't forget the previous titles in the series:

NANNY BODYGUARD
BEAUTY AND THE BODYGUARD
BODYGUARD'S BABY SURPRISE
BODYGUARD DADDY
HIS CHRISTMAS ASSIGNMENT

Get 2 Free Books,
Plus 2 Free Gifts —
just for trying the Reader Service!

"So, why you? Why Jamie?"

"Not everyone is rich like me," he said. "That would narrow down her options."

"You suspect Livia because she had a reason to despise Tess, but other than her nefarious character, I don't see enough to suspect her."

"If Livia survived that accident, she's desperate. Desperate people do desperate things."

Adeline nodded, folding her arms. "Desperation is valid." All this depended on Livia having survived the accident.

She went to the bookshelf along a side wall of the family room, where an electronic frame switched through several photos. Most included Jamie. His adorable, smiling face and bright blue eyes spoke of a happy boy. The pictures of Tess haunted her. She felt at odds falling for Tess's husband, especially knowing how much Tess had loved him. Although now Adeline questioned that love. If Tess had approached

Oscar with a proposal to start up their affair again, could she have loved Jeremy as much as she'd claimed?

Jeremy reached to the photo frame and pressed a button to stop its cycling. Adeline didn't realize he'd followed her across the room until then. He'd moved closer and she felt his warmth. She also sensed his absorption with one photo, in which Jamie must have been about two. He sat at a picnic table with a cake before him, and what looked like half his piece covering his face around his mouth. He smiled big.

"That was the first time he was really happy."

After Tess died.

"He had all his friends over. I set up an inflatable bounce house in the backyard and gave him his first tricycle for his present."

Adeline stared at Jamie's playful face and felt a surge of love. She'd helped to create such an angel. Now that angel was in the hands of someone evil, and they might not ever get him back. He could be killed. He could be dead already.

Unable to suppress the sting of tears, she turned to Jeremy for comfort. "Oh, Jeremy."

Jeremy took her into his arms. His hands rubbed her back, slow, sensual and firm. Then he pressed a kiss on her head. She felt his warm breath on her hair and scalp. With her arms under his and hands on his back, she snuggled closer, resting the side of her head on his chest.

"We'll find him," he said.

Don't miss
MISSION: COLTON JUSTICE by Jennifer Morey,
available October 2017 wherever
Harlequin® Romantic Suspense books
and ebooks are sold.

www.Harlequin.com

HRSEXP0917

THE WORLD IS BETTER WITH

Romance

Harlequin has everything from contemporary, passionate and heartwarming to suspenseful and inspirational stories.

Whatever your mood, we have a romance just for you!

Connect with us to find your next great read, special offers and more.